SEA TREMORS

EDWARD J. MCFADDEN III

SEVERED PRESS
HOBART TASMANIA

SEA TREMORS

WWW.SEVEREDPRESS.COM

ISBN: 978-1-922323-04-0

I have seen the dark universe yawning
Where the black planets roll without aim,
Where they roll in their horror unheeded,
Without knowledge, or lustre, or name.

-H.P. Lovecraft

1

It survived in the darkness, but was entranced by the light. And it was hungry.

Its purpose was to hunt and feed. It didn't know joy or happiness. It didn't feel fear, or pity. It couldn't be bargained with or cajoled. It had no companions, no family, and didn't know love.

It knew only one thing; killing prey.

For time uncounted its kind had lived in the cracks of the world, deep beneath the surface where sunlight was a distant memory, and where the residue of the hydrothermal vents far below provided the necessary elements for the chemosynthesis that supports life in the abyss.

Translucent anemone-like plants sway with the churning water, and bubbles surged around the beast, its white tentacles floating with the current. It hadn't moved in... It didn't know. Time ceased to flow in the cold depths surrounded by stone.

Did the leviathan remember? Or were the images that fill its skull dreams? Random snaps of its nerve ring's synapses? The creature doesn't remember the way humans do, in a linear fashion with benchmarks to help place the memories in the proper context and period. Its past is a series of dark episodes of survival and hunting. Some might call it instinct.

The crack in the oceanic crust it called home vibrated and quaked. The creature rarely strayed from its protective confines except to hunt, but something was happening. Something that had never happened in all its years.

The great rock slabs that held the world together cracked, and things moved that it had never seen move. Seawater flowed in new places, and the beast's normal exit from its lair was blocked as the oceanic ridge split and ground together. Shifting pressure pushed seawater and rocks, and the creature raised its two whip arms to shield itself, claws on each end snapping, looking for prey to drag into its parrot-like beak of a mouth.

A faint white glow penetrated the darkness, and the beast shifted its massive weight. Its translucent basketball-sized eyes were ultrasensitive, and could detect the slightest light, even at great distance.

It had known only darkness for so long.

It started upward, as water and stone trembled. Up. It didn't know what was above the darkness. It had never ventured beyond its own hunting ground, but the light...

There would be prey there.

Eight serpentine legs, smooth on one side and covered with spikes and suction cups filled with knife-like teeth on the other, snaked through shifting rocks, grabbing stone for purchase as the creature hauled its massive albino bulk from its hiding place. Without light in the depths, the leviathan's white body gave way to only a few sections of pink, the shade of a newborn child. The beast absorbed oxygen from seawater through its skin and pumped it over its gills and through its body with unmatched efficiency. The killer resembled a giant mutant squid-octopus, and somewhere in its evolution it had been a hatchling larva of a kind, though the creature hadn't been the same as the others.

Others? Had there been others? It recalled no companionship of any kind. It was alone, and it would always be alone. That was all it knew.

The sea grew warmer as it ascended. Giant eyes stared out from a milky armored carapace that tapered back over a teardrop torso. The light above grew brighter. Rock broke and separated. The beast hung in the depths, not unsure, but patient. It wasn't used to the unknown. It controlled its world.

Using its whip arms and tentacles, the beast pulled itself into open water. It pushed water through its siphon, and with a wag of its tail and stabilizer fins, it shot through the dark water. Creatures big and small fled before the beast, and it casually pulled fish into its maw as it climbed.

All living things were its food.

The ocean grew cold, then warm again. It let the sea carry it upward. The glow of light spread, and for the first time it truly saw its world. Color blossomed on rocks, and particles of vegetation and silt clouded the water. A great *boom* echoed through the sea and the light above faltered as a huge slab of rock slid into its new position, blocking its ascent.

It paused, unsure.

Bubbles streamed around the leviathan as its tentacles searched the stone for cracks, but there were none. It eased along the rock, pulling and pushing itself through the water, awkward in its movements, yet fluid. On it swam, as the Earth trembled and its world shook apart.

Light pierced the blackness again and the giant moved toward a crevasse in the stone. Above, the sleek white form of a shark glided through the sea. The great white flicked its caudal fin, surging through the water toward something unseen.

The creature dragged itself upward, its two larger arms before it, claws snapping. For a time, it was alone again, moving through the narrow crack in the sea floor, which was calm and familiar.

It exited the crevasse into a new world, an environment filled with vegetation and life. The sunlight penetrating the clear water hurt its large bulbous eyes, and for an instant the beast was blinded. A kaleidoscope of colors filled its view, and the sea shook like Jell-o.

Fish streamed by, but it was confused. Something gnawed at its insides, a feeling it has never experienced, a primal warning telling it to be cautious, but the overwhelming urge to feed washes over the creature. A burning and longing that eats at its mind and body, pushing it, driving it with a hatred and urgency it neither understands, or cares to understand. Its hunger is omnipresent, like another leg. It constantly feels the pull of starvation, the unease that comes from never being satisfied, never feeling whole. It knows no other way to live, as if a part of it was always missing, a piece that can only be replaced with flesh and blood.

It glides through the sea, boulders falling through the turbulent water.

Slowly. Inexorably. It floats upward.

2

Steep waves rolled across the inlet, and Cannon struggled to keep the twenty-six-foot SAFE boat on course. Sea spray drenched the windshield, and the twin Yamaha outboards whined and choked as the boat dipped into a valley between waves. Thick clouds obscured the sky, and a stiff wind blew out of the west, rank with the scent of rotten fish and salt. The Pacific Ocean stretched to the western horizon, its dark emerald water a chaotic mess of whitecaps. To the east, Devil's Rip inlet cut between the steep bluffs that separated Blackwater Bay from the anger of the sea.

Weather warnings scrolled across the main navigation screen, and GPS showed no other vessels. Cannon's responsibility as bay constable ended when he passed through the inlet into the Pacific, but he always patrolled up and down the coast along the bluffs to ensure no boats were hung-up on rocks or had slammed into the cliff face.

Despite the SAFE boat's thick blue pontoons providing stability, the vessel rolled and yawed as waves surged in every direction, the natural flow disturbed by the swirling wind. Cannon pulled back on the throttle and the engine whine reduced to a purr. He looked through binoculars, scanning the base of the bluffs where the Pacific pounded the shoreline.

A few harbor seals lounged on stones, but there were no boats. A small craft advisory was in effect, so he didn't expect to see any vessels, but he had to check, otherwise he'd worry. This was his backyard, and his responsibility, regardless of a line some suit in Sacramento had drawn. Nel told him this type of attitude was going to get him in trouble, and it had in the past, but he just couldn't leave things be. If something was wrong, or broken, or unjust, Cannon felt it was his responsibility to make things right, regardless of the situation.

The command console chirped, a steady beeping that rose in urgency and speed. Cannon searched for the cause of the warning he'd never heard before. This had been his patrol boat for six years, and whatever the SAFE boat was trying to tell him, he wasn't understanding.

The ocean trembled and shook, and the boat skidded over the turbulent sea. Cannon gripped the wheel as the SAFE boat speared the face of a six-foot wave. Whitewater crashed over the bow, and the aluminum pilothouse creaked.

The beeping changed to a steady bleep and ceased, like a flatline on a heart monitor going silent. That sound, along with the erupting sea, made Cannon remember.

The earthquake alert system cost the residents of California millions, all to get a warning of ten seconds, maybe less, but any notice helped when seconds could mean getting under a doorframe.

Giant boulders tumbled from the cliff face and crashed in the ocean, and slabs of stone cleaved from the bluffs. Waves jerked and broke in every direction as the seafloor split, and sections rose and fell.

Devil's Rip was a mile off.

Cannon turned the wheel, brought the boat about, and dropped the hammer. The patrol boat leapt from the water and drove through the rough sea, leaving a trail of whitewater and skipping over wave tops pulling thirty-three knots at 4200RPM. The shoreline ahead shook and twisted. Rock pillars surged from the ground and clifftops imploded, thick black dust clouds rising to the sky like the coast was being bombed.

The sea ahead disappeared, like someone had flushed the cosmic toilet.

Cannon spun the wheel, but the boat couldn't turn fast enough and dove forward. Swirling wind pounded the pilothouse as the SAFE boat fell over the edge of the abyss.

A whirlpool churned where the displaced water had been and the SAFE boat rode the side, the deck tilting at a forty-degree angle. Everything not secured slid across the dash, and chairs and loose items careened across the pilothouse and collected in a corner like garbage. Cannon's mug flew across the cabin, splashing him with cold coffee, and he almost fell as his feet slid out from under him. The command console was alight with warnings, and the ship's alarm klaxon shrieked.

Through the mass of water pounding the boat's windshield, Cannon saw the dark bottom of the spiral. The boat bucked as it slipped further into the swirling ocean, the outboards wailing as their water pumps strained to draw cooling water.

A surge of seawater jetted from below and pushed the boat up, driving it into the side of the whirlpool. Whitewater consumed the vessel as it was lifted from the sea, rising like a cork on an incoming tide. Cannon clutched the steering wheel, pain cramping his knuckles as he struggled to keep the SAFE boat from flipping over. The GPS showed the sea floor buckling and cracking, entire sections of the dark streak that marked the sea bottom falling off the screen like a video game.

The ocean erupted, and as fast as the whirlpool had appeared, it was gone. A mountain of seawater rose from the depths, shooting into the sky with such force Cannon couldn't tell how high it went. He turned the SAFE boat to starboard, waves pushing the twenty-six-foot vessel around like a rubber duck in a tub, the craft filled with water and bogging down in the rough surf.

To the east, the entrance to Devil's Rip loomed, a slit in the cliffside. Clouds of dust and silt hid much of the destruction, but thunderous booms and the shriek of rending and grinding stone echoed over the Pacific. He'd experienced tremors since coming to California, but nothing like this. His mind strayed to the old Superman movie with Christopher Reeves. How Lex Luther bought up all the land east of the San Andreas fault and tried to cause an earthquake that would drop half of California into the sea.

"Waterfront property," Cannon said, though there was nobody there to hear him.

The boat's bow surged up and came down with a smack, and Cannon fell, hitting the deck. The ship's wheel spun free, and the boat veered sharply to port, water pouring over the gunnels and further swamping the craft.

Water leaked beneath the pilothouse door as Cannon got to his feet. Blood dripped down his face, turning the sloshing water pink. He leaned against the command console as the bow was sucked beneath a wave, lifting the transom from the water along with the motors. The outboards shrieked, metal grinding on metal, propellers swinging in the air. The engines sputtered and stalled as the boat fell back into the sea.

"Shit," he said, turning the ignition key. Flywheels spun, and the engines coughed but didn't start. The bilge pump worked overtime, a steady stream of water shooting from the vessel's side. SAFE boats were equipped with self-bailing gaps where the pontoon gunnel meets the deck that allowed water above deck to drain away quickly.

A flock of gulls soared overhead, unconcerned with what was happening below.

Giant holes appeared in the ocean around the boat as the seafloor buckled and sank. Ten-foot waves broke in the shallows on both sides of the SAFE boat as it bobbed and drifted toward the channel that led to the inlet. Red and green buoys dipped beneath the sea, marking the passage. Cracks opened in the sea floor between the breaking waves as the sea retreated.

Cannon closed his eyes, asked his dead mother for help, and turned the ignition key.

The engines roared to life. He slammed the throttle down and the propellers tore into the ocean, fighting to push the boat forward as it got dragged beneath the waves. The bilge pump did its job and water no longer sloshed around the pilothouse. The boat was handling better, and as the vessel pulled free of the receding ocean, the boat came up on plane and passed into Devil's Rip. Sheer rock walls rose on either side of the boat as it tore through the inlet. The tide was going out, and despite the roiling sea the current was strong.

Devil's Rip was thusly named because of the intense currents in the inlet, and despite the earthquake, water still drained into the Pacific. The Yamahas were at full throttle, and the SAFE boat was barely making twenty-five knots.

The SONAR buzzed. Blobs of color raced across the screen as fish of every size and shape swam through the inlet, fighting to reach the sea. Dorsal fins streamed by and fish leapt from the water. Rocks and debris plummeted into the inlet, and ahead, Cannon saw Blackwater Bay, and beyond, the dark outline of Gullhaven.

Cannon's stomach went cold as he thought of Nel and her son. Nel fished her father's boat most days, but thankfully Joshua had an event at school, and she hadn't gone out on this day. Then a horrible thought burrowed into his head like a maggot; if the mountains were coming down, what would happen to the village? He had to get back. Find out where Nel was. Help Sherriff Locke deal with what was sure to be the largest disaster in the history of the three-hundred-year old fishing community.

The SAFE boat hit something, and Cannon fell onto the dash, his head hitting one of the navigation screens. The boat listed to port and slowed, propellers digging into the water. The vessel rocked, and Cannon realized something was ramming the boat. He backed down the throttle, and the craft slowed.

A five-foot dorsal fin knifed through the water, leaving a thick wake.

Cannon let his hand drop from the steering wheel to the Glock 19 on his hip.

The great white didn't appear to be fleeing like the rest of the marine life. The beast swam just below the surface, running behind the SAFE boat. Its torpedo shaped body glided through the turbulent water with ease, its caudal fin swaying back and forth, dark eyes focused on the boat as it kept pace.

Cannon cracked his knuckles and rubbed his neck. What the hell did this thing want? He knew apex predators put hunger above all else, but with the mountains crumbling into the ocean, Cannon was surprised the creature was hanging around.

Then the shark really surprised him. Without warning the great white came at the boat's starboard side and breached, jaws distended in a wide smile, gills flaring.

Cannon jerked the throttle arm, snapping it into neutral, and the vessel was yanked backward with the current toward the ocean. The shark landed short of the blue inflated gunnel, jaws snapping closed with a smack that was louder than the collapsing bluffs.

The shark crashed back into the sea, and Cannon pinned the throttle. The engines struggled and popped as they clawed at the water, fighting the current and pushing the boat forward again.

The great white crossed beneath the boat to the port side, and Cannon strained to see the beast through the pilothouse's side window.

The giant fish dove, its dorsal fin disappearing beneath the chaotic mess of blown out whitecaps. The boat rocked and swayed, the wet debris on the pilothouse floor sliding back and forth across the deck.

A stone the size of a basketball crashed into the water beside the boat, and the slap and splash made Cannon jump. He pulled on the steering wheel as he reeled back, and the boat arced to starboard, throwing spray and jumping over a wave.

A gray shape rose through the emerald water.

Cannon recovered and steadied himself, eyes locked on the emerging shark, nerves jumping, stomach ice. The beast's dorsal fin broke the surface. A great crack *boomed*, and Cannon looked over his shoulder and saw the south wall of the inlet collapse into the sea.

The great white's dorsal fin came at the SAFE boat. If the beast bit the pontoons, and they popped, he didn't know how he'd make port in the current conditions.

Cannon dropped the boat into neutral, drew the Glock, and headed out on deck.

3

Cannon exited the pilothouse and a gust of wind drove him backward. The SAFE boat's bow rose, and the pilothouse door slid closed on his arm as he braced against the doorframe. Pain lanced his shoulder and arm, the door like a blunt guillotine. He screamed, his voice blending into the wind and chaos of breaking stone. The deck tilted as a large wave rolled over the gunnel and whitewater washed Cannon down the deck like a piece of seaweed.

He held the Glock in his left hand and clawed at the gunnel with his right, but the blue inflated rubber was slick and had no handholds. He hit the transom feet first and used the momentum to right himself. The deck rose and fell as the boat was sucked out of the inlet by the strong current.

The five-foot dorsal fin was thirty feet away and driving, leaving a wake like the great white had a tiny outboard attached to its caudal fin. The rain picked up and Cannon lost sight of the shark, but only for an instant. The dorsal fin hadn't changed course as it speared through the sea.

He put his back to the pilothouse and brought up the Glock. With the boat heaving and falling there was no way he'd be able to get a good shot, unless it was at point-blank range. The weapon shook in his hand. He'd never fired his service weapon in the line of duty. He was normally a decent shot, but this wasn't the practice range and the great white wasn't made of paper.

The shark was twenty feet away, its gray body surfacing, when a large white amorphous blob passed beneath the boat. Cannon paused, his attention momentarily fixed on the oddity. He thought the seafloor was rising, but the shape moved like oil poured into water.

The great white's conical snout launched from the inlet, black eyes focused, gill slits flaring, extended jaws revealing rows of razor-sharp teeth. The beast clamped down on the starboard gunnel, thrashing its head, tearing the blue rubber.

Cannon fired, his primal scream rising above the gusting wind as he pulled the trigger until the gun clicked empty. Fifteen shots, and from what he could see he'd only hit the thing six times. Red dots appeared on the shark's white underside, dripping blood, but it didn't slow the beast. Its head whipped and pulled as it tried to sink the boat, but SAFE boats had their name for a reason. They were constructed to take a beating and were specially designed for law enforcement and rescue activities. So it was that the SAFE boat's inflatable gunnel had several chambers that allowed the boat to stay afloat and operate even with sections deflated.

The boat trembled and shook as the shark tore a piece of the gunnel away. The great white eased back into the sea, jaws half open in a smile as it slid beneath the waves.

The inlet erupted like an explosive charge had detonated, and rocks and vegetation fell from the bluffs as the earthquake's crescendo shook the channel.

Cannon glanced at his watch: 2:27PM. Eight minutes had passed since the warning klaxon had sounded. Somewhere in the depths of his mind he remembered hearing that the longest earthquake in California history was fourteen minutes. He hoped this one didn't last that long, or there might be nothing left when... if he made it back. He gazed west toward the Pacific, then back east to the bay. With the SAFE boat damaged and moving like a brick, he didn't know if he could escape the inlet before its walls collapsed.

He went back in the pilothouse to the command console, and considered calling for help, or sending out a mayday. He was the main rescue team, and with Gullhaven shaking apart he doubted he'd get a response, but his worry got the best of him and he tried anyway.

"Command, this is Cannon. Kathie, do you read me?"

Static.

"Command, this is—"

"Hang on a second, Cannon," came a voice from the comm.

It wasn't Kathie, he was sure of that.

"Cannon, this is Sheriff Tanya Locke. What is your situation? We're a little busy here." Her gravelly voice made Cannon think of her shapely body and her mane of blonde hair.

"I'm in the inlet. Not good out here, Tanya. What's—"

"You're on your own until further notice. Locke out."

Cannon stared at the command console, his nerves stinging the bottom of his feet and the palms of his hands. Things on land must be worse than what he was experiencing, and again his thoughts went to Nel and Joshua. If they weren't safe, he didn't know what he'd do. He'd finally come out of his twenty-two-year sleep, and he couldn't lose Nel and her son.

He said 10-4 into the comm anyway. Protocol was protocol.

The shark was back. Its dorsal fin glided through the raging sea, circling the SAFE boat. The beast left a trail of blood.

Cannon eased the throttle forward and the boat fought to move through the thick chop. With the boat swamped and a section of the starboard gunnel deflated, the craft was hard to control, and Cannon couldn't bring the vessel on plane.

The great white circled and watched.

Sharks are common in Blackwater Bay. Cannon saw them hunting regularly. They swam up from the red triangle, one of the hottest shark grounds on the planet. San Francisco Bay opened to the Pacific, and whales frequented the area, which meant apex predators came in great numbers to dine at their equivalent of a five-star restaurant.

The SAFE boat was doing eight knots, and piloting the craft was like driving a car with a broken power steering pump. Waves crashed over the bow, and seawater poured through the rent in the gunnel. The boat wouldn't sink, but at the rate the vessel was flooding it wouldn't be long before the outboards bogged down and were unable to push the boat.

Like a switch had been flipped, everything stopped. The wind eased, the water flattened, and the cracking and booming of breaking stone lessened. For half a heartbeat everything was still and calm.

Cannon took a deep breath. With the earthquake over he could wait for help.

He remembered the shark. The beast was on a collision course again, its dorsal fin slowly rising from the calm sea.

Then the dorsal fin was gone and the scent of bleach stung Cannon's nose.

A white serpentine appendage shot from the water, hung in the air for a heartbeat, then fell back and slithered beneath the waves.

Boom.

The air vibrated and the water trembled and shook.

Aftershock.

He was almost through Devil's Rip, the town of Gullhaven in the distance. Boulders fell, and the mountainside to the north slid into the inlet, fully blocking it and sending a massive surge of whitewater across the bay.

Cannon braced for impact.

A fist of water lifted the SAFE boat and drove it forward, whitewater engulfing it. Churning water filled the windshield as the vessel got tossed around and he clung to the steering wheel. The engines whined but didn't stall.

The bow dipped, diving nose first, but Cannon spun the pilot's wheel, turning the craft to port and pulling the boat free of the dive. The boat surfed the face of the surge, sea water shooting through the gap in the gunnel, blasting the windshield. Cannon kept the wheel steady, riding the momentum of the surge, throwing a wall of spray. If he turned at the wrong time, at the speed he was traveling, the SAFE boat would be launched off the wave.

Heart pounding in his chest, eyes burning from focusing, Cannon only made course adjustments that kept the boat in the flow of the water. There were no sandbars or low areas in the center of Blackwater Bay, and the surge diminished as it rolled on.

Dingmans Warf was coming on fast. How would he stop? He was going to smash into Gullhaven along with the wave and there was nothing he could do about it.

He opened a comm channel and hoped Sheriff Locke was still there. "Locke. Do you copy? I have information you need. Do you copy?"

Static.

Cannon went on anyway. "To anyone listening, head for high ground. There is a massive wave heading for town. It will arrive in seconds. Seek higher—"

The boat rocked violently to starboard and Cannon was tossed across the pilothouse and smashed into the bulkhead. The wheel spun free, and the windshield filled with the churning sea.

Cannon got to his knees and pulled himself to his feet, the deck heaving beneath his feet, adrenaline giving him one last jolt. He was exhausted, hungry, blood dripped into his eyes, and his lower back ached. He clutched the wheel, steadying the SAFE boat as it was hurled toward the wharf.

The water stopped shaking.

Ten minutes had passed since the warning klaxon sounded.

Dingmans Wharf jutted out into the bay at the end of Main Street. It was a chaotic mess of fishing trawlers and pleasure crafts. Beyond, Gullhaven waited to be pounded. Several buildings had been reduced to rubble, and people stood on rooftops. Perhaps they'd gotten his warning. Or they had eyes. The mountains to the east were crumbling and landslides cascaded toward town; dust, smoke and steam obscuring much of the devastation.

The wave surge was dying out, losing its force, and Cannon found he had better control of the boat. He turned the wheel hard to avoid hitting a large sailboat that had broken from its moorings and threaded through the maze of destruction.

Once through the wharf, Main Street opened before the boat as the knot of water broke and dissipated, giving Cannon and his ride one last push.

He worked the wheel as the boat skimmed down Main Street atop the whitewater. Cannon had driven on the road that morning, and as the vessel flew past The Bean coffee shop, he caught the faint scent of French roast.

The boat slowed as it passed the bank, town hall, and his favorite bar, Gloria's. He was feeling like he might make it when a sharp scraping sound made him look back just in time to see the outboards snap off the transom and fall into the floodwater.

"Oh shit." With the motors gone he had no control of the boat. He considered jumping overboard, but quickly decided against it. Though the mountain of water had dissipated, the retreating sea tugged at everything in its path. With part of the starboard gunnel gone, and the boat continually taking on water, Cannon had nothing left to do but wait, like a passenger on a doomed flight.

He spotted his lifejacket in the pile of items gathered in the corner of the pilothouse, and went to retrieve it, but didn't make it. Seawater engulfed the SAFE boat and tossed it through the air. The vessel landed with a crash as the whitewater drained away.

Everything went still.

Cannon peered out the windshield.

The SAFE boat rested on the roof of Century One Office Plaza, a three-story building. Tallest in town.

The floodwater withdrew.

4

Cannon slid open the pilothouse door and the SAFE boat wobbled. He froze, keenly aware the boat was on a roof three stories high. The deck tilted away to his left, and he worked his way along the pilothouse, easing his way aft. The motors had broken away, along with part of the transom, and Cannon stepped over the destruction and off the rocking boat. He walked around to the bow, wet gravel set in tar crunching under his feet, the sound of the retreating sea white noise in the background. The boat's keel sat on a crushed HVAC unit and the bow pressed against the building's main exhaust duct.

A gust of wind tore across the rooftop, and the boat shifted and almost tipped. Cannon reached over the gunnel and grabbed a coil of line tied to the bow cleat. He looped the other end over the exhaust shaft, then did the same with a rope on an aft cleat. The SAFE boat was probably garbage because fixing the transom and starboard pontoon wouldn't be worth the expense, but he didn't want the boat to fall onto the road below and injure someone. Plus, he needed his stuff from the pilothouse.

A thin wail that sounded like a woman in pain echoed over the rumble of rushing water and whistling wind. Cannon ran to the roof's edge and looked out on the devastation. The streets of Gullhaven were mostly flooded, but the water was pulling back like a receding tide, dragging cars, debris and… Cannon gaped and put a hand over his mouth like a southern belle who's seen a frog scampering about her kitchen.

Corpses floated in the flotsam, and seagulls dive-bombed the dead bodies, pecking and pulling at exposed skin. Whitewater flowed down Main Street toward the wharf, which was underwater. Blackwater Bay was a roiling mess of whitecaps and dirty foam, as everything sloshed and settled like a pond that been disturbed. To the east, boulders tumbled down the mountainside, leaving a trail of dust and pebbles. County Road 19 looked blocked, which meant there was no way to reach Gullhaven by land.

Another wail of pain broke Cannon from his reverie. He ran back to the SAFE boat and carefully climbed back onboard. The deck slanted and moved beneath his feet, but the ropes he'd used to secure the vessel did their job. He steadied himself against the pilothouse bulkhead and slipped through the door.

He retrieved his backpack and opened it. The inside was damp, but the items within weren't soaking wet. His lunch was the worst. The brown bag was stained with water, and his sandwich was soggy. He pulled a sweatshirt from the pack, along with a spare magazine for the Glock, his wallet and phone.

Cannon shivered. He was wet, cold, and his stomach growled from lack of food, so he woofed down the wet sandwich, pulled on the sweatshirt, and checked his phone. It was off, so he turned it on and put it on the pilothouse seat as it powered up.

The spare magazine was wet, and Cannon flicked out the fifteen bullets with his thumbnail, checking each round and drying it on his shirt. The bullets looked fine, but the only way to know for sure was to fire the weapon, but he couldn't waste ammo, and it didn't matter anyway. It wasn't like he had another gun. He pulled the Glock 19 from its holster on his hip and replaced the clip. The gun could fire underwater, so said the manufacturer, but Cannon had never tested the weapon under such conditions.

A handheld radio sat in its cradle on the side of the command console, and Cannon grabbed it. He twisted the on switch and static burst from the small speaker. He pressed the transmit button and said, "Command, this is Constable Leonard Cannon, does anyone copy?"

Broken static, thumping sounds, then more static.

Cannon repeated his hail two more times and when he didn't get a response, he left the radio on, tuning it to the emergency channel and clipping it on his belt.

Wailing and screams of pain made Cannon pick up his pace. He padded the blue rubber gunnel. "Sorry, bud," he said, and headed for the door that led to the emergency staircase.

There was a cigarette urn next to the door, which was propped open with a stone. Cannon hesitated at the top of the stairwell to check his watch. Nineteen minutes had passed since the earthquake warning system sounded.

The stairwell was dark, and he used the handrail to guide himself down. Emergency lights lit each landing and he'd only gone down one floor when he ran into a throng of panicked people.

Century One Office Plaza was the only professional building in Gullhaven, and it held accountants, doctors, and engineers. Cannon's accountant, Barry Liberman, was in the group, along with his foot doctor, Clarissa Marluqe. When they saw him, their eyes widened like he was Santa Claus on Christmas morning.

"Oh, Lee, thank god it's you. What should we do?" Clarissa said. She stepped back and looked at him. "Are you OK?"

The crowd stopped chatting, like animals that've sensed a predator.

He looked down at himself. He was drenched, his dark blue uniform pants ripped in several spots, his badge gone. Blood dripped into his eyes, and he wiped it away with the back of his hand. "I'm fine. Got tossed around out on the bay. Don't do anything. Wait here for a bit and let me go see what's happening. It's over. Don't go back to your offices. The emergency stairwells are reinforced just for this type of situation."

"It's over?" said a blonde woman Cannon didn't know.

"There's a lot of water moving around out there still, but the worst of it is done," he said. One of the hardest parts of his job was soothing folk's angst and consoling them when they needed compassion, and he'd come to understand over the years that public service truly meant serving the public.

"How bad is it?" Doc Pepperton asked.

"Bad. Devil's Rip is blocked, and the falling rock sent a surge of water over the town. It's not pretty out there." The images of floating bodies circled in his brain like a turd going down the toilet. "Stay in here until someone comes to get you."

Nodding heads. Cannon waved down offers of help and continued down the stairwell, following the wails of pain, hand on his Glock. His nerves danced on a wire, and he couldn't get the image of what he'd seen out on the water out of his head. The tentacle thing that had gone after the shark. Was he losing his mind? He knew the brain fabricated strange things during and after trauma, but this was beyond weird.

Another scream of pain, and gurgling, like someone was breathing water… or something thicker.

Cannon reached the first-floor landing and waded into the floodwater. It was deep, and he paused when the water reached his waist. He drew his gun and held it above his head as he continued, paper and personal items drifting with the flotsam.

He stopped when the water was chest high. To continue he'd have to swim, and the memory of the tentacle and the idea of great white sharks swimming the streets made him head back up the emergency staircase.

A shrill cry, then nothing.

Cannon found a window on the west side that was feet from the building next to it. The thin service alley between the two buildings was only four feet, and Cannon broke down a door and used it as a bridge to cross to the building next door, where the screams emanated from.

He found no people. Cannon knew the building's first floor had a small reception area flanked by a bakery on one side and a nail salon on the other, and the second floor was apartments. The home he entered looked untouched, and from the pictures on a shelf above the TV, he could tell a single woman lived there.

"Meow. Meow."

Cannon jumped. A cat eased out from behind a couch, its green eyes glowing from within a mound of black fur.

Cannon headed for the door, but stopped and looked back at the cat, the memory of bodies floating in the floodwater rushing back. What if the cat's owner was dead? How would the animal eat?

He sighed and went to the kitchen. A tall cabinet pantry contained every flavor of cat food imaginable—tuna bits, salmon in water, pork and chicken stew. Some of the pictures on the cans looked better than what Cannon ate. He opened two and put them on the floor, then partially opened two more cans and put them on the counter. Then he put the stopper in the kitchen sink and turned on the tap. Nothing came out. Cannon frowned and went back to the pantry and retrieved three bottles of water which he emptied into the sink. He'd never had a cat, but he knew they were smarter than dogs and wouldn't consume every morsel of food available within five minutes of him leaving.

Cat taken care of, he exited the apartment into an orange wallpapered hallway. He found the staircase and headed down; the sound of splashing, the wet slap of meat being torn, and the crack of bones splintering echoing up the stairwell. Gun above his head, Cannon waded into the water, down the stairs and through an archway into the lobby. The water was up to his waist and filled with trash.

Floodwater broke on the reception desk in tiny waves as something thrashed and splashed behind it. Cannon waded into the floodwater, gun held out before him. A planter with a large tropical bush sat next to the reception desk and Cannon used it as cover.

A ten-foot great white shark ripped at a corpse, the beast's head thrashing as it tore away an arm. There wasn't much left of the body, but Cannon saw blonde hair and then a face. He reeled, tripped over something hidden by the floodwater, and fell headlong into the drink. The Glock went flying and hit the wall by the front door and fell beneath the cloudy water.

The splashing stopped and the *pop* and *snap* of floodwater slapping against the lobby walls filled the silence. A two-foot dorsal fin came around the reception desk and Cannon hoisted himself onto the desk. He spared a glance for where he thought his gun might be, but it was too far away, and the shark was in the way.

He stared down at what was left of Cindy Becker, a young school teacher who'd come to Gullhaven for the job. She hadn't been Joshua's teacher, but there were only two teachers for each elementary school grade, so he'd met her several times while attending events.

Her blonde hair was matted with blood and a chunk of her head was missing. Both arms and a leg had been severed, and where her clothes were torn away, there were deep bite marks.

He looked away.

The shark paced, looking up at Cannon as he stood atop the five-foot desk. He looked around for a weapon and saw a freestanding coatrack, but it was in a corner several feet away.

The shark's black eyes were unblinking, its jaws open in a smile. It had him, and it appeared to know it.

A row of shelves behind the desk contained information on the building, a couple of pictures, the alarm company sign, and an award from the chamber of commerce in the shape of a glass teardrop.

"That'll do," Cannon said to the shark.

He grabbed the award. It was heavier then it looked.

The fish wagged its caudal fin, building up speed as it circled, and breached from the floodwater, jaws flexing open.

5

Cannon threw the glass Gullhaven Chamber of Commerce award like a football. It spiraled through the air and hit the shark on the snout as it drove from the floodwater. The ten-foot white shark slammed into the desk, unfazed by the five-pound piece of glass that bounced off its face. Jaws snapped closed inches from Cannon's legs as he jumped behind the desk. Blood, fat, and strands of blonde hair floated in the water next to what was left of Cindy Becker and Cannon gagged.

The great white slid back into the water and Cannon climbed back onto the desk. The beast's dorsal came into view, the shark searching for him. Cannon leapt across the room, landing hard on his side in the floodwater. His face and arm stung, but he slogged toward the coatrack, ignoring the splashing behind him.

He went under and stroked hard, closing the ten feet between himself and the coatrack in a flurry of frantic strokes. He grasped the metal pole that made up the coat tree's core, and relief washed through him.

His Glock was underwater by the front door, but he couldn't see it with all the debris floating in the floodwater. The shark's dorsal fin came around the reception desk, its lateralis system picking up the vibrations in the water as Cannon moved.

The coatrack was an old school affair. The base of the five-foot metal pole had three legs splayed out in opposite directions, with four pins protruding from the top at odd angles. Cannon braced himself, holding the coatrack before him like a lance.

The shark was undeterred. It rose from the shallow water, dorsal fin leaving a wake, mouth opening.

Cannon waited until the beast was almost on him and thrust the makeshift spear forward, aiming for the fish's left eye. He missed, but the blow stunned the shark and it paused, shaking its head and thrashing. Cannon stabbed again and again, beating the shark with every bit of strength he had left, which wasn't much. His legs ached, his arm where the SAFE boat's pilothouse door caught him pulsed, his head pounded in rhythm with his heart, he was starving, and his mouth was dry as paper.

The great white backed off, a thin stream of blood leaking from its head where one of the pegs atop the coat tree had punctured the beast's slick gray skin. Cannon waited, breathing heavy, tiny stars sparkling across his field of vision. The floodwater was dropping. It was at Cannon's waist.

Sensing it was outmatched, and with barely enough water to swim, the fish wiggled its caudal fin and swam out through the broken front window into the flooded street. Sharks are always moving, keeping water flowing through their gills. The great white would die if it couldn't swim freely.

Cannon remembered the Glock and he searched the floodwater, reaching down into the brackish water. He couldn't find it, so he went underwater. His eyes stung when he opened them—oil, sheetrock dust, and an abundance of dirt and other contaminants clouding the water. He came up empty handed, took a deep breath and went back down.

It took four tries, but finally he found the weapon wedged between a bookshelf and a wall. He held the weapon up and examined it. It looked fine, but it had been underwater for a long time and he doubted it would fire, promises of the manufacturer notwithstanding.

Thoughts of the gun not working made his hand go to the radio clipped to his belt, but it was gone. "Dang," Cannon said. Now he had no way to communicate with the sheriff and command. Then he remembered his phone. It was in a life-proof case and could survive being in the drink. He patted his pockets, but no phone. Then he remembered he'd left it on the command chair in the SAFE boat's pilothouse.

He had to go back and get it, but first he had to do something he was dreading. The wails of pain that had led him here had stopped some time ago. He sloshed toward the reception desk, blood-red water flowing from behind it. There wasn't much left of Cindy Becker, but she deserved better than to float around with the trash.

Tall curtains were pulled back to either side of the broken plate-glass window that looked out onto the street. He tore one down and wrapped what was left of the blonde woman in it, then placed her shredded corpse atop the reception desk out of the water. At least she'd be safe from scavengers. He'd come back to collect her when he could.

Cannon headed back the way he'd come, up the stairs, and over the door that served as a bridge to Century One Office Plaza. As he climbed the steps to the roof, Cannon considered what to tell the crowd he'd find on the second-floor landing. He was covered in blood from handling Cindy's corpse, he'd learned nothing, and had no plan, so he decided to say as little as possible.

"Oh, my," said Clarissa when he arrived at the landing. Everyone turned, chatter ceased, and there were several gasps.

"I'm fine. It's OK. Just heading back to the roof to get my cell phone," Cannon said. He didn't stop walking as he moved through the small crowd.

"But what… what… happened?" said a young man who couldn't stop biting his nails long enough to spit out three words.

"That screaming you heard? Not good," Cannon said.

Silence.

When he got to the roof nothing had changed other than it appeared the water had gone down significantly. The streets were still flooded, but no longer ran with whitewater. The Warf and eastern edge of town were still underwater, but things looked better than they had a few minutes ago.

Cannon glanced down at his watch. 2:54PM. Thirty-five minutes since the earthquake warning.

He retrieved his phone, and as feared, it had zero bars. Cell coverage in Gullhaven wasn't great—there was one tower on the western face of the mountains, but clearly it was down. He had no way to get in touch with the sheriff or Nel.

With nothing left to do on the roof, he went back down to the crowd on the second-floor landing. "We're screwed," he told the crowd as he arrived.

Nobody said anything. They just stared at him. This was his job, to know what to do when nobody else did.

"There's no cell signal and I lost my radio. I've got no way to contact the sheriff, so perhaps it's best if we all just hunker down here and—"

"You need a two way?" said an older man from the back of the group. The frail olive-skinned man shuffled forward, and Cannon recognized him, but didn't know his name. He was the building janitor/handyman. Cannon had seen him in Gloria's Pub, though they'd never spoken.

"Yeah. You have one?"

"Sure. Doubt you'll be able to get the sheriff on it, though. The repeater is probably down," the man said.

"Most handhelds can go radio to radio, especially on the emergency channel," Cannon said. "What's your name?"

"Denson, Roberto Denson."

"Well, Roberto, you might have just saved us from sitting in this stairwell overnight. Can you get the radio?"

"It's on the charger in my office. I need it for fire drills. Haven't used it in months, but it should be charged. I'll go get it."

Cannon nodded, and silence fell as everyone waited.

The sounds of rushing water and commotion had died away, and an eerie silence had settled over Gullhaven. What was there to say? They were alive, and these folks hadn't seen the devastation, and didn't fully understand how screwed the valley was.

"Maybe we need some fresh air," said Doc Pepperton. "Clear our heads."

Cannon shot him a harsh look. What was the man thinking? Yeah, fresh air would do their worried psyches some good, but what would seeing the destruction do? He decided they'd have to face it soon, and who the hell was he to tell them what to do anyway? He was the bay constable, not the mayor.

"Sure. Go up to the roof if you want. Just stay away from the boat and prepare yourselves. It's not pretty out there. I'll wait for Roberto," Cannon said. As he spoke, he realized being away from the group when he called the sheriff was a good thing. Now he could have a semi-private conversation if he managed to reach her.

The crowd shuffled up the stairs and disappeared around the switchback landing between the second and third floors. Cannon was alone with his thoughts, and as usual they tormented him. His mind conjured images of Nel and Joshua in peril, fighting for their lives and screaming for his help, but he wasn't there. They were alone. He had to find them.

Roberto returned with the radio. "Here you go. It's on channel four."

Cannon and Roberto headed to the roof where they found the crowd gazing out over the parapet wall at the destruction below. Roberto joined the group and Cannon hid behind the SAFE boat as he switched the radio to the emergency channel and hailed the sheriff. Nothing. He tried several times but got no response. Exactly what Roberto had feared. With no repeater, the signal wasn't str—

"Lee, is that you?" The voice of Sheriff Tanya Locke boomed over the radio, static filling the background.

"10-4, sheriff, I'm here with a group of people on the roof of Century One Plaza."

"How the hell did you get up there?"

"Long story... well, short story really, but my boat is up here, and I'll leave it at that."

She chuckled. Her smoky voice softened, "Well, I'm glad you're OK."

"Thanks," he said. "You too. What are we looking at?"

"It's bad. Devil's Rip looks blocked, as you know, CR19 is covered in boulders, and Gullhaven's been put through the ringer. Comm is down, so I have no idea what the situation is in the rest of the state. It looks like we're on our own for now."

"What's the plan?"

Sheriff Locke sighed. "I haven't found the mayor yet, but I'm setting up a triage and evacuation center in the high school. Thankfully it didn't take any major damage in the quake and is still structurally sound according to the fire crews. It's above the flood line and has an emergency generator. I'm going to set up a command center there."

"What of the station?"

"City Hall and the Sheriff's Office is..." Silence. "No longer functional." Cannon heard tears behind the sheriff's voice and that worried him more than anything else. Tanya was a tough bird and she didn't get rattled.

"How can I help?"

"Trevor Krisp is picking people up in his boat and bringing them to the high school. I'll send him your way, but there are emergencies and trapped people all over town. Ask the folks at Plaza if they can stay there a few more hours until we get things under control."

"They can. Oh, and..." Cannon couldn't find the words.

"What is it, Lee?"

"I interrupted a shark attack in town here. Great whites are swimming in the streets, and I saw..."

"What?"

"Cindy Becker's corpse is wrapped in a curtain on the reception desk in the lobby of the apartment building next door."

"The one next to the bakery?"

"Yeah."

"Very sorry to hear that, but based on what I've seen, we're in for more bad news on that front."

Cannon didn't tell her about the bodies floating in the streets. They were dead and what they all needed to do now was to concern themselves with the living. There would be plenty of time to mourn.

Tiny mouse feet scurried up Cannon's back and the ice cube in his stomach became a block. The sheriff was right. Whatever the death toll was it would forever shape Gullhaven. He thought of Nel and Joshua again. The smell of Nel's hair, the way Joshua looked at him like he was God. He loved them both, Joshua like a son, and Nel... He didn't know exactly how he felt about Nel. He knew he loved her, but Sherri's ghost always rested on his shoulder, reminding him that she'd been his first love.

"See you soon, Cannon out."

It was 3:09PM.

6

Century One Office Plaza was on the east side of town, and as Cannon headed down the stairs, he found the water had receded to only a few inches. With Roberto in tow he sloshed across the lobby and out the thick glass door. In the distance the sound of an outboard echoed off the buildings and rose like a buzz saw.

"Damn," Roberto said.

Trash, seaweed, overturned cars, broken lampposts, clothing, silt and sand covered the streets, and in some places eddies in the floodwater had created sand spits around corners and turns in the road. The air smelled fresh and salty, with an undercurrent of rotten eggs.

"Yeah," Cannon said.

Several buildings had significant damage, but most structures still stood. As Cannon stared, he envisioned what the street had looked like just that morning. He also saw what it would look like after everything was fixed. He felt confident Gullhaven would spring back, even if it took several years.

"We should walk up the road a clip. Trevor won't be able to get up here anymore with the boat," Cannon said.

Roberto's eyes narrowed, and his lips formed a tight red line.

Trevor Krisp was an unpopular man. He was a rich real estate developer from San Francisco who had a second home in Gullhaven, and he cruised up the coast on his fifty-foot sailboat on the weekends. Cannon figured he'd been on an extended vacation, it being Tuesday. Krisp was part of a community of non-locals who called Gullhaven their second home, and while many people hated the presence of the outsiders, nobody could argue with the money they brought to the valley. Without them, Gullhaven would lose a large chunk of its economy.

Cannon said, "Looks like the folks upstairs can walk up to the high school."

"Seems so. You want me to go tell them?" The man's eyes shifted to the west toward the wharf and flooded portion of town, and he shifted his weight and looked down at his feet.

"Yeah," Cannon said. "You do that. Lead them up to the high school. You can handle that, right?"

"Sure thing, Mr. Cannon."

"Cannon is fine, or Lee."

Roberto nodded. "You stay safe now, you hear?"

Cannon saluted and said, "I'll see you later."

"10-4."

Cannon walked up the street and he'd only gone three blocks before he reached deeper water. Tiny waves rolled across the road and lapped against buildings. He saw Krisp waiting two blocks up. He trudged through the deepening water, his legs protesting each step. He needed food, water, and rest, but he wouldn't stop until he found Nel. Regardless of what Krisp thought they were doing, priority one was finding Nel and Joshua.

"Yo," Krisp yelled.

Cannon sighed. The man wore cream colored khaki slacks and a blue dress shirt with the collar open, a red sweater tied around his neck. The standard uniform for assholes worldwide.

"Hey," Cannon said. He reached the boat and leaned on the bow.

"You look like shit," Krisp said. He tossed Cannon a towel.

"Then I look how I feel," Cannon said. He climbed onto the boat and dropped onto the bench seat before the command console.

Krisp's boat was a nineteen-foot Boston Whaler with a ninety horsepower Johnson. Boom arm clips were attached along the gunnel so the tender could be lifted and placed on a sailboat's deck. Across the transom in black letters, the name "Spare Change" was stenciled.

Bile rose in Cannon's throat.

"Tanya said to come get you and bring you to her, but the water has receded. You still need me? You can probably walk t—"

"Yeah, I need you. You got someplace to be?"

The man's head jerked back like he'd been slapped. "Excuse me?"

"I need you to take me to the wharf. I…" Cannon realized he didn't want to tell the man they were going looking for his girlfriend, but he hadn't prepared a lie, so he made one up quick. "Sheriff wants me to take a look. Survey the damage."

"Funny, she didn't mention anything to me," Krisp said.

"Last time I checked, you weren't a law officer."

Krisp chuckled, but said nothing.

Cannon knew what the man was thinking: neither are you. The part-time residents didn't fully understand what Cannon did. They saw him as the guy who chased them and told them to slow down in the inlet, or the pest who wrote tickets for taking undersized striped bass. In reality, he had similar authority to the sheriff, but technically not on land. Tanya treated him like a deputy, and everyone in town knew it.

Krisp nudged the boat into drive and the Johnson buzzed and popped as the Whaler slid through the shallow water. When they reached the wood archway above the road that read Dingmans Wharf, the water was eight-feet deep and it didn't look to be receding.

"Looks deep here still," Cannon said.

Krisp scanned his depth finder. "It's been at this depth for the last twenty minutes or so."

The harbor was a mess. Boats sat piled like children's toys, and the floodwater got deeper as Spare Change eased through the brackish water toward Blackwater Bay.

Nel had been scheduled to be at the elementary school in the morning, but would've been done by 10AM. Knowing Nel as he did, he figured she'd taken Joshua out to brunch at Monkey's Play Palace for pancakes, then maybe played some games and went on a few rides before returning home. So that placed her back at her apartment by noonish. She lived on a second floor in an old house that had been built back when things were done right. All these thoughts didn't ease his worry. That wouldn't happen until he hugged Joshua and kissed Nel.

Her apartment was on the north side of town, a couple of streets back from the bay. The streets there were sure to be flooded. "Take us out into the bay and head north toward Razor Point."

"What for? I've been over there. Same as here. Shouldn't we head back to the sheriff? Start helping rescue people trapped by the flood?"

The man had a point. People were trapped in buildings all over town, and his job was helping them, but wasn't Nel a citizen of this town? Didn't she deserve to be rescued like everyone else? He knew that was thin shit, but he didn't care. "That's what we're doing."

Krisp nodded, pushed down on the throttle, and the Whaler cut through the water, weaving in and out of sunken boats, debris, and patches of kelp and seaweed churned up from the bay bottom.

Razor Point was named such because the sand spit, which extended out into Blackwater Bay five hundred yards, resembled the old school shaving blades used by barbers. Krisp slowed the boat and brought it to a stop as he scanned his depth finder. "We're over the spit now," Krisp said.

Cannon looked over the side and sure enough he saw the sandbar fourteen feet below the surface. He lifted his gaze toward the shore, looking for the corner of Nel's building. Sometimes on night patrol he'd beach the SAFE boat and setup a folding chair on the sand when the tide was out. He'd sit there for hours, staring at the small rectangle of light that marked Nel's kitchen until it went dark for the night. It was his way of looking out for her. Like Batman, except without the money, costume, and cool gadgets. So not really like Batman at all, more like Patheticman.

"Where to now?" Krisp said.

"Head over there." Cannon pointed at a group of buildings that surrounded the house Nel lived in.

Krisp stared at him, but said nothing as he slipped the Whaler into gear. Once over the sandbar the water got deep. Blackwater Bay was over a thousand feet deep in spots, and there were trenches and crevasses on the bay bottom, but a complete survey had never been completed.

The motors whined as Krisp brought the boat up to speed, but he didn't bring it up on plane. Wood, pieces of boats, even a car floated in the bay, and Krisp was careful as he picked his way through the flotsam.

"WTF?" Krisp said.

"What?" Cannon said. He looked around but saw nothing unusual.

"Something big down there," Krisp said.

Cannon got up, went around the console and stood over Krisp's shoulder.

The SONAR screen showed dark lines marking the bottom, with yellow and white splotches representing creatures and other debris. Off to port, a large blob rose from the bay bottom, moving slowly east toward the Whaler.

Cannon said nothing. His stomach was trying to climb up his throat, and his lower back throbbed with pain as it always did when adrenaline flowed. Should he tell Krisp he'd seen something like this before? He hadn't told anyone what he'd seen in Devil's Rip for fear of people not believing him, yet here the thing was again.

"What do you make of that?" Cannon said.

Krisp's eyes narrowed. "No idea," he said, very slowly. He turned the wheel and the Whaler arced to starboard toward the mystery.

"What are you doing?" Cannon asked.

"I'm gonna check this thing out."

"No you're not. Get back on course. We've got people who need our help. We don't have time right now to chase imaginary sea monsters," Cannon said.

Krisp looked at him, defiance carved on his tanned face. His eyes burned, and he didn't adjust the throttle control.

Cannon knew rich dudes like Krisp didn't like being told what to do, so he softened his tone. "Look, I want to see what the thing is too, but we've got more import—"

A serpentine white tentacle shot from the water and just missed the boat. Its white skin glistened, suction cups filled with teeth puckering and searching.

"Whoa," Krisp said. He spun the wheel to avoid the tentacle as it fell back into the bay.

Another tentacle shot from the water and hung over the boat. The Whaler raced on, and the arm came down and crashed behind Spare Change as it arced toward shore. The center console rocked and listed, and Krisp pressed the throttle arm all the way down. The Johnson dug in and the Whaler listed further, and Cannon braced himself against the gunnel.

Krisp clung to the steering wheel, feet sliding out from under him. The boat was jolted from below and Krisp was tossed overboard, disappearing beneath the whitewater of the Whaler's dirty foam wake.

Cannon dove for the throttle, pulled it back and it snapped into neutral. The boat rocked as its wake slammed into the transom. Cannon searched the sea but couldn't find Krisp. Everything was quiet for a heartbeat and then Krisp's head poked above the surface.

"Over here! Here!" Krisp yelled.

Cannon looked at the fish finder. The massive blob moved away from the Whaler toward Krisp. The scent of bleach spread over the water like sewage.

Krisp was making so much noise. If he would just shut up and stop splashing.

Two tentacles sprang from Blackwater Bay.

Cannon spun the wheel, turned the Whaler around, and brought the boat up to speed. He put the nose of the vessel on the tentacles and drew down, sighting the serpentine legs.

The Whaler skipped over the water, the Glock's barrel shaking and moving in small circles as Cannon tried to sight the tentacles. He was afraid he'd hit Krisp if he missed, but the tentacles were almost on the man and the Whaler wasn't fast enough.

He fired.

Click.

He pulled the trigger again.

Click.

The third time a bullet spit from the gun and threw-up a tiny water spout when it hit the surface.

One of the tentacles wrapped around Krisp and the man screamed as he was crushed. The snake-like appendage lifted him from the water, twisting his body as it hung in the air, and plunged him back into the sea.

Cannon yelled and called, but Krisp didn't come up.

Cannon searched, but there was no sign of the man, so there was nothing to do except flee the area, and that's what Cannon did.

He'd seen two people die since this nightmare began and it was only 4:06PM.

7

It had fed, but the tiny odd creature hadn't satisfied its hunger. A deep hollow pain consumed the beast, and it continued its hunt. It had never consumed human flesh and blood, but the creature felt new energy coursing through it as it drew seawater into its mantle, jetting it out through the siphon in its torso. The beast surged through the bay, pushing waves before it and leaving a wake.

Its senses were swamped with new impulses; live prey, dead prey... strange sounds and shadows. Things floated in the water, and it detected more of the unusual creatures. It burned with energy and life, its new surroundings bringing with it the fading dark images of its past. There was more prey in the light, but even as its instincts made this primordial connection, a horrible metallic whine vibrated through the water.

One of the creatures was on the move above.

It swam up, searching for the rumble and screeching, but found nothing but a trail of whitewater and the peculiar smell that told the creature his new prey was near. Because the prey was unfamiliar, instinct told it to retreat to the darkness, hide within the cracks and catch unsuspecting sea life, but all its senses tingled, its tentacles flared, heat and hunger burning through the leviathan. It was a hunter, and it would feed. There was too much fresh prey. Too much of the new blood that nourished it, but made it lust for more.

More... Always more...

Its large eyes still adjusted to the light as it detected fish and other sea life streaming around it. The beast ignored them. Why sift through the sea when better prey was available? Hunger tugged at the beast, as it always did, its last meal already forgotten.

It was agitated, realizing there was a bounty of prey above, but also danger. The creature pulled in water and expelled it, driving itself through the sea. It moved within tall green kelp-like plants that swayed back-and-forth, brushing against its white skin as it drew in the water it needed to breathe. The fear of danger retreated as it floated within the forest of green, waiting for new prey to feed its growing hunger.

8

Cannon struggled to control his angst, the memory of Krisp's death planted firmly in his frontal lobe and a vague unease gnawing at him as if the leviathan in the bay was watching him. He brought the Whaler down to a crawl, and the Johnson sputtered and popped and almost stalled. He passed Kensington's Warehouse, large pieces of its aluminum walls torn away, opening it to the floodwater. A corpse floated in the flotsam, and thankfully Cannon didn't recognize the person. He considered fishing the body out, then decided against it. For the next few hours he needed to think about the living. About Nel and her son. They were all that mattered.

The old house's porch was underwater, but the second story looked undisturbed. If Nel had been home, she and Joshua should be OK. Everything would be alright. All he needed to do was keep telling himself that, but part of him, the cop part, knew he was bullshitting himself. Until he saw Nel and Joshua alive, the worm in his stomach wouldn't stop wiggling.

He dropped the boat in neutral and went to the bow. The boat bumped against the porch railing and came to a stop. The water was clear, and he saw white paint peeling from the deck boards below. Several of the first story windows were broken, and water flowed freely through them.

"Nel? Nel? Joshua? You here?" he yelled.

Nothing. The wind whistled, and water lapped against the house.

Not good. His stomach sank. She wasn't here, or worse.

He had to search the house and make sure, so he leaned into the floodwater and tied the Whaler off on the railing. The whine of the hydraulics echoed over the water as he brought up the motor. Cannon swung his legs over the gunnel and balanced himself on the porch railing a foot below the surface, using the gutter above as a handhold. He inched his way to a corner where a column supported the porch roof. He climbed, struggling, legs wrapped around the pole. It was only six feet, but it was the hardest climb of Cannon's life. The pole was slick with moisture, and it took him several tries before he was able to pull himself onto the roof, scratching his belly on the coarse roof shingles.

He lay there, panting. Maybe he'd never get up? Just go to sleep. His hand fell to his Glock. If he found Nel or Joshua, or...

The front bedroom window was broken, shards of glass protruding from the wooden frame like teeth. He pulled his Glock and used it to break out the rest of the window. He kept his weapon out as he entered Nel's apartment.

Her bedroom was dark, the red glow of an unseen battery powered device sending daggers of red light across the room.

"Nel? Joshua?"

The house creaked.

Cannon froze, and his brain started working through scenarios, but none of them were good. If it was Nel or Joshua, why wouldn't they answer him? Then he realized he'd assumed Nel and Joshua would recognize his voice and he hadn't announced himself. Recent events would have her on edge, and everyone had seen enough disaster movies to know not everyone acted ethically during emergencies.

"Nel, it's Lee. We had chicken for dinner last night. Teriyaki, the way I like it."

Footsteps in the hallway.

Cannon put his back to the wall, gun in both hands, weapon pointed at the ceiling over his right shoulder.

The door pushed open, hiding him behind it.

"Lee?" The voice was feeble and small and Cannon recognized it immediately.

"Joshua!" Cannon leapt from behind the door and gathered the boy in his arms.

The boy was skin and bones, but he hugged Cannon so hard he knew something else was wrong. "Where's your ma?"

The boy looked at the floor and cried, deep sobs that made Cannon put his arm around the boy.

"What is it? What happened?"

The boy cried, but said nothing.

"Joshua." He took the boy's shoulders and turned him so he could look into his eyes. "Where's your mom?"

"I... don't.... know."

"What do you mean? She left you here alone?"

The boy shook his head no.

"What then?"

The kid shook like he'd seen a ghost.

"Come on. Let me get you something to drink so you can calm down and tell me what happened. Sound good?"

"O... OK," the boy said.

They went to the apartment's kitchen where Cannon retrieved a soda and sat the boy at the kitchen table Cannon had bought as a house warming present when Nel moved in. The child took several sips and put the can on the table. Cannon waited, his stomach a firepit, his hands shaking with nerves, worry, and weariness.

The boy stopped weeping and looked up at Cannon, who smiled. "You want to tell me what happened?"

Joshua nodded. "We were coming home from Monkey's, I got pancakes with chocolate chips and maple syrup."

"OK, then," Cannon said.

"We were coming up the street when the fire whistle blew, but we didn't know what was going on. So we just walked. Then the ground shook, and bricks started to fall from buildings, and I saw..." The boy broke down into a crying jag.

Cannon waited.

"A brick landed on a lady's head. Then the water came. We were almost home, and we were running... you know, I was afraid, but ma said everything would be OK once we got home." The boy stopped there, like it was too painful to go on.

Cannon put his arm around the kid and pulled him in. "It's alright. Everything will be OK. What else?"

Joshua wiped his eyes with his sleeve. "We were going up the porch steps and... and... we heard it coming."

"What?"

"The water. It was loud and scary, and we stopped and looked back. Just for a second. All we saw was white and mom screamed, and I was so scared."

"You're safe now," Cannon coaxed. His hands trembled, and his legs shook. "What happened next?"

"I... I don't know," the boy said. He cried again.

Cannon said, "Don't know? When was the last time you saw her?"

"The sound of the water... I was so scared. Mom jumped on the porch railing, and next thing I knew I was on the porch roof and everything below was filled with water."

"And your mom?"

"She was gone." The boy's head fell to the table and he wept.

Cannon dropped into a seat next to him and let his head fall in his hands. The surge of water that had rolled over Blackwater Bay had killed many. He'd seen the corpses in the streets, but that didn't mean Nel was dead. He had to keep telling himself it was possible she was alive. For Joshua's sake, if nothing else.

"Listen," Cannon said.

The boy lifted his head, hope and despair fighting for control of his face.

"We'll find her. You and I. She's a good swimmer and she's probably fine and waiting for use at the evacuation center."

The child's face brightened. "You think so?"

"I do," Cannon lied. On some level he knew lying to the boy might make things worse down the road, but was it a lie? For all Cannon knew, Nel was alive and waiting for them. Stanger things had happened in the last hour. "You ready to go find her?"

Joshua nodded and took a long pull on his soda.

It was 4:27PM, and sunset was around 8:30PM, which meant he only had three-and-a-half hours of daylight left. Navigating the floodwaters in the dark would be a fool's business.

Cannon held the boy's hand as they climbed out the broken window onto the porch roof and down into the boat. Joshua looked much better sitting on the bench in front of the control console. He'd stopped weeping, and he looked around eagerly, his tiny brown eyes shifting back and forth as he searched.

What if they found Nel dead in the water? Did he want Joshua to see that? The boy was only four and seeing his mother's corpse floating with the garbage could harm him in irreparable ways.

"You know what?" Cannon turned the wheel and made a right down Tipper Avenue because he thought he saw something floating in the road ahead. "I know a shortcut."

The boy turned to look at Cannon through the plexiglass spray-shield mounted on the center console.

The road narrowed ahead. It was one of several sections in Gullhaven that displayed a lack of city planning. Two sections of development came together, but each road had been off by a few feet so when they met, the road narrowed three feet and the buildings were set closer together.

"You really think my mom is OK, or are you treating me like a little kid?" the boy said, hope filling his voice.

"She might have been rescued already, buddy. She could be worried about you and waiting at the school."

The child looked confused.

"That's where everyone is going until we get stuff fixed."

The boy nodded and went back to searching the floodwater.

Sunlight peeked through the cloud cover and the wind lightened. It was cool for June in northern California, and Cannon breathed deep, trying to ease his nerves and beat back the angst that was crushing him and making his chest hurt.

The current picked up as the road narrowed and Cannon pressed down on the throttle and the Johnson whined. Buildings loomed on both sides of the road, and tiny rapids rolled over parking meters and cars. A thin waterfall cascaded into the street from the front window of a hamburger joint to the east, and Cannon steered the boat away from it.

The floodwater hadn't gone down much in the last half an hour, and Cannon gazed over his shoulder, but his view of Blackwater Bay was blocked by buildings. Pain lanced Cannon's back, and the bruise on his arm pulsed. He needed food and knew he should have searched Nel's kitchen, but it was too late. He had to get Joshua to the evacuation center, so he could search for Nel.

More rapids bubbled in the floodwater as the current picked up and the Whaler slid through a narrow gap between a building and a pile of rubble. The current grabbed the boat like a leaf on the stream, and the eddy pushed the Whaler to port and Cannon's hand slipped off the wheel. The boat jerked and rubbed along the brick façade of T's Dry Cleaners. The crunch of fiberglass made Cannon cringe. Red bricks fell, slapping the water and pounding the Whaler's deck.

Cannon brought the boat back to starboard, but overcompensated, and the nineteen-foot center console bounced off a submerged car and rammed the building across the street, Jody's Diner. The front glass window shattered, and Joshua dove out of the way to avoid the glass and fell in the water.

Cannon slammed the boat into neutral and jumped into the floodwater. He searched the water, his unease growing when the boy didn't surface. Then he remembered the child couldn't swim. Cannon went under, but there was so much debris, and the falling bricks and breaking glass had disturbed the silt and sand on the road below and clouded the floodwater.

He swam around, feeling with his hands, panic rising in him. Cannon's hand touched fabric and he grasped it and surfaced. He dragged a lifeless Joshua from the water and lifted him over the Whaler's gunnel onto the deck.

The boy's chest didn't rise and fall.

9

The last hour and eight minutes had turned Cannon's world upside-down. He stood in the floodwater next to the Whaler, staring at Joshua's lifeless body, fear paralyzing him. This was his fault. Then he heard Nel's soothing voice through the static that threatened to drive him mad. "Deep breaths, then bring him back." The words were so matter-of-fact Cannon shook his head, the haze of fear and worry lifting like fog.

He vaulted over the gunnel and knelt next to Joshua. He bitched every year about having to spend a half day in the hospital getting recertified for CPR, but as Cannon tilted the boy's head back and held his nose, he made a mental note to send nurse Kathy a dozen red roses.

Cannon breathed in the boy's mouth, counting and spacing his breaths. Then he moved to Joshua's chest and started pumping. He recalled Nurse Kathy telling him with children you had to be easy, not press as hard. Their ribcages are soft and developing, and there were many cases of CPR doing more damage than good when it came to children.

"Come on," Cannon coaxed as he pressed on the boy's chest.

A minute passed.

Joshua still wasn't breathing.

Cannon picked-up the pace, blowing stronger breaths, pushing on the boy's chest a bit harder.

Nothing.

Cold perspiration dripped down Cannon's back. It was happening again.

He breathed, then pumped. Breathed and pumped.

Panic rose in him as it had the day Sherri died. She'd been his only love. The person he'd planned to spend the rest of his life with, only to lose her like he was losing Joshua. He'd pounded on her chest as well, breathed into her mouth, but it had done no good.

"Come on, Joshua. Breathe goddamn it!" He pressed harder on the boy's chest.

Sherri and Cannon had been at the river, swimming and messing around when he saw the rope hanging from a tree over the water. He'd dared her to swing on it and jump in the river. Made fun of her. Told her she was a wimp, and when she'd climbed the river's embankment he'd laughed, never expecting that his life would be destroyed within the next minute.

Another minute had passed, and terror filled Cannon as he performed CPR. Just like he had on Sherri.

The rope had snapped, and she'd plummeted thirty feet to the river's edge where she'd landed hard and didn't get up. She never got up. Nel was the first women he'd dated since that day twenty-one years ago.

Tears leaked down Cannon's cheeks, Joshua staring up at him with glazed eyes.

Rage welled in him, a white-hot anger that scorched his mind and drove out all rational thought. He beat on Joshua's chest, pounded on the kid like he was a side of beef. Then he was blowing air in his mouth.

Nothing.

"Come on you little shit!" Cannon yelled. He pounded the boy's chest and slapped his face. "Come on!"

Water spit from Joshua's mouth and he coughed.

Cannon laughed, a wild unhinged bellow that made the boy look up at him with worry.

Cannon turned the boy on his side and he spit-up seawater, his chest heaving, muscles trembling.

"Are you alright?" Cannon asked.

The boy nodded as he caught his breath.

Cannon leaned back against the gunnel, stars filling his vision, pain cramping his neck and lower back. "Holy shit. Holy shit."

Joshua put his small hand on Cannon's knee. "It's OK. I'm fine. We don't need to tell mom."

Cannon threw his arms around the boy and pulled him in, laughing.

"Ouch," Joshua said.

"What is it?"

"My chest hurts."

"Yeah, you're gonna have some bruising. I had to hit you pretty hard. You were almost…"

The boy looked at him and nodded.

Cannon asked the boy several questions, and he answered them all correctly. He was worried about lasting brain damage, but the child seemed fine. Tough little sidewalk weed.

"Let's head to base and get you checked out," Cannon said. He got to his feet and swayed, dizziness overtaking him as the Whaler rocked in the floodwater. He sat on the gunnel and closed his eyes, taking deep breaths.

"You OK?"

"Yes, Joshua, I'm fine." He tussled the boy's hair and went to the command console.

During the commotion the Whaler had drifted into a gap and wedged itself between two buildings. "Joshua, take a seat so I can get moving."

The boy climbed onto the bench in front of the command console.

"Cross your fingers," Cannon said. He turned the ignition key and spun the Johnson's flywheel. Metal rubbed on metal as the motor coughed to life. Cannon inched up the throttle control, but didn't put the boat in gear. The motor popped and wheezed, then steadied out. He put the boat in reverse, twisted the wheel hard to port and fiberglass scraped and cracked as the boat came free. The bilge pump didn't come on.

He made a left on Arbor Road and the water got deeper and the current stronger. Seawater still ran in the streets on the west end of Gullhaven, and it didn't look like the floodwater had gone down in the last hour.

A gray two-foot dorsal fin slid by on the starboard side, but the shark paid them no attention and disappeared around a corner. Cannon and Joshua looked at each other, the boy's eyes wide as quarters.

"It's alright. We're safe." Cannon padded his Glock in its holster. The boy didn't need to know the gun might not fire.

"Did you know there are snakes in Devil's Rip?" the boy said.

Cannon stared at him. "What do you mean?" The boy had made the statement without provocation.

"I had a dream... at least, I think it was a dream, when I was uncontacted," Joshua said.

Cannon contained a chuckle. "You mean when you were unconscious?"

"Yes."

Cannon said nothing. The sound of rippling water, the pop and crack of tiny waves breaking on buildings, and the faint screech of a seagull filled the silence.

"And what did you dream?"

Joshua put his fingers in his mouth and looked at the deck, rocking back and forth.

"You can tell me. Go ahead."

The boy looked up at Cannon with wide eyes that just about stopped his heart. "You and I were fishin'. That spot you like by the big rock?"

"Gibraltar east. Yeah. I love sitting up there."

"We were pulling out fish like we never have, but we had to stop." The boy looked troubled.

"Stop. Why?"

"Because of the big snakes."

"There are no big snakes in our waters." Cannon's hands trembled.

"These were big snakes. White and pink. And there were a bunch of them."

"What were they doing?"

Joshua looked at the deck. "They were trying to get us. One wrapped around your boat, and… and…"

"What?"

"It pulled you under. Somehow I ended up watching from the big rock. You know how weird dreams can be. One minute I was standing next to you on your patrol boat, then I'm up on the rock."

"What happened to me?"

The boy said nothing.

This was too weird. Cannon hadn't told anyone what he'd seen in Devil's Rip, and he hadn't had a chance to tell anyone what happened to Krisp. There was no way the boy could know what was out there. The dream twisted and burrowed into him like a disease, but he had to let it go. It was a coincidence, nothing more. Or maybe he'd said something the boy picked up on?

The outboard churned through the floodwater and Joshua was spared the sight of floating bodies. Cannon turned onto Main Street and headed for the school. The water got shallow and he was forced to turn off Main Street and work his way along low-lying backroads until he ran out of water.

"End of the road," Cannon said. The sound of hydraulics echoed off the buildings as Cannon brought up the motor and tied the boat off on a parking meter. He lifted Joshua from the boat and carried him the last fifty feet to the flood line where water lapped on blacktop.

The school was still a mile away, perched on a lower ledge of the eastern mountains surrounded by green grass and trees. They came across people as they walked. Most were dazed and wandering about confused. After a couple of blocks, Cannon had collected a crowd behind him like the pied piper. He knew a couple of them from out on the bay, but not well. The group was content to follow him after he explained where he was heading.

"Can't wait to see my mom," Joshua said.

Cannon's stomach sank as he remembered the lies he'd told. Like all falsehoods, his were about to come home to roost, and as he looked down at the boy, he struggled to smile. He told himself again it was possible. Nel might be there just like he said, but if she wasn't, he didn't know what he was going to do. He'd be needed on rescue teams, but he couldn't leave the boy alone. Cannon took Joshua's hand and squeezed it.

The high school was a two-story brick structure built in 1943, back when they did things right. The horseshoe shaped building had a long driveway that wound up the hill the school sat on and ended in a large parking lot that Cannon had never seen full. Though he had no kids, he knew the place well. The high school served multiple functions, and he'd been there many times, even before he started attending Joshua's events with Nel.

A crowd milled in the parking lot. A car beeped behind them, and Cannon and his throng got off the road and cut across the grass up to the school. Flies and cyclones of gnats filled the air, unaware that the valley had just been punched in the jaw.

Deputy Sheriff Terrance Day spotted Cannon and came to greet him. "Lee, all good?"

"We're alive." Cannon winced, remembering the bodies that still floated in the floodwaters. "Sorry, I didn't mean it like that."

"I know what you meant. Don't sweat it. We've all been through a lot."

Cannon nodded but said nothing. He didn't mind the distraction because it was delaying going up to the school and breaking Joshua's heart.

"That your boat on top of the Plaza?"

"Maybe."

"Dang. You're one lucky bastard, Cannon."

"Says who?"

Deputy Sheriff Day chuckled. "Not me. Look. Get up there. The sheriff's putting rescue teams together. There are people trapped everywhere."

"10-4," Cannon said.

"See you tonight. Looks like we're gonna be sleeping in the school for the foreseeable future."

"Yup."

Day turned to walk away, and Joshua said, "Sir? Have you seen my mother?"

Day's eyes shifted to Cannon, who said nothing.

"Haven't seen her, buddy. She tell you she'd be here?"

"Lee said she's probably here waiting for me," the boy said. His innocence made Cannon's stomach hurt.

"Yeah," Day said, understanding washing across his face. "I'm sure she's up in the school."

Cannon nodded to Day and he and Joshua continued up the hill, brushing away flies as they went.

Dorothy Ann Toll High School was etched in stone above the school's main entrance. The large wood double doors stood open like the gates to Rivendell and Cannon smelled the aroma of food and heard the murmur of people. It was like coming home, and that idea settled into the front of Cannon's brain as an unlikely person joined them.

10

"Mom!" Joshua was a blur as he threw himself at his mother who braced herself and caught the boy in her arms. Nel hugged him tight and lifted her head to look at Cannon. She mouthed "thank you" and he nodded and smiled.

The pain in Cannon's chest eased and he breathed freely for the first time in over an hour. His knees grew weak and he sat on the concrete bench in the garden around the flagpole. Head in hands he closed his eyes, letting the cool breeze sooth his nerves. His hands trembled less, the nail in his head had reduced to a tac, and he no longer felt the chilling nausea in his stomach. The worst was over.

"Cannon?" It was Nel, and at the sound of her voice he looked up. Joshua and Nel stood before him, both wearing masks of concern. "Are you alright?"

He stood and took Nel in his arms. "I am now."

"You gonna tell mom what happened?" Joshua said.

"Thought that was going to be our secret, buddy?" Cannon looked at Nel and smiled.

The boy shifted on his feet and put his hand in his mouth.

"Get your hand out of your mouth." Words spoken by every mother a thousand times since the beginning of time.

Cannon winked at Nel. "Why don't you tell her?"

Joshua did, in amazing detail. Nel's smile fled halfway through the story and the glances she fired Cannon's way were less than loving, but when Joshua got to the ending, she hugged him again.

"Does your chest still hurt?" she said.

"A little. Lee said Doc should check me out."

Nel wagged her head. "Yes, Doctor Pepperton just got here. He can take a look."

"Oh, good," Cannon said. "I saw him and some others when I... landed on the Plaza."

She laughed. "Landed on the Plaza?"

"How did you get here? We were worried," Cannon said, changing the subject.

"Got sucked under and clung to an awning until I was picked up. They checked the house, but I guess you'd already gotten Joshua. Let's go sit."

"Later. I've got more work to do before the sun goes down."

Nel said, "You look exhausted. Have you eaten?"

He shook his head.

"Let me get you some food."

"Don't worry about me. I'll grab something. Take care of Joshua," Cannon said. "I'll hook up with you later. I've got to see the sheriff. You and the boy get settled in. Save me a spot in the gym."

She leaned in and kissed him.

He entered the school through the front entrance and met Deputy Sheriff Day again. "Yo, where's she at?"

"Room 119. She's commandeered a media classroom and set up base," Day said.

"10-4."

"Hey, Cannon," Day said.

"Yeah?"

"The mayor is in there with her."

Cannon sighed. "Great. Thanks for the heads-up."

"I meant to ask you before. Isn't that Krisp's tender you came in on?"

Cannon had almost forgotten about Krisp. He needed to report the man's death, but what would he say? "Oh, no biggie, sheriff, the watcher in the lake from The Lord of the Rings plucked him from Blackwater Bay like a shiner." They'd lock him up, but he had to tell the sheriff something.

"He didn't make it," Cannon said.

Dorothy Ann Toll High School was named after the founder of the school. Mrs. Toll ran Gullhaven's first school, a one room shack with no HVAC. She'd started her campaign for a new school building by inviting townsfolk to visit the one room school in January, and by the end of the meeting she had the town's support. Fourteen years later the front wing of the current building had been constructed. As the town grew, two side wings were added, one in 1962 and the other in 1984.

The door to classroom 119 was closed, and as he reached for the doorknob he paused and listened. The low buzz of chatter and the static bursts of radio communication leaked from the room, but he couldn't make out what was being discussed. He pushed open the door and strode through like he owned the place.

"Cannon. About time," Sheriff Tanya Locke said. She was smiling, so he didn't take the barb to heart.

"Had a couple of delays."

"I bet."

"Where's the mayor?"

"You just missed her." The smile on Tanya's face couldn't be wider.

"Krisp didn't make it," he said.

That stopped the room's chatter, and everyone stared at him awaiting further explanation. When he said nothing, Tanya said, "Well, what happened?" She was no longer smiling.

The moment of truth. He decided to go with a lie of omission, at least for the present. "I don't know for sure. The Whaler was hit, he ended up in the water, and..." He stopped and waited to see if he'd be pushed for more information. Cannon figured everyone knew there were sharks roaming the floodwater, so an assumption of a shark attack made sense.

But the sheriff was the law. Tanya said, "And what?"

"He went under and didn't come up," Cannon said. That was true.

Tanya frowned, but said nothing.

"You didn't see anything?" said Tanya's right hand, Gloria Pesch. She was a civilian, but she was the longest tenured member of the department and that held sway in Gullhaven.

"You wouldn't believe me if I told you."

"Try me," Gloria said.

Cannon sighed and said nothing.

Tanya crossed the room, moving around tablet-arm desks strewn about the room in a haphazard mess. She put her hand on Cannon's shoulder, and said, "He's been through a lot. Give him a break."

Cannon's cheeks grew hot, and he smelled the musky scent of Tanya's perfume, felt the heat building between them.

"He'll fill us in later, right Cannon?" Tanya said.

He stepped away and Tanya's hand fell to her side. "Yeah. Everyone needs to hear."

Gloria sighed and went back to her work.

Tanya smiled at him and said, "You hungry?"

Cannon nodded.

They went to the cafeteria where Cannon got a large coffee and two ham sandwiches. He looked around for Nel and Joshua, but they weren't there. Cannon ate while Tanya talked.

"We got a real problem here and I need your help."

Cannon said nothing.

"All communication is down. No idea what condition the rest of the state is in, but if our experience is any indication it's going to be a while before the staties can help us," she said. "I've got people keeping the hospital limping along with the emergency generators, but the building took major damage."

"We'll be OK."

"Yeah? What about food? Water?"

Cannon said nothing.

"And there's been some strange sightings in Blackwater Bay," she said.

He cocked an eyebrow. "Do tell?"

"Ms. Carveie, she lives down by the wharf, says she saw a white tentacle pull a boat under," she said.

"When was this?" Cannon asked.

"Right after the quake."

"Where the hell is Mayor Dennison? All this is her responsibility, no? We need to get back out there and rescue the folks still trapped by the flood."

Tanya sighed. "Many have made their way here, but most of the west side of town is still unaccounted for. The people in the hills and up on the mountainside should be fine, but we might need to ration food which means every house will need to be visited."

"Some folks might not like that."

It was her turn to say nothing.

The radio on her hip came to life. "Sheriff. You copy? Sheriff Locke?"

Tanya's eyebrows rose. She slipped the radio from its holder on her belt and pressed the comm button. "I'm here, Chuck. What you got?"

"I've got the backup generator for the repeater up and running, but I guess you figured that out."

"10-4. Get back here and bring any spare radios you've got," the sheriff said.

"That's a 10-4. Out."

"Finally, some good news," Tanya said.

Cannon nodded, but said nothing.

Tanya said, "What didn't you want to say in front of Gloria and the others?"

"I saw something... what it was... I was stressed and wasn't seeing clearly. Let me think on it a bit. It'll come back."

"Sure," she said. She got up, her eyes narrow slits, her lips a thin red line.

She was pissed he wouldn't confide in her, talk it out. "Tanya, you know—"

A burst of static from her radio. "Mayday. Mayday. Anyone? This is the Second Chance and we are in need of assistance. Mayday. Ma—"

She sighed. "This is the sheriff. What's your position?"

"We're off Razor Point."

Tanya looked at Cannon, who nodded.

"10-4. Constable Cannon coming out to you." She closed the channel and said, "I'll have Chuck bring a base station up here. Now that the repeater is up, we're gonna start getting calls on the emergency band. I'll have Day meet you at the flood line. He can go with you."

"I don't—"

"That's an order."

Cannon knew it wasn't clear if she could give him orders, but he stuffed the last of his second sandwich in his mouth and got up. Through a mouthful of food, he said, "Need a gun."

She eyed his Glock in its holster.

"It was underwater a long time and misfired twice. Ammo is wet, and it needs to be cleaned well before it can be used again. The thing almost got me killed."

Tanya lifted an eyebrow. "I'll have Day bring you a weapon with ammo."

"10-4, Sheriff."

Tanya put her hand on Cannon's shoulder. "Be careful."

"Count on it."

"Oh, take a quick survey of the bay and inlet if you can while you're out there."

"Got it."

The school hallways were getting crowded as more people arrived, and Cannon did some quick math in his head as he walked. If half the people in Gullhaven needed lodging, that would mean the school needed to accommodate over one thousand people, and the high school couldn't fit that many. He made a mental note to speak with the sheriff. Perhaps the younger folks and males could construct a camp of sorts on the athletic fields, but that was an issue for later.

As he left the school, he stopped in the gymnasium to say goodbye to Nel, but she wasn't there so he left word with a friend to tell her where he'd gone.

It was 5:32PM, three hours until the sun went down.

Day joined Cannon and they headed for the flood line. Day handed Cannon a Beretta 9MM with a spare clip. "We're down to using civilian weapons."

Cannon lifted an eyebrow.

"Armory at the station is underwater."

"Great." He examined the Beretta. The Italian-made M9 looked to be in good condition, but there was only one way to tell. Cannon hated relying on a weapon he personally hadn't maintained and fired. Civvies tended to put their weapons in a drawer and forget about them, and that was fine ninety-nine percent of the time, but it was that pesky one percent that worried Cannon.

Seeing his apprehension, Day said, "I know what you're thinking. Did whoever owned this thing maintain it? Will it fire when you need it to?"

Cannon leveled the weapon at a cloud and fired. The *pop* echoed off the buildings and Cannon said, "Well that settles that."

"Indeed."

When they reached the flood line, Day said, "Why did you tie the boat out so far?"

Had he? Cannon looked around, and to him it seemed like the boat had drifted out further. "I'll get it. Keep your panties on."

He waded into the water that lapped on the blacktop, and he was waist deep when he reached the Whaler.

The side of the boat was scraped and gashed where it hit the building, but the bilge was dry. Cannon walked the boat over to Day and the man inched into the floodwater like a child afraid of the ocean.

They went aboard, and Cannon lowered the motor. The Johnson cranked to life on the first turn and the Whaler slid through the silent water, the tall shadows of the fading day falling over Gullhaven, cracked and broken buildings looming on both sides of the flooded road. Cannon turned on Main Street and threaded through the flotsam and jetsam clogging the wharf.

Bodies still floated in the floodwater. The living took priority, but that didn't make passing the corpses any easier. Day, like Cannon, knew most of the people in Gullhaven, and seeing the glazed dead eyes of people he'd known turned the deputy sheriff a milky shade of white. Cannon knew how the guy felt. His stomach churned, and his nerves jumped like he'd had ten cups of coffee.

They eased out into Blackwater Bay, and Cannon cycled up the motors.

Day yelled, "What the hell is that?"

A mile out, the large dorsal fines of orca circled something unseen.

"We'll take a look on the way to Razor Point." Cannon pushed the throttle control down and headed for the orcas.

11

The Whaler skipped across Blackwater Bay, the center console having no problem pushing through the light chop. The sun started its descent to the horizon, and the glare off the water made it difficult to see. Thin clouds trailed across the sky, and the sunshine felt good on Cannon's face. The air was sweet, the scent of salt and the bite of the chilled air reviving him. The boat was cruising at thirty-eight knots, throwing spray, and he took a deep breath, savoring being out on the sea.

Deputy Sheriff Day was having a different experience. He clung to the stainless-steel handrail on the side of the control console, his fingers red with strain, face a mask of pain and fear. His body tensed and stiffened each time the Whaler smacked a wave.

"You alright? You're looking a little Kermit."

Day turned his head, but Cannon couldn't see his eyes through his mirrored sunglasses. "Kermit?"

"The frog? He's green," Cannon said.

Day nodded, but didn't laugh or smile. He turned back into the wind.

Holding the wheel with one hand, Cannon lifted binoculars to his eyes with the other.

He couldn't see the Second Chance or Razor Point. With the water in the bay higher than normal, the sandspit was submerged, but he knew the area well. Closer and to the west, four orcas circled, their black sail-like dorsal fins creating a whirlpool. Two of the fins were small. Those were the females, whose dorsal fins were considerably shorter than their male counterparts. Orca were common in Blackwater Bay. The deep water and bountiful fish made it a popular feeding ground for beasts brave enough to risk passage through Devil's Rip.

The apex predators were known as the wolves of the sea, because they hunted in packs. One of the beasts breached, its pectoral side fins driving the creature from the bay. Patches of white on slick black skin glistened, tongue lolling out. The twenty-five-foot beast crashed back into the bay and continued circling its unseen prey.

"What do you make of that?" Day said.

"Looks like they're feeding on something. Probably a…" Cannon didn't want to finish the thought because he didn't want to think about corpses floating in his bay. "Like great white sharks, killer whales have no natural predators, which leaves them free to hunt the sea at will." Cannon lifted the handset on his marine radio. "Second Chance, do you copy?"

"Yes, we copy."

"This is Constable Cannon. What is your current condition?"

"Taking on water, got two injured people."

"That's a 10-4. Will five minutes make a difference? We've got something here that might be gone in thirty seconds."

"I don't think so." Static.

"We'll be right there. Cannon out."

He adjusted course three degrees northwest and put the Whaler's bow on the orca pod. He wanted to see what they were noshing on, and he wanted to do it without a boatload of rescued people.

Day said, "The sheriff tell you she wants you to take a look at Devil's Rip?"

He'd forgotten. "Yeah, we'll blow by there on our way back if we can. Depends on the condition of the injured."

The dorsal fins were five hundred yards off the starboard bow and Cannon pulled back on the throttle and brought Spare Change to a crawl. Whitewater slammed against the transom and bubbled up around the Johnson.

Cannon examined the SONAR. The orcas circled something big, a dark shape that shifted and changed size and color. The blob began to rise, thick blue lines extending away from a lightening center mass.

Tentacles shot from the whirlpool between the orcas; white, slimy arms with suction cups and spikes. The tentacles dove and writhed in the bay like sea serpents, and one wound itself around an orca's dorsal fin. The orca bucked and rolled, its pectoral fins struggling to push through the water.

Cannon pulled the Beretta and sighted the vortex in the center of the orcas. He fired four times, taking his time, squeezing the trigger like he was at the range. Slow and easy. As the shots rang out over the water, Cannon asked himself why he'd fired. To save the orcas? They'd attack the boat if they had to, so it wasn't love for killer whales. It was fear of what Cannon knew was below but couldn't see.

The tentacles pulled back into the bay and the orca scattered like a flock of birds after a car backfires. Cannon looked over at Day, who stared out at the bay where the scene had unfolded. He hadn't said a word through the entire ordeal. His face was Wonder Bread white, and now Cannon thought the guy really did look green around the edges.

The Whaler rocked on the turbulent sea created by the thrashing orcas and diving leviathan.

"You saw that, right?" Cannon said.

Day nodded, but said nothing.

This was good news. Day had seen the beast. "What do you think it is?"

"Octopus?"

"Not that big and strong."

"Giant squid?"

"At the upper depths?"

"We did just have a massive earthquake," Day said.

Cannon cranked up the outboard and turned northeast toward the Second Chance. It was a spec off the starboard side now, bobbing on the chop that rolled across Razor Point like a surf break. Cannon zoomed in on the chart of the area. Krisp had gone down not far from his current location, and he and Joshua had also passed this way.

Cannon looked through the binoculars. "She's drifting into the point."

"It'll get pounded there," Day said.

"Thanks for the information."

Cannon dropped the throttle, and the Whaler leapt from the water as the outboard whined and clawed at the sea. As they got closer, Cannon saw the sailboat's mainmast tilted toward the waterline. Waves pounded the boat's port side, which looked to be underwater.

"Why didn't they abandon ship on their tender?" Day said over the swirling wind.

Cannon scanned the sailboat with the binoculars. "I don't see one. Probably got washed off deck when the quake hit."

The Whaler was two hundred yards off the sinking boat's port bow, and Cannon drew back on the throttle and the motor fell to a low hum. Their fishtail chased them, and Cannon moved around to the starboard side, which was still above water.

"How you gonna handle this? Have them jump in the bay and we fish them out?"

It was a good question. The Whaler was only nineteen feet long, and if the sailboat went under and the Whaler was too close... Then he remembered there were injured people aboard. "Can't do that. We've got injured."

"Right. Right." Day turned his way, but said nothing as he waited. They were on the bay, Cannon's territory.

They had to dock with the sinking vessel. They had no choice.

Cannon inched the Whaler around to the aft gunnel where a rope ladder with wooden steps hung into the bay. He maneuvered the boat against the ladder, and said, "Day, get the bow line tied off."

Day looked at Cannon as if he was speaking Swahili.

"Tie that rope…" He pointed toward the bow at a coil of black, double-braded, 3/8 line. The rope had a nylon core and a breaking strength of five thousand pounds, "…onto that cleat."

Day let go of the handrail and flexed his hand as he headed forward.

Cannon shut down the motor and a young girl hung her head over the Second Chance's tilted starboard gunnel. "Oh, thank God you're here. Let me get dad."

Day fumbled with the knot on the bow line, and Cannon ended up tying off the boat before he jumped onto the Whaler's gunnel and grabbed the rope ladder. "Hold down the fort. I'll call you if I need you."

Cannon was halfway up the ladder when a man with dark hair graying at the temples appeared above. "Constable?"

"Yes, sir."

"Nice boat. We were worried you were…"

"What?"

"Not nice people."

"Where are your injured?"

"Below. My wife and son. I think she has a broken leg and my son took a bad fall as we got tossed around. Hit his head on the bulkhead. He's dizzy and sick to his stomach."

"Probably just a concussion," Cannon said.

"That's what his mom thinks."

"Can we move them topside, you and I? Or do we need help?" Cannon said.

"We can do it. By the way, I'm Trent Collie, and this is my daughter, Alex."

"Nice to meet you. Wish it were under better circumstances. Never seen you out here before?"

"We don't get out much. Sometimes I think I'm just making a contribution to Izzie's son's college fund."

Cannon chuckled. He knew Izzy. His marina was the biggest in the Dingmans Wharf.

"Have you seen the marina?"

Cannon nodded. "Not good. You'll see it for yourself on the way in."

Over the following half hour, Cannon and Trent moved his wife, Linda and their son, Trent Jr. to the Whaler. Once onboard, Cannon positioned Linda and Trent Jr. in the bow before Trent Sr. and Alex, who sat on the bench seat.

Cannon cycled up the motor and the Whaler jumped across the light chop of Blackwater Bay. "Everyone alright?" he asked.

Nods and wagging heads.

"I need to take a short detour. That OK with you guys?" Cannon said.

Trent Sr. looked at Cannon with a face that said, "Haven't we been through enough?"

Linda said, "I'm fine and Trent will be too. Do what you've got to do."

Cannon nudged the wheel and changed course, the Whaler arcing gently west as they made for Devil's Rip. The sun was falling, and he was blinded by the direct sunlight. He fumbled in the console for sunglasses, but all he found was a pink pair of kid's glasses with rainbows for eyebrows. He put them on and turned to Day. "Go ahead. Say something."

Day said nothing. The man still hadn't gotten his sea legs, and he was back to clinging to the control console like a child confronting his first jump into a pool.

From afar the inlet looked normal. Tall cliffs rose on both sides of the channel, but even from two miles away Cannon saw chunks missing from the bluffs. As the Whaler crossed the last section of open bay before the start of the inlet, he slowed the Whaler to a crawl. He was concerned there could be large sections of the fallen rockface unseen just beneath the surface.

He killed the motor and let the boat drift toward the mouth of Devil's Rip.

Cannon lifted the binoculars. "Damn," he said.

Boulders, dirt, and dead vegetation filled the gap that Cannon had motored through a thousand times. He examined the waterline, and there didn't appear to be any water leaking into or out of the bay.

Devil's Rip was completely blocked.

That meant the orcas and great shite sharks trapped in the valley would be cut off from the Pacific. He didn't know if that was good or bad, but he figured it was important, so he opened a channel to the sheriff.

"Sheriff, this is Cannon, do you copy?"

"Go ahead, Cannon."

"Rescue complete. They're OK. I did a fast tour of the north bay during my rescue. Saw some weird stuff we'll tell you about later. Devil's Rip is totally blocked. Nothing is getting in or out of the bay anytime soon. Have there been any other calls out here on the bay?"

The marine radio crackled, and the sheriff said, "Hold a second, Cannon."

Cannon looked back over his shoulder to the northeast, toward where the orcas and the unknown had appeared. The bay looked flat and silent.

"Cannon, we've got nothing else for you. Bring those folks back here."

"10-4. Cannon out." He was surprised to hear there hadn't been any other marine calls. He'd seen several boats bobbing on the bay, but the folks were either waiting things out, or... The or. Cannon hated the word or.

"Everyone hold on, we're heading in."

Day smiled so wide Cannon thought his face might crack.

Cannon brought the Whaler up to speed and set course for the wharf. He felt heat on his neck as the sun dropped, and the Johnson screamed.

12

Back at the high school, Cannon found controlled chaos. Reunited families consoled those whose loved ones hadn't been found, children cried, and infants wailed as the crushing weight of humanity took its toll on the school. The east wing bathroom toilets weren't flushing, the trash was overflowing, and the school was already showing signs of over population. People rested in hallways, classrooms, anywhere there was a dry, clean, flat surface.

Weeping and wails of pain and sorrow drifted through the building as folks dealt with their losses and the uncertainty of what tomorrow would bring. Collective anxiety had drained the town of its energy, and as sundown approached, Cannon worried for the people still trapped by the floodwaters. Calls had come in from all over Gullhaven, and many people would have to hunker-down for the night. The mayor and sheriff had decided search and rescue efforts would be suspended at sundown because in the dark it was too dangerous with so much debris in the water.

Cannon wandered the halls of the high school, slowly making his way in a roundabout route to the command center in room 119. The mayor waited for him there, and she was sure to find some reason to bust his balls. Nel and Joshua waited in the gym, and his rack was calling. He was dead on his feet, his eyes burned, and his arm where the cabin door had caught him throbbed with pain. He rubbed his eyes and wished he had a drink.

The last rays of the setting sun cut through the lobby windows, and light danced off the brass trophies in the display case. He searched for the large cup given to the winners of the 2001 Mendocino County Championship in women's basketball. He peered through the dirty glass, looking for Nel's name on the black plastic square at the trophy's base. He tried to imagine her then, in high school, stalking these halls with her friends. Boyfriends. She'd told him so many stories of this place. All stories he wasn't part of.

He sighed. He'd put off meeting with the mayor long enough. He headed to the new wing and entered room 119 quietly, but despite his effort, the door creaked, and every head turned his way.

The mayor resembled Ann Coulter, except she had black hair. Racoon eyes stared at him from darkened sockets. Her clothes were slightly disheveled, which made Cannon raise an eyebrow. She'd be put together in the center of a hurricane.

"Where you been? It's almost dark and you've been back a half hour," she said. Her thin body was hunched, and she looked like the weight of the world rested on her shoulders.

"Needed to splash some water on my face," Cannon said.

"For half an hour?"

"Been a long day."

"No shit. You think you're the only one who's had a rough day? You're a civil servant," she said.

The command center grew quiet, and Tanya stared at the paperwork on the desk before her.

"Thanks for the information. How may I help you... my lady," Cannon said, and he bowed with a flourish.

"Stand up, you jackass," she said. Someone chuckled, but he couldn't tell who it was. "We've got people still stranded all over town. What's the situation out on the bay?"

Cannon sighed. "Warf and west side of town are still flooded pretty bad. There's some boats bobbing around on the bay, but nobody hailed us, so I assume the boats are derelict or everyone onboard is..."

"Is what, constable?" Her eyes blazed like he'd caused the earthquake.

Mayor Katy Dennison was tough, but when it came to Cannon, she was a viper. She'd hired him, convinced him to move to Gullhaven, said he was the perfect fit, even though he was an outsider. They'd met in college and had a brief romantic relationship, but he'd broken it off, suggesting they remain friends, which they had. He'd been on the job in Gullhaven a few months when she'd made a pass at him. Kissed him one night when they were working late on the marine budget down at town hall. It had been before he met Nel, but his visceral reaction to pull back and push her away had brought on a rage, an anger that never abated. He hadn't known she still held a torch for him. If he had, he probably wouldn't have taken the job.

Nobody in town knew why the two didn't get along, except Nel. Katy had tried to fire him several times, but each time the town council stood behind Cannon. That support and his threat to tell everyone what she'd done kept her at bay, but didn't stop her from abusing him whenever she saw fit, and she loved to make him look like a fool in public.

"And the rip?" she said.

"Totally blocked," Cannon said.

The mayor said, "What does that mean? Nothing, really, right?"

Cannon said, "The long term effects of the elimination of the tidal currents will be devastating to marine life, but in the short-term I can't think of any dangers the blockage might cause."

"What did you and Day see out there? He's been staring at a wall in the nurse's office since he got back," the mayor asked. "Won't talk. Like he'd seen a ghost. And there's been more strange tentacle sightings in the wharf."

At this, the sheriff lifted her head, and Cannon felt the stare of everyone in the room on him. He wasn't a marionette on her strings, and he didn't perform on command. "I need something to eat. I'll provide a full report after I gather my thoughts."

The mayor glowered at him and Cannon thought he saw a thin smirk on Tanya's lips.

"I'm holding a debrief at 10PM in the teacher's lounge. I expect you there with a full report and suggestions about moving forward. We've got a lot of work to do tomorrow and we need a solid plan," the mayor said.

"Good thing you're here then, huh?" Cannon said. He didn't wait to hear her response and pushed out through the door into the hall.

Cannon made his way down to the cafeteria and found Nel tending to Joshua and several other children. She was trying to get them all to go to sleep, but the kids were wound-up, and the gym was noisy with the sounds of humanity preparing to shut down for the night.

Nel hugged him and said, "How you doin', cowboy?"

"Hanging in. Who are all these kids?"

She leaned into him. "Their parents are missing and I'm looking after them until they're found."

He said nothing as he looked at the kids. Some of them were most likely orphans, and Cannon felt a surge of sorrow wash over him as the children looked at him with wide, trusting eyes. Eyes that said, "You'll make everything right, won't you?"

"You are superwoman. How are you holding up?"

"As best as to be expected." She looked down at Joshua, who stared up at them listening to every word. "What's it like out there?"

Cannon's eyes shifted to the boy, and he said, "Later. I've got a few things to do before my day is over. There's a debrief at 10PM and I'll be down after that. Do you need anything?"

She shook her head no.

"I'll see you later." He kissed her on the forehead and went to the cafeteria to see what he could scrounge up. There wasn't much left of the night's spaghetti dinner, but he got a cold bowl of pasta and a couple of meatballs. As he ate, he was joined by his buddy Clint Weston, the local can-do guy.

"Yo. My brother." Clint slapped Cannon on the back. "You look like shit."

"Thanks. You too."

"You look like you could use a drink."

Cannon's eyebrows lifted.

"I got a bottle stashed on the roof. Care for a nip?"

Cannon laughed. "Let me guess. You ran from your house without clothes or food, but you managed to remember a bottle. That right?"

"You want a hit or not?"

"I do."

Clint laughed. "I gotta hit the head and then I'll meet you up there."

"10-4."

Clint slapped him on the back again and left. Cannon finished eating and washed his plate and placed it on the giant pile next to the sink. He looked down into a sink that looked bigger than his swimming pool as a kid. They needed to start thinking about survival. Conservation. Wasting water washing dishes would have to end. Males would have to urinate outside. All the small day-to-day conveniences they all shared had become crutches and now the town needed to walk on its own two legs.

Cannon's nerves jumped, and the bottoms of his feet hurt as he climbed the emergency staircase to the roof. The door at the top stood open and Clint sat on the western parapet wall. The sun had set, leaving a bruised sky, and the gray of dusk spread over the valley. The bay was black as ink, and the distant mountains that separated Gullhaven from the Pacific Ocean were dark and seemed far away. A gentle breeze pushed across the rooftop and brought the scent of smoke and salt.

As Cannon approached, Clint handed him a pint of Jack Daniels. "Oh, how I love you," Cannon said as he received the bottle. He took a long pull, the sharp bite of the whiskey burning his throat and settling in his stomach like a firebrand.

"Always knew you had a thing for me."

"You and only you." Cannon took another swig and handed the bottle back to Clint.

"What's happening down in the situation room?"

"The mayor and sheriff are telling people still trapped by the flood to hunker down for the night and they'll be rescued in order of priority tomorrow. She said it's a long list. The wharf and west side got pounded and are still underwater."

"Nel told me about... your day." He handed the bottle back to Cannon.

"You don't know the half of it." He handed the bottle back, and said, "I'm good. I've got a meeting in a bit." Cannon gave up drinking because he'd felt the slow creep of addiction, but that was before Nel. He had his act together now and enjoyed the occasional cocktail, but like an ex-smoker who craves a cigarette during stressful situations, Cannon's mind still cycled to booze when his nerves jumped, and the pit of his stomach turned to ice.

The two men sat there for what seemed like hours but was only twenty minutes.

"Clint, I saw something out there. Something..."

Clint lifted an eyebrow.

"First in Devil's Rip when the earthquake started, then again on the inner bay."

Clint watched him but said nothing.

"The thing was... Well, I don't know what the hell it was."

Clint waited.

"The SONAR showed some type of major anomaly, then I saw... I saw a giant tentacle go after a great white shark. Then the thing took Krisp and attacked killer whales," Cannon said. "And there's been several reports of a strange tentacled beast terrorizing the wharf."

"You must be mistaken. Nothing attacks orca."

"This thing did." Cannon gazed at the bay to the east. "I felt... You know how you feel when you're falling, or really excited?"

Clint nodded.

"A feeling of dread washed over me, but I couldn't run. I had to see what it was."

"That why Day's unresponsive?"

"I think so. In shock, maybe?"

"What do you plan to do?"

"First I've got to tell the mayor and sheriff."

"You haven't told them yet? Bitchy woman gonna be pissed," Clint said.

"And? What could I have done to stop that?"

Clint said, "Good point. Someday you're going to have to tell me why that woman hates you so much. I mean, she hates all men, but she despises you. What do you think it is? Something the earthquake dragged in?"

"Maybe." Cannon's face grew hot with whiskey burn and his stomach growled as he paced along the parapet wall. It was odd seeing the town with no lights sparkling along the streets, no blue TV beams leaking from windows, no green and red road lights or car headlights meandering through the mountains. There was a certain peace to the scene, but something unnatural as well.

"Listen, you think you can help me out the next few days? I'll ask the sheriff if you can be my deputy? Day is useless out there." Clint was single, and his ex-wife and kids lived in San Diego. That thought made Cannon feel like a total ass. He hadn't said anything about Clint's family, but what was there to say? Without communication he had no way to contact them. "Hey, I'm sure your boy and Grace are alright. Judging by the strength of the earthquake here we must have been close to the epicenter, which means San Diego might have had nothing more than tremors."

Clint nodded, but Cannon could tell his friend was worried.

The darkness thickened as Cannon looked out over the valley. A three-quarters moon hung in the sky, and stars blinked against an inky background. His watch chimed. 10PM. Seven hours and thirty-nine minutes since the earthquake started. He sighed and headed down the stairs to the meeting to see what tomorrow would bring.

13

Its confrontation with the odd giant fish had weakened the leviathan, but the orca it had eaten restored its strength and energy. The beast rested for a time, letting its arms flow with the current as it digested its prey. The bay darkened when the bright eye in the sky disappeared, and the beast's natural instincts took over. It never felt peace, for it was constantly consumed with hunger, but its brief moments of rest replenished it, allowed the creature to grow.

The silence was broken by sound vibrations, which stirred the beast from its near sleep within tall sea grass. The strange sound urged it forward, tentacles floating in the bay before it. The creature snapped its claws, its color shifting and brightening with reds and pinks, then fading back to white as it calmed.

This wasn't a danger. It was prey.

The leviathan surged through the water, rising as it wagged its stabilizer fins and shot water from its siphon. The sky above was black, white dots peering down like a million fish eyes. The water was dark, but its eyes adjusted, and it saw as it had in the abyss. Everything was clear and sharp, the slightest glint of light registering.

The creature surfaced, pulling seawater into its mantle and over its gills.

It sensed blood beyond an impregnable wall of... was it stone? It attached its forward tentacles to the rock, its suction cup teeth digging into the material, which gave way beneath the force of the beast.

Crashing and splashing, and something bellowed.

The beast roared as it shifted its girth, lashing out with its two claws. The tentacles slithered through the water, finding prey and pulling it toward the creature's parrot-like beak of a mouth.

Warm red blood burned through the beast.

It fell back into the water, aglow with the energy and satisfaction of the kill.

Snap! Snap! Bubbles, something cutting through the bay. It recalled that sound, knew—

Hot pain pierced one of its tentacles, and the beast roared again, shooting spray and submerging.

Snap!

Vibrations in the water and air, the rank scent. Its claws searched the destruction, seeking out the source of the noise. Rage grew in the beast, its primal hunger tensing every muscle as it absorbed the foreign projectile into its soft skin. Black ink pumped from the beast and filled the water, as heat coursed through the creature, its color changing, its blood leaking into the sea.

The beast's serpentine arms attached to anything they could find, tearing down everything in its path as it jerked its girth through the wreckage toward its prey.

Its prey. That was all that mattered. Satisfying its hunger.

The sounds stopped when its right claw found one of the odd creatures. It snapped the thin animal in half, felt the vibrations as its body fell into the water. Then it was feeding, pulling the pieces of its prey into its mouth, reveling in the taste of human blood.

The beast breached from the floodwater filled with new strength and hatred. It felt the hole in its tentacle, tasted blood, and came to the closest thing it knew to pleasure.

Baywater surged around the creature and pushed it inland. The beast's warning systems went off. The odd structures above the waterline would protect its prey and be a danger to it. It eased through the floodwater, sensing the rising water and more helpless prey just out of reach.

14

The teacher's lounge smelled of feet and baloney, and when Cannon arrived, there was no coffee left. Candlelight flickered on the walls like dark waves, and Cannon blinked when he thought he saw a writhing tentacle in the dark shadows. Mayor Dennison sat at the end of a lunch table, the sheriff at the other. Gloria, the sheriff's assistant was there, and two deputies Cannon didn't know very well. He didn't remember their names. One was Jim, or John, the other Brian? Between the two deputies was Nathan Pearlman, a local science teacher. Cannon had no idea why he was at the meeting.

"About time Cannon. Your watch broken?" the mayor said.

Cannon glanced down.10:04PM. Seven hours and forty-three minutes since the earthquake began. "Didn't realize I was on the clock. You got someplace to be?"

"You're on the clock until I say you're not. Sit down."

Cannon's stomach burned and when he looked at Tanya, the sheriff looked away. Cannon took a moment to think up a witty comeback, but when nothing came, he sat down.

"You want to start by telling me what the hell you saw out there?" the mayor said. The dark bags beneath her eyes shined, her makeup long washed away.

When Cannon said nothing, the mayor said, "What's our status, Tanya?"

"Not good. I've been unable to reach the Coast Guard Station at Point Reyes, and Travis Airforce Base has gone silent. Power is out and will be for the foreseeable future. Russ over at the station says the blast of water the facility took caused major damage. Could be weeks before he can get the juice back on. They're working to get a line to the outside world. The emergency broadcast system is saying standby. Information forthcoming."

"Any word from Jesse Draper or Toby?" the mayor asked.

"I saw the top of Toby's copter down in the wharf. It's underwater," Cannon said.

"And Jesse is up coast until next week," the sheriff said.

"So no whirlybirds. Great," the mayor said.

"There's more," the sheriff said. "Hundreds of people are trapped above the floodwater on the west side of town. Many we've been in contact with, others we have only distress calls."

"What've you done to notify folks we're coming?"

"We've been speaking with those who reach us, and I've had every boat I've got ride through the streets with bullhorns."

"Good. That will help. We've got time," the mayor said.

At this, Nathan Pearlman cleared his throat.

"Yes, Mr. Pearlman?"

"We may not have as much time as you think, mayor."

Mayor Dennison sighed. "For those who don't know him, this is Nate Pearlman. He teaches science here at the high school. He asked to be here because he said he had something important to tell us. Nate?"

"Yes, well, I do teach science, but one of my hobbies... not really a hobby because I use the weather stations as labs for my kids and the data I get can be—"

"Mr. Pearlman, we've got many things to get through before we can hit the rack tonight, so if you would, the important stuff only."

"Yes, of course, mayor. Sorry." Pearlman straightened like he was standing before his class. "I have three weather monitoring stations around Gullhaven. One up on the bluffs to record the sea conditions and El Niño, a second in the mountains to the east, and a third on Blackwater Bay's shoreline down by Izzy's. Data on the earthquake shows what you'd imagine, it scored an eight on the Richter Scale and lasted roughly ten minutes with one small aftershock. But that's not what's important." He paused for effect and looked around the table, making eye contact with each person. "Blackwater Bay is rising."

The faint tap of a clock ticking, the whoosh of the watercooler tank filling, and the hum of the refrigerator compressor filled the silence.

"You heard me, yes?" said Nate.

"We heard you, but I guess no one believes it," Cannon said. "The inlet is blocked, Nate, the tidal flow has stopped."

"And unless the earthquake changed the tides, it's low tide. Bay can't be rising," the sheriff said.

Cannon remembered Razor Point being covered in fourteen feet of water, when it should be exposed at low tide.

"But it is. Look." Nate spread a piece of paper out on the table. "I only have six hours of data from one station, but it clearly shows the bay rising, and at a decent pace."

"How could that be? Are you sure your sensor is functioning properly?" Cannon said.

"I'm sure. There's nothing to break. It's a temperature depth sensor. Nothing complicated."

"There's no way you could be getting a false reading?" the sheriff asked.

"That's what I thought so I went out and checked. Didn't need to see the sensor to know the water's rising."

"And the hits just keep on coming," said the mayor.

"How long do we have?" Cannon said.

Everyone stared at him, late to the realization of what the rising water meant.

"Hard to tell," Nate said. "The exact typography of the ground and valley walls is unknown, so all I can do is estimate the volume of the valley. But at the rate the water is rising, I'd say we've got three more days, give or take twelve hours."

"Care to fill us in?" the mayor said.

"Poor choice of words, ma'am," Cannon said.

"We have three and a half days until everything in the valley is underwater, including the high school," Nate said.

"You're sure?" the sheriff asked.

"Sure as rain," Nate said. "Sorry."

Nobody spoke. The clock ticked. The frig buzzed.

"What could possibly be causing this?" the mayor asked. She looked like she'd aged ten years in the last five minutes.

"Not sure, but the quake was bad. There's been talk about the next big one breaking tectonic plates, which could shift the very foundations of Earth," Nate said.

"So, what are you saying? There's a crack somewhere in the valley that's letting in seawater?" Cannon said.

"That's my working theory. The fissure is most likely on the bottom of Blackwater Bay," Nate said.

"Is there any way to stop it?" the mayor asked.

Nate said nothing.

"OK. We need to start thinking about evacuating the valley," the sheriff said.

"How are we going to do that? Roads are blocked. Inlet is blocked," one of the sheriff deputies said.

"We have no choice. Start putting together a plan, but keep this quiet for now. We don't need a town full of panicked people. Let's get through tomorrow, rescue—"

Every radio in the room squawked, and the sheriff took control of the communication. "Go ahead, base."

A male voice Cannon didn't recognize said, "Ma'am, we just got two more of those calls. Kim Pepper and Des Brek both just called—separately—to report a giant octopus tearing the wharf apart. Kim said she saw the thing pull someone from a second story window like a giant snake. What the hell is going on, sheriff? Third one of the day."

"10-4, base." Tanya closed the channel

"You're not going to have them investigate?" Nate asked.

"What do you expect them to do in the dark?" Cannon said.

"We'll see what the day brings." Mayor Dennison pulled back a lock of her long black hair with a finger and put it behind her ear.

Cannon sat in silence, processing the report about the creature and Nate's news about the rising water. He'd suspected something was off with the floodwater. "I've seen it," Cannon said.

When Cannon didn't continue, the mayor said, "What? Spit it out."

Cannon only half believed what he'd seen with his own eyes, so how would he describe something he didn't fully believe he'd seen? "Krisp was... killed."

Frustration flooded the mayor's face when Cannon didn't continue. "We know this, Cannon. What—"

"You don't know shit," Cannon said. He breathed, upset with himself that he'd let her get his blood pressure up. "Krisp was plucked from the sea by... by..."

"What?" the mayor shouted.

"I don't know. When I came through the inlet during the earthquake, something big showed on the SONAR, and whatever it was scared off a great white shark."

"Could have been anything, Cannon," the sheriff said. "The orca were—"

"I saw them. This was something else."

"How can you be sure?" the mayor said.

The skepticism in the mayor's voice burned Cannon's cheeks and turned his stomach to fire. "I can be sure because a tentacle wrapped around Krisp and dragged him into the water like a frog plucking a fly from the air," Cannon said.

"A tentacle? Like what's been reported?" the sheriff said.

"It's hard to say exactly what I saw. And these reports? People see strange shit when they're hungry, afraid, and trapped by floodwater teeming with great whites. I know one thing. I saw something, and it's killing people," Cannon said.

The mayor sighed. "The last thing we need with the bay rising are more predators in the water."

The room fell silent again and the refrigerator's compressor hit a high note.

"So, don't get pissed, but you're saying you saw a sea monster?" Nate said.

Cannon said, "Day saw the thing too... plus four other people at least. The thing is terrorizing the flood zone, and with the water rising, it'll be here next."

"Giant squid have been written about for hundreds of years," Nate said. "You've heard the term kraken?"

Cannon nodded.

"It's Swedish for 'uprooted tree.' That's what sailors thought the things looked like, all the roots writhing. In my text books they're called cephalopods."

"What do you propose we do?" the sheriff asked.

Cannon sighed. "Look, I know how crazy this sounds. I wouldn't have believed it myself if I hadn't seen the thing. Normally it's best to leave apex predators alone. Ignore them and they'll go away, but this creature is trapped in the bay."

"Cut off from its food supply," Nate said.

"And the water is rising," Cannon said.

The clock chugged past 10:30PM and Cannon's eyelids drooped. He'd been going nonstop for over fifteen hours, and if he didn't shut it down soon, he'd collapse. The welt on his arm throbbed in rhythm with his heart and his eyes felt like sandpaper.

"OK. One thing at a time," the mayor said. "We need a fleet of boats to do rescues. That's priority one. Tanya, you and your team round up as many functioning boats as you can. Sailboats, kayaks, you name it. Also, figure out how to protect our fuel. Without gas for the boats and generators, we're really screwed."

"Any clue how to do that? Izzy's pump is underwater already," Cannon said.

"There's usually a few empty tanker trucks waiting to go haul gas," the mayor said.

"Saw Beth Greorge last night, so her rig should be here," Cannon said.

The mayor shot icicles at Cannon with her eyes. Beth Greorge had been seen around town with many men. "Good. Fill it and bring it up the mountain road as far as you can."

"10-4. I'll get someone on it," the sheriff said.

"Cannon, I want you to take Mr. Wizard here out to his weather station in the morning and see how bad things have gotten. We're going to have to tell people in the morning if Nate's right... especially if we have unknown predators hunting in the floodwaters."

"Center square will be flooded tomorrow. I'm sure of it," Nate said.

"Tanya, tell your people to have their heads on a swivel. Keep trying to contact Point Reyes Coast Guard Station. I need to know if there is any hope of help. Sweet dreams, folks," the mayor said. She got to her feet.

As the group broke up, Nate said, "Cannon, you got a minute?"

He nodded.

When they were alone, Nate said, "Sounds like a giant squid."

"What would bring it?" Cannon asked.

"Food."

Back in the gymnasium, Cannon found Nel watching over her brood of children. There were more than earlier in the day. "Looks like you've picked up a few," he said. He kissed Nel on the forehead and rubbed her neck. He didn't know how she did it. He didn't blame her for wanting to be out on the water. Taking care of little children whose parents were missing was much more difficult.

"Katy and Jack's parents showed up, but those six there," she pointed, "three more families torn apart."

He hugged her and kissed her neck. "Mayor says there are many people still trapped. Their parents are probably fine. I'll get them tomorrow."

She said, "You promise?"

Cannon didn't answer. Instead, he told Nel *almost* everything, but he didn't want to worry her. She had dark bags beneath her eyes and red blotches on her face. Her makeup was smudged, and the front of her shirt was dirty with food.

Nel sat in silence, the good listener she was, and Cannon poured it out. She nodded, smiled, but her face grew pale as her lips thinned and her eyes narrowed.

When he was done, she said, "Shit."

"Understatement of the year."

He lay back on his cot and it was Nel's turn to massage him. The large cafeteria windows were dark, and no lights twinkled in the town below. Cannon's stomach churned, and the sting of Clint's liquor crept up his throat.

He felt better now that everything was out on the table. The hand they'd been dealt sucked, but at least now he knew what they were dealing with. But did he, really? The valley was filling with water and they didn't know why, an unknown creature was stalking the bay and floodwaters, they had no way out of the valley, no way to get food, and they had a limited supply of water. He closed his eyes and was asleep in minutes.

15

Day two dawned chilly and gray. Cannon gazed out on Gullhaven from the high school roof as he sipped his coffee. Thick stratus clouds pushed over the bluffs in the west and snaked into the valley like smoke. Capsized boats bobbed on Blackwater Bay and the town's scars were many. Cannon chuckled weakly when he saw his patrol boat atop the Plaza building, where it would stay until all the important things were taken care of. He frowned. The steeple on town hall had toppled, chunks had broken off several of the large buildings, and complete structures had disappeared into a crack that ran through the mountains down to the bay.

He turned away from the devastation and leaned against the parapet wall, watching the orange glow of daybreak fight through the gloom that hung over the mountains to the east.

He'd slept decent considering the circumstances. As miserable as the prior day had been, Cannon knew he'd spend this new day dealing with the extremes left behind by the quake. He'd have the thrill of rescuing people, hearing how he was their savior. What would they have done without him? He'd get to see that look in their eyes when they realized they were going to be OK, and every dark possibility they'd spent the entire night worrying over wasn't going to come to pass.

He also knew the rising sun would bring home all the things he was able to ignore in the darkness. For every person he rescued, there'd be a corpse for him to fish from the floodwater. That was if the sharks, orca, and… Sigmund didn't get to them first.

Cannon took a pull of coffee and glanced at the exhaust vent where Clint had his bottle stashed. Just a little dip would do him right, but he couldn't. There was too much to do. Too many people who needed his help. He chuckled. Where the hell had he pulled Sigmund the Sea Monster from? He hadn't thought of that show in thirty years, but he figured the nickname made sense. Kraken, giant squid, colossus, hydra, leviathan, all seemed too strong and powerful, and Cannon didn't want to think of the thing that way.

"What'cha doin'?" the Sheriff said. She leaned in the stairwell doorframe with an unlit cigarette between her lips. "Got a light?"

"I quit ages ago. You know that."

"I know you said you did," she said. She took the cancer stick from her mouth and held it between her forefinger and index finger, displaying it for him as though he'd never seen one before.

"Why would I lie?"

She came toward him, smiling. "How's everyone in the gym?" she said. She leaned against the wall and took an imaginary drag on her burner.

"You really don't have a light?" Cannon said.

"Oh, I don't smoke it. I just like to hold it, feel it between my lips," she said. She sat next to him.

"What for?" Heat baked between them and Cannon felt the left side of his face grow hot, like he was roasting in the sun. This happened whenever he was near her, which was why he tried not to be near her. The attraction he felt brought on guilt he didn't know how to deal with. He loved Nel, but Tanya was gorgeous, and he was only a man.

"I imagine I'm smoking it. Pretend I taste the smoke. It's not the same thing, but it's better than nothing."

"Ever try a vape?"

"I'm not it in for the nicotine. I enjoy the smoke."

Cannon got to his feet. "Did you need me for something? Otherwise I'm going to get my day going."

"Yeah, I wanted to tell you I've got a man up in Pikers Peak keeping an eye on the entire valley. He'll report in if he sees anything." She took an imaginary drag off her unlit cigarette.

"That all?"

"No."

Cannon was getting pissed. She always did this. Dragged things out.

She slipped the cancer stick into her breast pocket and sighed. "Bad news, constable." Her entire demeanor had changed. Pits of ice replaced puppy dog eyes, and her posture stiffened. "There are reports of looters in town. Hitting the shops. Trapped folks have been calling the thefts in. I need you to deal with that first, then join the rescue crews."

"Theft? Why aren't your boys going after them?"

"The looters are in boats, Cannon. On the floodwater, and if it's on the water, it's on you." She lifted her chin. "Any questions?"

Cannon said nothing.

She eyed him, the corners of her mouth drooping, her eyes narrow slits. "Be careful now, you hear?"

Cannon hit the stairs.

The building was coming awake, and the sweet scents of bread and coffee wafted from the cafeteria. He went and got Nel and helped her bring her children, which had grown to a group of eight, to eat.

"How'd you sleep?" she asked. The children sat at a lunch table and Nel and Cannon waited in line.

"OK." He stared down the long line of people then looked at his watch. 7:49AM.

Seeing his impatience, Nel said, "What is it?"

"I hate to do this to you, but I've got to roll."

Her mouth fell open and her eyes widened.

"I know. But the sheriff says there's looters ripping off the stores in the flood zone and I need to get down there."

She smiled. "I'll let you go if you eat first. You can cut the line. Nobody will mind."

He nodded and kissed her. "I'll try and stop in and see you for lunch."

She sighed. "See you tonight. Be careful."

Cannon saw the dejection, and said, "What is it? I told you most of these kid's parent's will be back by tonight. It's going to be—"

"That's not it." She bit her lip.

"What?"

"I feel like an old lady, stuck back here while the men go save the world. Everyone is saying you guys need help out there. Shouldn't I be helping? I want to help."

Cannon took her by the shoulders. "My father says the people who helped most thought they did the least, and the shits who did nothing took all the credit." He pulled her close. "What's happened in the last twenty-four hours can be a major scar that affects these kids for the rest of their lives, or it can be a pebble on the roadway to a happy future. You are making the second option possible. There is no more important job right now."

She nodded, kissed him, but didn't look convinced. He'd never admit it to her, but Cannon was happy she was safe up in the high school, away from what was going to be a gruesome day, but he understood how it felt to be left behind. He said, "Look, let me help get these kids off your hands and then we can talk about you getting out there, but keep in mind you've got Joshua to think of. What would happen if something happened to you?"

"You've got Joshua to think of too," she said.

He nodded. "See you later."

He slipped into the kitchen, grabbed an egg sandwich, and ate it as he made his way down the high school's long driveway.

On the outskirts of town, the destruction caused by the quake became more profound. Parts of buildings had fallen away, and rubble comprised of stone, wood, concrete, and broken glass littered the streets in neat piles made by the eddies of the receding floodwater. Sorrow crept through Cannon. Stores he'd shopped in, restaurants who'd feed him. All the people who'd worked there. He'd seen some of the folks who worked the area, but many were missing and feared pulled out to sea and drowned in the flood surge.

He'd left his boat tethered to a lamppost at the flood line, which had been halfway up Newbark Street. Now the entire road was flooded, and the water lapped on the cross street.

"Shit," he said.

"Yup," Nate said.

Cannon jumped. "Where the hell are you hiding?"

"Just waiting for you. Any doubts now?" Nate stepped out of what was left of the Pizza Palace.

Cannon looked up the road. Nobody had moved his boat. It was right where he'd left it, so that meant Blackwater Bay was rising. There was no other explanation. "Is the rate what you expected?"

"Maybe a little slower, but I don't see any reason to tell anyone that. Especially since I'm not sure."

Cannon nodded. "The Scotty principle from Star Trek. Always over estimate, that way you look like a hero when you're on time. Extra time could slow things down. Paralysis by analysis. You're right. Let's keep this between us until you have more data. Don't want to provide time that may not exist."

Nate nodded.

The teacher watched Krisp's Whaler bob on the floodwater. Cannon said, "Why are you here, Nate?"

The man looked at his feet, then met Cannon's eye. "I want to come out with you. Help."

"No way, man, this is—"

"An extreme situation. I know. That's why you need as much help as you can get," Nate said.

"Try not to get yourself hurt or killed. You know how much paperwork I'd have to do?" Cannon said.

Deputy Sherriff Day and Clint came around the corner and came up short. "Dang," Clint said.

"And as if on cue the peanut gallery arrives," Cannon said.

"Sheriff sent me to help you," Day said. "Thanks for telling her..." Day looked at the ground.

Cannon looked to Clint.

"She deputized me," Clint said. He let his hand drop to the Colt 45 on his hip.

That made Cannon think of his Beretta M9 and he pulled it from its holster and handed it to Clint. "Don't want it to get wet."

16

Cannon waded through the water to the boat. The trash of humanity littered the floodwater; papers, wood, the scattered remnants of Styrofoam. Cannon stepped on something and looked at his feet. The water was murky, and a thin sheen of oil undulated around his waist.

Sweat dripped down Cannon's forehead as his mind ran through all the possible things he might step on and he grimaced. To his left a red shirt floated on the floodwater, its arms extending as if asking for help. He was halfway to the boat when he remembered his radio.

"Shoot," he yelled.

"What?" Nate's voice echoed down the flooded street.

"Forgot to take my radio off my belt. Now it's a paperweight," Cannon said.

Nate said, "Day has a radio. We're good."

The mayor said Day had been mentally out of it following his encounter with Sigmund, the unknown sea monster. Cannon's stomach burned. The guy appeared OK, but if the shit started flying… He reached the Whaler, untethered it from the light post, and pulled the nineteen-foot center console through the trash-filled water. When the floodwater was two feet deep, he said, "OK, ladies, your chariot awaits." Cannon nudged the boat and turned it bow out. The crew waded into the water and climbed the stainless-steel ladder that hung off the transom.

Onboard they fidgeted and dried off as Cannon pumped the fuel primer bulb. "We good?"

Day stood beside him, eyes glazed, and said nothing.

Clint raised an eyebrow and took a seat next to Nate on the bench in front of the control console.

"Hey, Day, you with us?" Cannon said.

Day turned his head and looked at Cannon, but said nothing.

"Look. We got some serious shit to deal with and if you're not up for it, then maybe you should get off the boat?" Cannon said.

Day said, "What are you talking about?"

"You. You OK? You seem… in space, man. Can I count on you when the bullets are ripping? We've got looters to deal with and they're most likely armed."

"I'm fine," Day said.

"Alright then," Cannon said.

The sound of hydraulics filled the silence as Cannon lowered the Johnson into the floodwater, leaving it angled up slightly. He didn't want to bang the lower unit on unseen debris. The engine roared to life with one turn of the key and spit water out the cooling ejection port, spraying the oily floodwater and creating dimples like thousands of insects crawling over the slick surface.

He nudged the control arm and put the outboard in gear. The Whaler eased through the water, the destruction of the earthquake sliding by on both sides of the street. Cannon made several turns as he wound through the flooded section of Gullhaven, searching for the looters. As he looked on his town with fresh eyes, his heart ached. The Gullhaven he loved was no more, and the new town that would spring up in its place would be forever changed.

"What's that sound?" Nate said.

Cannon didn't hear anything, so he cut the motor and the Whaler glided silently through the floodwater. He heard it, the low rattle of an outboard to the south.

"Give me your radio," Cannon said.

Day looked at him, "Use the boat's UHF."

"It's broken."

Day shrugged and unclipped the radio from his belt and handed it to Cannon.

"Give me the clip. I'm keeping it." Cannon wasn't normally so tactless, but he didn't have time to nurture feelings.

Day stared at Cannon, eyes narrowing, as he tried to figure out whether he had to listen to Cannon's commands. The mayor said it herself, if it's on the water, it's on him. Day came to the same conclusion because he handed Cannon the clip and looked away.

"Base, this is Cannon. Do you copy?"

Static. Broken words, then, "Go ahead."

"Do you have any rescue boats working in the Fitzpatrick Street area? Over."

"One moment, Cannon."

Wind gusted, and the chill breeze made Cannon shiver. He wore his blue uniform pants and short shelve blue uniform shirt. In his haste he'd forgotten to bring his rain slicker, a sweatshirt, food.

"Cannon, nope, we've got nothing going on over there that we know about. Copy?"

"That's a 10-4. We'll go check it out and report back. Cannon out."

Cannon went to start the motor, then hesitated.

"What?" Nate said.

"They'll hear us coming," Cannon said.

Nate nodded.

Cannon pulled a wooden paddle from its holder on the gunnel and held it up.

Clint sighed. "That'll take a long time. They'll be gone."

"True." Cannon put the paddle back.

He had no choice. They had to go in guns blazing, that was the only way.

"OK. We go right at them. Day, take a seat next to Nate and be ready. Clint with me," Cannon said.

Day looked at him, said nothing, and went and sat.

The breeze blew the Whaler up the street, and Cannon spun the wheel and used the wind to turn the boat around. He let the current carry them until they hit Clover Lane, where he turned the wheel again and headed toward the sound of the engine.

Buildings loomed up to Cannon's left, and the wind fell to a sparrow's fart. "OK. You girls ready?"

Nate said, "You have an extra weapon?"

He didn't, but then he had a thought. He bent and retrieved a boat pole from its elastic straps on the gunnel. He handed it over the plexiglass windshield atop the command console, and Nate accepted it, looking at it like it had come from space.

"That's all I got right now."

Nate's eyes shifted to Day's gun, but Cannon shook his head. Day may be flaky at the moment, but he wasn't handing a Glock over to a science teacher. Not yet.

Clint said, "Locked and loaded."

"Don't get itchy. Remember those forms," Cannon said. He felt like shit after he said it. People had died, and he shouldn't be making jokes. "Sorry, just be careful, please. Last thing I want is an innocent getting shot."

Clint nodded. "No worries, brother."

Cannon tossed his head side-to-side, cracking his neck. He looked behind him, did a fast visual inspection of the Whaler to make sure nothing would fly overboard when he punched it, and lit the fuse.

The Johnson screamed to life and Cannon dropped the hammer. The boat jumped from the water, spitting a fifteen-foot rooster tail. Buildings flew by in a brown and white blur, and sea spray pelted the storefronts along the road. Waves rolled through broken windows, sucking out seat cushions, garbage and two corpses.

People waved and called from windows above the flood line, their haggard faces excited and afraid. He waved to let them know he'd seen them and powered on. His list of backtracks was getting long, and that made him remember the teacher, Cindy Becker, whose corpse he'd left on the reception desk in the apartment building next to the office plaza.

Fitzpatrick Avenue was coming on fast, but Cannon didn't slow. He needed the element of surprise. With the Johnson screaming, the other motor could no longer be heard, and he worried they'd taken too long and the thieves had escaped, but his fears were for naught.

Piper's drug store appeared on Cannon's right and that was his cue. He spun the wheel hard, the Johnson choking and yelling, the Whaler jerking over the floodwater. He straightened the boat and drew his Beretta, but there wasn't much to see.

Cannon killed the outboard and the Whaler continued up the flooded street as the wake slammed the transom and pushed the vessel forward.

A crusty old open hull sailboat with a 10HP motor with a painted cover was tethered to a railing out front of Demigods Jewelry and Pawn. There was nobody in the boat. The engine rattled, and a broken mast stuck from the center of the deck and flew a pirate flag. Cannon had to chuckle.

The front window of the pawn shop was blown out, but nobody was visible through the large opening. Surely whoever was in there had heard the Whaler approaching? The boat slowed to a crawl. Cannon left the engine down and turned the wheel, putting the portside against the building next to the pawn shop. It was an apartment building that had once been a department store, and the old red bricks were flecked white with seeping lime. Clint tied the Whaler off on an awning that hung over the building's entrance.

"What do you think?" Clint said.

Cannon said nothing. He peered around the broken window frame into the pawn shop. Shadowy reflective waves danced on the walls as the floodwater roiled and slapped against display cases, but Cannon didn't see anyone. "Whoever it is must be in the backroom." Cannon checked his M9. "I'm going in. Nate, I want you to stay here, ready to fire up the Johnson if we need to get out of here fast. Clint, give me five then follow me in. Day, you follow five minutes after that if you don't hear from us."

Clint and Day nodded.

"Please be careful," Cannon said.

"Yeah, yeah. I know. The paperwork," Clint said.

Before today Cannon hadn't dealt with the possibility of discharging his weapon in the line of duty since he was in the Navy, and that was years ago. He was a range boy. His father, a retired detective from LA, called him that all the time. He said it to be funny, but Cannon knew it was his father's way of telling him he was less than he'd been. A bay constable in a backcountry town was equivalent to a meter maid in LA.

He vaulted over the gunnel and eased through the broken window, being careful not to cut himself on the tiny shark-like glass teeth sticking from the splintered frame. A low buzzing sound and the scent of bleach filled the pawn shop. Cannon waded through the waist high floodwater, keeping his back to the glass cabinets that lined the eastern wall, Beretta held high and pointed at the ceiling.

Cannon slipped behind the counter and a *bang* reverberated through the store. He looked down and saw he'd walked into a wire stretched across the opening between counters that was tied to a vase that sat on a high shelf. The old piece of pottery landed in the water with a crash and busted on the countertop just below the surface.

The buzzing stopped, and Cannon heard water sloshing around. He leveled the Beretta at the backroom door, bracing himself against the wall the way he'd been taught, trying to make himself small.

He waited a five count. Nothing. Another five.

Cannon swung into the open doorway and panned his gun across the backroom. A figure in a black shirt slipped out a back door into an alley. He gave chase, half swimming, half running through the water. A small electric drill sat atop a cabinet, and a dusting of metal shavings floated atop the grease slick on the surface of the floodwater. From floor to ceiling, safety deposit-type boxes lined the wall, and several of the copper colored doors were open.

He exited into the alley, getting low in the water, gun before him in a double handed grip. He flicked the safety to off position with his thumb and took a deep breath.

"Hold it!"

Cannon turned to see a red-haired teenager pointing an old six-shooter at him.

A ray of sunlight cut across the alley, and time stretched out. Clint would be along, so all Cannon had to do was wait and not get shot.

Something glinted in the water behind the kid. A searching white tentacle rose from the floodwater, slithering down the alley like it was the Mariana Trench. The scent of bleach stung Cannon's nose, and a low rumble echoed down the alley. Waves broke against the buildings, but the kid was lost in his fear and didn't appear to notice.

Sigmund was coming, its arms searching. Cannon started to level his Beretta.

"Don't." The punk sighted his gun, arm out straight, oblivious to the chaos building behind him.

If Cannon saw the kid's arm shaking even the slightest bit, or if the gun barrel appeared unsteady, he would have dropped his arm and taken a shot. Could he put the kid down? Cannon wasn't the greatest shot and targeting arms and legs might get him killed. It was center mass with one shot or do nothing. Cannon raised his hands. "All cool."

The slithering tentacle was five feet behind the looter.

"Naw, man, not cool." The kid thrust the gun forward like he was going to fire.

The white tentacle wrapped around the kid's waist, jerking him backward, and he fired into the air. The white arm squeezed the thief as suction cups filled with teeth bit into flesh and bone. Bricks fell like rain at the end of the alley as the leviathan pulled its massive albino girth around the corner of the building. The tentacle thrashed and fell back into the floodwater.

The kid went under and didn't come up.

Blood bubbles popped in the whitewater as the beast came on, the sound of cracking bone and tearing meat making Cannon stagger. Blood and chunks of skin and fat covered the surface of the water, and Cannon retched.

17

Cannon leveled his Beretta at the writhing tangle of white tentacles advancing up the alley and put his back to the brick wall of the pawn shop. A finger floating in the floodwater brought up the rest of the egg sandwich Cannon had for breakfast. He coughed and puked, acid stinging his throat.

The corner of the building at the end of the alley fell away, crashing into the water and sending a debris filled wave rolling down the alley. A basketball sized black eye set in a white carapace peered through the wreckage and locked on Cannon. The leviathan grunted, pushing and pulling its massive girth through the shallow water.

The back door to the pawn shop was ten feet away, and Cannon dove for it, no thought for the noise he was making or whether he'd make it.

A thick white tentacle swept left and came at Cannon, tooth-filled suction cups opening and closing. He planted his feet and fired the Beretta, three shots in fast succession. The tentacle stopped whipping back and forth, three holes leaking blood in the brackish water.

The leviathan stopped advancing, its tentacles disappearing beneath the floodwater.

Cannon pointed the Beretta at the sky, breathing heavy. The blood, skin and fat slick on the water left a ring of nastiness on his shirt and pants, and the smell of blood filled his nostrils. Vomit came up his throat and he couldn't hold it down. He threw up again, bits of egg and bacon joining what was left of the looter.

"You OK out there?" It was Clint.

"Yeah, don't come out here."

Cannon pushed through the turbulent water into the pawn shop's stockroom where Clint waited.

"What the hell happened out there? We heard—" Clint said.

"We've got to get out of here, fast. You can listen in while I give my report," Cannon said.

They raced back to the boat and Cannon fired up the outboard and spun the Whaler around.

"What hap—"

"Not now!" Cannon piloted the boat down the street, glancing over his shoulder every few seconds, but the beast was nowhere to be seen. After they'd gone a few blocks, Cannon slowed and called base to fill in the sheriff.

"So there's no doubt left. We've got a giant mutant octopus-squid terrorizing Gullhaven. Just what we need. I'm glad you guys made it out. Did you recognize the kid?" the sheriff said.

"Not definitively. But he had red hair and freckles and sure looked like Joey Murphy's kid," Cannon said.

The sheriff harrumphed. "Would make sense. Apple don't fall far from the tree."

"I need to continue our patrol. Pick up people as we go? Or do you want me to try and track this thing? Knowing where it is would help us avoid it while we continue rescue efforts."

A pause. Static. Then, "No. Rescue as many people as you can. We can't waste time searching for this thing now. There are too many people still trapped by the floodwaters."

"Well aware of that, base."

"10-4. Keep me informed. Sheriff out."

Cannon sighed, clipped Day's radio on his belt, and let his hand fall on his Beretta in its holster.

"You OK?" Nate asked. The young man had stayed silent throughout his report, his eyes wide as quarters.

Cannon had to laugh to himself. The guy had been all gung hoe two hours ago, but now the creature and a dead looter had him rethinking things. Cannon knew the look well. Most people had a version of it: a mixture of confusion, fear, and anger at the loss of control. But for all that, Nate was a good man. A guy he'd be proud to call friend going forward if they were lucky enough to make it through the quagmire of crap they all faced.

"Yeah. Just a bit shook up. The way the thing… it looked at me, you know? Like we had a moment," Cannon said.

Clint and Nate exchanged a glance.

"I know, sounds crazy, but right before the thing came at me, I felt like we had some connection. Like it was looking to me for answers."

"What it was looking for was its next meal," Clint said.

"You're right," Cannon said.

"It was most likely confused by the unusual surroundings and paused with shock when it saw you. I'd wager that's what you perceived as your moment," Nate said.

"I don't know. Didn't feel that way. It was like… it was trying to talk to me. That's crazy, right?"

Clint and Nate said nothing.

"OK, then," Cannon said.

Clint said, "Anything need to be done about…" He looked down at the deck of the Whaler. "Anything need to be done about the death?"

"I'll take care of the paperwork at some point, but I'm afraid whoever it was will go down as missing. I'd rather not tell someone their kid was killed by a sea monster while thieving. What purpose would that serve?"

Clint shrugged.

Cannon piloted the Whaler up and down the flooded streets, and Clint suggested starting a makeshift morgue on the second floor of Tina's Gym on the edge of the wharf district. So Cannon, Nate and Clint spent the next two hours searching for looters, survivors, and piling corpses.

Most of the wharf was turned upside-down, but there was a crew working to find useable boats. Cannon didn't see any other looters, and as mid-day approached, he radioed the sheriff with an update. She ordered him to give Nate and Clint their own boats and continue rescue efforts. Over three hundred people had been rescued.

"Tanya," Cannon said, but winced. She hated when he used her first name when discussing business. "Have you considered sending out a scavenger party? We're going to need tents, camp stoves, lights, tarps, you name it."

"Was waiting on more vessels," she said.

"Got it. Cannon out."

Cannon transferred Clint to a twenty-one-foot Grady White walkaround with a 175HP Yamaha and step-down cabin. Nate was given an old sailboat. It was underpowered, but they didn't need speed because it could carry a lot of people. Cannon dubbed it the Bus.

People heard the boat motors roaming town and waded out into the flooded streets to be picked up. It always amazed Cannon how much confidence the light of day brought.

Cannon made several trips to the flood line with boat loads of people, all of whom looked tired, hungry, and depressed. As the fear wore off and reality sunk in, the survivors were seeing their destroyed home and thinking about all the money they'd lost and all the work it would take to get things back to normal. Most of the folks he transported didn't want to talk, and that was fine with Cannon. What was there to say? He had no real answers to give them, so he appreciated them not asking.

Cannon saw Clint once, and Nate several times as residents were shuttled up to the waterline, which had crossed Clover Lane and was working its way toward Hillside Avenue, only eight blocks shy of the high school driveway entrance. Nate moved more people than Cannon and Clint combined with his old sailboat, so Cannon decided it made more sense for Cannon and Clint to collect people and bring them to the Bus.

The Bus disappeared around a corner with its latest load of passengers, and Clint took off for Nel's neighborhood where the old houses and apartments were. Cannon brought the Whaler up to thirty knots, weaving in and out of giant pieces of rubble sticking from the floodwater like forlorn monuments of a lost city. There was a lot of debris in the water, and Cannon had the motor tilted up and his eyes never left the sea ahead.

Something splashed next to the metal warehouse on the south side of Izzy's boatyard. Cannon arced the Whaler toward it and brought binoculars to his eyes.

Something white slithered from the bay and wrapped around a six-foot brown lingcod fish.

Cannon pushed down the control arm and the Johnson screamed, lifting the Whaler as it skidded over the floodwater. He headed toward the boatyard, setting a southern course toward the tentacle as it disappeared with its fish.

He slowed the boat, the faint scent of bleach the final clue that Sigmund was in the area. Chilly fingers of fear walked up his back. He was alone, in a nineteen-foot boat, with twelve bullets left in his gun and one spare clip.

The Whaler rolled on the gentle chop, sea spray soaking the deck and draining into the hold. He sat behind the wheel, a sudden barrage of exhaustion washing over him. The bruise on his arm throbbed, and his ankles and knees hurt. Then he remembered the pile of bodies they were making, people he'd known. People whose only crime had been being in the wrong place at the wrong time, and they had received the ultimate sentence. The one you couldn't get paroled from.

It was 2:19PM when Cannon heard it. The deep, air splitting *womp womp* of an approaching helicopter. He shielded his eyes and looked to the horizon, the bluffs rising like a giant wall, blocking out the Pacific.

Cannon brought up the binoculars.

A copter hovered over Devil's Rip. It was low, two hundred feet or so above the pile of rocks that stopped the tides from flowing into Blackwater Bay. The whirlybird hovered there for several minutes before dropping its nose and cutting across the bay.

Rotors hammered the air, and as the copter got closer, Cannon read the name Viking Industries on the bird's side. The helicopter was an Airbus H125, and could carry six people 350 miles without refueling. The black fuselage shined, even in the gray overcast light. The bay reflected off the underside of the chopper, and then Cannon remembered where he'd heard the name Viking Industries. That was Vikram Singh Kahn's company. The millionaire had a house up on the hill and owned homes in San Francisco and New York.

The copter dropped low, leaving a fishtail of water, mist and wind behind as it tore over the bay.

Cannon waved as the whirlybird flew overhead, and the pilot dipped the copter's nose and Cannon gave him a thumbs up. The sound of rotors clawing at the air was deafening, and Cannon covered his ears.

The black helicopter changed course and headed for the high school.

18

Instinct drove the beast forward. It pulled itself around a square rock, reaching out with its eight tentacles and two long whip arms. Claws snapped and searched as scattered signals flooded the beast's brain, white hot heat coursing through its complex nervous system, its skin shifting like a red sunset as it worked itself into a frenzy. It sensed new prey and focused like an arrow, and it knew nothing else.

The square rock splintered and cleaved, shards of stone falling about the beast, impaling its sensitive skin. It pulled itself through a narrow gap, rocks falling around it like the steep valley was collapsing in on itself.

Its forward arm grasped its prey, and the simple organism broke like a shrimp shell. The beast struggled to pull its prize into its maw, the floodwater sloshing and pulling at everything between the giant square stones.

That sound, the scent of fire, and pain.

Danger.

Fear drenched the creature in fury, and the great beast bucked and heaved, slipping back the way it had come.

This feeling, the ache. The beast still didn't understand that the new sensation was pain.

It had left its kill behind, and hunger ate at it, blinding the creature to all other things. It sucked in water, jetted it out, and wagged it stabilizer fins as it rocketed through the bay, cutting in and out of the oddly shaped rocks and the metallic multicolored turtles that never move.

It sensed fish in the bay… and something else. A sound louder than the danger sound that brought the ache. It dove deeper, for the moment retreating to the depths to hunt.

19

The copter flew low over Gullhaven and disappeared behind a building. Cannon started the engine and dropped the Whaler in gear, heading for base. He'd met Vikram Singh Kahn several times, and he thought the man wasn't like the rest of the weekenders that came up from San Francisco to "the country." He was always respectful, and once Cannon saw the man in line in the drug store like a normal person. Most of the rich folks who lived on the hill had their stuff delivered.

The Johnson whined as the boat pushed through a patch of debris. Usually Cannon would've stopped and cleaned the intakes, but he was in a hurry. If that was Kahn flying his bird, he'd have information about the outside world. What was happening down state in Sacramento. He also didn't want the mayor and sheriff filling the man's head with all kinds of bullshit before nonpolitical voices could be heard.

The flood line had consumed Hillside Avenue, and Cannon slowed as the floodwater lapped against the blacktop, creeping ever closer to the high school. The water had encroached thirty feet since morning.

The motor rumbled, then fell silent. Cannon jumped into the floodwater and tied the Whaler off on a No Parking sign. When he was free of the water, he stomped his feet and shook himself like a dog, trying to dry himself as he headed for the school.

He arrived to find a crowd five rows thick around the Airbus H125, which had landed in the half-empty school parking lot like a spaceship. The sleek black craft sat with its rotors spinning slow, both cockpit doors standing open. A beautiful woman with cream colored skin, long silky black hair, and striking green eyes stood next to the copter speaking with the sheriff. She wore a blue pantsuit that looked high-end, but Cannon knew that was the woman's attempt at causal sheik. He'd met Mrs. Priva Kahn, or as she was known in Gullhaven, The Ice Queen, and found her shy, despite her jet set looks. The townies called her Ice Queen because they mistook her shyness for arrogance and elitism, but that's not how Cannon saw it.

He felt the same about Mr. Singh, who stood on the opposite side of the helicopter, speaking with the mayor. Singh wore faded blue jeans, a white t-shirt, and running shoes. He looked nothing like the billion-dollar electronics magnate whose picture had been featured on the cover of Forbes and in the New York Times Magazine, who'd selected him as man of the year in 2018.

A chill breeze tore at Cannon as he headed for the crowd. A dark line of clouds marched across the horizon to the east, and they looked fat with rain. He looked around for Nel, but didn't see her. His stomach sank.

"There he is," Clint said when Cannon arrived at the mayor's side.

Singh and the sheriff stopped talking when he joined them.

"That you over by the wharf when we came through?" Singh asked.

"Yes, sir," Cannon said.

Singh made a show of looking over his shoulder. "My dad here?" His accent was true blue Americana; Indian mixed with southern Californian with a dash of northeast drawl.

Cannon shifted on his feet and looked at the ground.

"Easy, just busting your peanuts. Sir and Mr. are what people call my father. Please call me Vik."

"Yes, s... Will do, Vik." Cannon smiled.

The mayor looked like she'd just taken a swig of three-month-old milk. "We were having an important discussion," she said.

Vik looked at her, then back to Cannon. The question on his face was easy to read: what's the deal with you guys? He said, "Ms. Mayor, I think Constable Cannon should be in on this. He needs to know what's happening out there." Vik smiled at Cannon as if that settled it.

And it did.

Seeing the easing tensions, Clint wandered over with Nate in tow. Clint knew Vik well. He'd done some work over at his house. "Clint, glad to see you up and around."

"All good, Vik," he said. "You look like you need a drink."

Vik laughed.

"What happened out there? How'd you end up here?" Clint asked.

The mayor sighed. "We have to debrief. Is this the best place?" She looked around at all the expectant faces watching them.

Vik followed her eyes and scanned the crowd. "This seems like the perfect place. Everyone needs to know what's happening. We're in for a long, tough time. California is—"

"Sir... I mean Vik, can I have a word?" Cannon said.

A brief flash of anger passed over Vik's face. He was a man not used to being interrupted. Vik's face softened, and he said, "Of course."

Cannon leaned in and whispered, "She's got a point, Vik. These folks are tired, hungry and scared, and they have a long, hard road ahead. Shouldn't we wait to brief them? Why worry everyone with things we're unsure of? At the very least we need to get our ducks in a row so we can answer questions and not sound like fools."

Vik leaned away from Cannon and said, "They're adults. They deserve to know their situation."

"And they will. After we put together a neat package to lay out for them. We can do that as soon as the briefing is over, and we agree on what's next. With big groups like this the discussions turn to shouting matches fast."

"You going to tell them?"

Cannon stepped back. "Folks. We've decided that Mr. Singh is right." The mayor began to protest but Cannon put up a hand. "There will be a general meeting at 6PM in the gym after chow. Give us a little time to get our facts in order," Cannon said.

Vik cracked his knuckles and sighed.

"Let's go inside, get you some coffee, and—" the sheriff said.

"Coffee?" Vik turned to find Clint. "I thought I was promised a drink. I think I need it."

Clint stepped forward. "Coming right up. I'll have some of Tennessee's finest in your coffee ASAP."

"Tanya, let's go to the teacher's lounge. We can talk there," the mayor said.

The sheriff nodded, and she and Priva started for the school. Clint and Nate fell in alongside Cannon, and the mayor said, "Where do you two think you're going?"

Nate stopped walking, but Clint ignored her and continued on.

"What do you mean?" Cannon said.

The mayor rolled her eyes like Cannon was the dumbest shit alive. "This is a high-level meeting for senior staff. These two aren't even low-level staff."

At this, Clint stopped walking and turned. "I'm a deputy," he said and let his hand fall to the Colt on his hip.

"Says who?" she said.

"The sheriff," Cannon said. "And Nate is our key science person, and he understands the situation better than us."

Coming up behind them, Vik said, "The more the merrier. We need all the help we can get." He slapped Clint on the back. "Besides, Clint here is on a mission for me. You got a problem with that?" Vik's tone had changed, and he looked at the mayor with eyes that said, "Go ahead, challenge me."

Mayor Dennison looked at the ground, and said, "Very well."

Cannon smiled.

The crowd dispersed, and Cannon asked Clint, "Anything I need to know about Vik?"

Clint shook his head. "We've had a couple of drinks. No biggie. I help him out time to time, keep an eye on his... interests when he's not here."

Cannon said nothing. He knew his friend was into stuff he couldn't know about, but he'd believed Vikram Singh to be clean. He pushed the idea from his mind. "Alright, you better double-time it to the roof and get him his sniff."

"Yup." Clint peeled off and headed for the stairs in the high school's main lobby. He'd taken five steps when he turned and said, "Oh, Nel was looking for you."

Damn. Cannon almost slapped his forehead like in the old movies he'd watched with his father. He'd check on her after the pow wow. He hit the head, splashed some water on his face, and recalled what he knew of Vik's boat.

Vik's yacht, the American Dream, was the biggest luxury liner in Gullhaven. The two-hundred-twenty foot single stacked, five level floating hotel had a gym, a pool, and was equipped with all the toys required for playing on the sea.

"The American Dream is anchored just outside the break line to the north of Devil's Rip," Vik was saying when Cannon entered. The millionaire sipped a cracked mug with relish, the words Don't Worry, Be Happy painted in red on the white ceramic.

Cannon was last to arrive, and once again all the coffee was gone. He took a seat, holding in the anger fueled by lack of caffeine.

"We were on our way back from French Polynesia. Beautiful flat sea, not so much as a breeze. Right, honey?" Vik turned to his wife, who nodded.

"Then we hear a *whomp*, like half the air just disappeared, and the sea turns into a churning mess in seconds," Vik said.

"The earthquake warning system didn't go off?" the sheriff asked.

"Yeah, about two seconds after I heard the sound. But I have eyes, sheriff. I saw the bluffs crumbling so I stayed away until the tremors stopped."

"Tremors? That what you think they were?" the mayor said.

Vik turned his gaze on the mayor and smiled, but said nothing.

The room grew quiet and the buzz of the compressor on the faculty frig buzzed and rattled.

Vik took a deep breath and looked at Cannon and Clint. "Where I was the quake was little more than tremors. I was in five hundred feet of water."

"You were lucky there wasn't a tsunami," Nate said.

Vik nodded.

"What do you know of the rest of the state?" Cannon asked.

"Not much. The epicenter was up this way, but San Francisco took a pounding. They felt tremors all the way down in LA... yes, mayor, tremors," Vik said. "The plate responsible for the recent quake completely split apart, and a tremendous amount of energy was released. Nobody knows for sure why this type of event occurs, nor do they know the total ramifications of its effects. The quake sent tremors across such a large area because it was unusual."

"How so?" Cannon said.

"Normal faults can only rupture where the slab is being extended. This quake… this bastard spread to deeper parts of the tectonic plate that should be compressed," Vik said.

"So, the very foundation of the Earth has cracked?" Nate said. He looked around at everyone as if to say, "I told you so."

"Pretty much, and it gets worse. The emergency channels are packed. It's going to be a long time before you get help by sea. I'd suggest we try and get help through the mountains."

"No can do," the mayor said. She seemed to relish being able to upstage Vik, even if her news was bad. "Roads are blocked."

"We can open them," he said.

"That will take time we don't have," the mayor said.

"Time? Are you shitting me? We got nothing but time," Vik said.

The mayor sighed. "Nate? Fast, please."

Nate gave Vik the details.

"You're sure?" Vik said.

"No question," Cannon said. "Nate here thinks there's a crack at the bottom of Blackwater Bay, and the Pacific is seeping into the valley. Jives with what you just told us."

"We need to search the bottom for the fissure. See if it can be sealed," Vik said.

"That's nuts," the sheriff said.

"All this earth shifting stuff might explain where this strange beast came from," Cannon said.

"Beast?"

Ruh, roh, Cannon thought. The way Vik's eyes lit up with the possibility of real danger told Cannon he didn't know danger. "There's something odd in the bay. We're not really sure what it is," he said.

Vik's right eyebrow lifted.

"The thing ripped down a building in town. It's tangled with orca, sharks. We've seen tentacles," Cannon finished weakly.

"Giant squid disturbed by the quake?" Vik said.

"We're wasting time," Nate said. "We don't have good enough SONAR to investigate the bay bottom, at least that I'm aware of."

"I can possibly have something transferred from the American Dream, but at that depth we'll get general information. I think we need to put our eyes on this thing," Vik said.

"I'm willing to risk the creature attacking, but without adequate SONAR I don't see how we're going to search the bay bottom, which is a thousand feet deep in spots and covers over fifty square miles," Cannon said.

Vik smiled. "You've never met Pearl," he said.

20

Pearl was a two person, million-dollar luxury submersible designed to turn the ocean into a millionaire's personal aquarium. "Pearl can go deeper than a thousand feet. We'll have no problem finding the fissure," Vik said.

Cannon had seen the sub sitting on the American Dream's deck from a distance several times. It had two large ballast tanks for a base and a glass globe as a cockpit. "No problems? Have you heard a word I've said?" Cannon said.

Vik looked at him like his was nuts, but said nothing.

The sheriff said, "I have to agree with Cannon." She brushed her mane of blonde hair away from her face. "The creature is out there. We have no idea what it is, or what it might do if it sees the sub."

"And even if you find a fissure. So what? What can we do? How could we possibly close it?" the mayor said.

Nate said, "We have no idea what we're dealing with. We need data before we can even have that discussion."

"And to get said data two people need to go into the bay with nothing between them and the beast except a thin piece of glass," Cannon said.

"Not glass, Lexan. It can withstand pressures up to—"

"Yeah? Up to what?" the sheriff said.

"You all just told me the biggest threat to our valley is the rising water. So what's the deal? Anyone got any better ideas?" Vik said.

Nobody did.

"I volunteer to go. I know how to pilot the submersible, and I want to be the one to catalog and photograph whatever this thing is." There was the gleam in Vik's eyes again. "Nate, you want to come with? As the scientist of the group?"

Nate looked to Cannon for help, the edges of the man's face turning a slight shade of green. Measuring water from the surface was one thing, but going a thousand feet deep where sunlight fades and there's four hundred and fifty pounds per square inch of pressure always trying to kill you was something else altogether. "I... I..." stuttered Nate.

Cannon sighed and let the man off the hook. "If anyone goes down with you, it will be me," Cannon said.

"Says you," the mayor barked. "I'm in charge here, and I say who goes."

Vik laughed. "Katy, why don't you zip it? You're not in charge of shit. It's my sub, and if I want to drop her in the bay, that's what I'll do. I don't need anyone's permission."

"But you do," the mayor said. "We're under a state of emergency, which gives me—"

"Cannon, you up for this?" Vik said.

Katy stopped talking and looked at Cannon for help, her face lined with pain and anger.

"Nate, can you help topside?" Cannon asked.

"Sure," the man said. His face brightened at the thought of not having to go down in the sub. "But I think you guys have forgotten something."

Everyone stared at Nate, waiting for him to deliver his edict.

"You said you can drop it in anywhere you want?" Nate said.

Vik wagged his head.

"How do you plan to get the submersible into the bay with Devil's Rip blocked?" Nate said.

Doubt spread over Vik's face, but turned into a wide smile. "Not an issue. The Airbus can haul it over the bluffs."

"Really?" Cannon said. "The Airbus H125 is a good copter, but it's designed to carry passengers long distances, which means it has a large fuel tank, but can only carry a useful load of twenty-five hundred pounds or so."

"Useful weight?" the mayor said.

Vik said, "The amount of weight the copter can carry in addition to its own weight."

"What does the sub weigh?"

Vik did the math in his head and a frown spread across his face. "About sixty-five hundred pounds." He rubbed his chin and looked at the ground. Then he snapped his fingers. "I've got it. The H125 can haul about twenty-five hundred pounds, as you said, counting fuel weight. So if we bring the fuel level all the way down, and have only the pilot in the fuselage to maximize the lift capability, we should make it."

"How do you figure? We're still way short," Nate said.

"Not if we take the sub apart," Vik said. His smile almost split his face.

Cannon said, "You can do that?"

"No worries. My crew can break Pearl down into its four major components," Vik said.

"That'll take forever," the mayor said.

"Nonsense. It's quite easy. The ballast tanks and their support assembly detach, and the tanks can be separated. Then we'll remove the cockpit bubble and related electronics. All that's left is the main fuselage. Should weigh between fifteen hundred and two thousand pounds, the other components less."

"We'll need a ship in the bay," Cannon said. "A big one."

"Where are we going to get one with a gantry arm that can haul over six thousand pounds?" Clint said.

Vik said, "No worries. The Airbus can't lift Pearl when fully assembled, but she can drag her stubborn ass."

The mayor sighed. "And while you're running around doing this, who is going to run the rescue operations?"

"You said yourself the rising water is top priority," Vik said. "Shouldn't you have your best people on it?"

"And I can take care of things here. Get the scavenger parties going and start putting together a tent city out on the ball fields," the sheriff said. Tanya looked at Cannon and bit her lip, her eyes filled with worry.

"The weather doesn't look good," Clint said. "You want to get caught 1,000 feet deep when a storm hits?"

"The rain will make things worse," the mayor said.

"Don't see how we can wait," Cannon said. He turned to Vik, "How long before you can have the sub over the bluffs and reassembled?"

"The sub will be ready by morning. I'll see to it," Vik said.

"And all you need is a ship with a big deck, so your people can put the sub back together?" the mayor said.

"Yes. I can have the sub over the bluffs in about six hours I'd think," Vik said. "We can monitor the mission from the American Dream and topside on the launch vessel. We'll bring the necessary equipment."

"Need anything else from us?" the sheriff asked.

Vik drummed his fingers on the table and looked at the ceiling. "What am I going to pump all my copter fuel into? I've got 379 gallons in there, and three hundred needs to come out."

"Fifty gallon drums?" Cannon said.

"Toby over at All State heat and cooling has a supply of new tanks behind his shop. Good ones with double linings. The Airbus can bring a couple out to the American Dream and we'll lash them to the deck," Clint said.

"Can you see to that?" the mayor asked.

Clint looked at Cannon, who nodded.

"Sure," Clint said.

The mayor harrumphed, but said nothing.

"Cannon, any ideas about this ship we need?" the sheriff said.

"A ferry would work best, if there are any still floating," Vik said.

"I saw the Albatross when I was coming in. It was against the south side of the market, a hole in its side," Cannon said.

"How big?" Clint asked.

"Three feet by three maybe."

"I can fix that. Weld a patch over it. Will it run?"

Cannon said, "No clue, but I can check it out and let you know. The bigger issue is how will we float the mother? She was on blacktop."

"That area should be flooded by now, no?" the mayor asked.

"Should be a couple of feet of water at least. Don't know if that'll be enough," Nate said.

"That rust bucket weighs a ton, but there might be enough water to float it enough for us to pull it," Cannon said.

"Can you have the ferry by Devil's Rip within six hours?" Vik said.

Cannon looked at Clint, who nodded. "We'll try."

The pow wow broke up, the mayor and sheriff huddling-up in the corner, throwing furtive glances his way.

"Cannon, where to first?" Clint said.

"I've got to go see Nel before I'm single," Cannon said. His gaze strayed to the mayor and sheriff who were in a heated discussion. "Can you handle getting the tanks to Vik? Assign somebody to help him and his crew get the thing onboard the American Dream."

"Sure. You want me to meet you out by the Albatross?"

"Could you? Bring the welder. You've got a boat, right?"

"Naw, but I'll team up with someone. Nate going with you?"

Cannon looked over his shoulder. The science teacher waited by himself, like a child lingering around to see if he'd passed a test. "Yeah, I might need a hand."

"Alright then. See you out there."

"10-4." Cannon turned to Nate. "Go get something to eat and meet me at the boat in forty-five minutes."

Nate pursed his lips and then opened his mouth to speak, then shut it.

"What?"

"You're really going down in the sub?" Nate said.

Cannon said nothing.

***

The gymnasium was half empty and Cannon headed outside and found Nel kicking around a soccer ball with four kids. When she saw him, she kicked the ball to Joshua and went to him. "You look tired." They embraced and Cannon kissed her on the top of the head. She frowned.

He had to stop doing that. Treating her like a sister, not a lover. He pulled her in and kissed her hard. She stiffened, looking back at Joshua who watched with a smile on his face. "You miss me?"

"Always. Sorry I've been MIA, but…"

"You're doing your job, and pretty darn well. I'm down to three orphans."

"I see that. The Minter kids and the Fedrick boy."

She frowned.

The Minters ran a mom and pop shop at the edge of Izzy's Marina called Oasis that sold coffee, breakfast and lunch. They were probably both working when the quake hit. Tony Fedrick was a fisherman whose wife had died of breast cancer three years prior. Tony had probably been out fishing or working on his boat when the earthquake hit. If his guesses were right, those three kids would be permanent orphans.

The question was, should he tell Nel all this? Hope was holding her together—just like everyone else—and snuffing out that hope wouldn't help anyone.

"You OK?" she asked.

"Yeah, just thinking."

"I know." She looked back at the kids. "Joshua's been asking for you."

Cannon smiled. With no family of his own, he'd taken Joshua under his wing, and it pained him that he hadn't spent enough time with the boy during the crisis.

"What's up, sport?" He approached the kids.

"Nothing," Joshua said. When Cannon didn't ask another question, the boy said, "Is it true there are bodies floating in the water?"

"Where did you hear that?"

Joshua looked at the ground.

"Here, let me see that." Cannon kicked the ball around with the kids for a few minutes as Nel watched, beaming.

A thin sheen of sweat covered Cannon's forehead when his radio chirped. He pulled it from his belt and opened a channel. "Go ahead base, Cannon here."

"Cannon, we just got a call from up on the hill." He didn't recognize the voice of the person speaking.

The mansions up on the hill started at the mountain top, where Vik had his place, and the houses got closer together and cheaper as the development snaked into the valley and ended with a row of super mansions at the edge of Blackwater Bay. Cannon said, "Go ahead base."

"Ms. Chandrey, you know the old lady that lives in the big old green house on Fifth Street?"

He didn't know her, but he knew the house. "What about it?"

"She spends a lot of time looking out her window as you might expect, and she says she just saw…" The voice ceased.

"Don't tell me? She saw what she believes to be an octopus tentacle pulling something into the water," Cannon said.

"How'd you guess?"

"Clairvoyant."

21

The clouds to the west encroached on the valley, a thick dark line above the bluffs. Cannon piloted the Whaler and Nate stood by his side staring into the mist that rose from the cool water. The bay was a chaotic mess of light chop, the sea dark as oil under an overcast sky. Gulls fought and squawked, divebombing shiners that leapt from the water. The scent of salt filled Cannon's nostrils, and his skin felt tight and itchy.

The Johnson purred, the Whaler doing a pedestrian twenty-five knots, slicing through the two-foot waves with ease. Nate said, "You think the thing will still be there?"

Cannon turned to look at Nate's face. The thirty-something's eyes were red as cinders, and dark black bags hung beneath his eyes. He shrugged and said, "Probably not."

Nate relaxed like a deflating balloon. "Why are we bothering?"

"I want to hear what she has to say. Any information we can get on this thing might help," Cannon said. He turned to Nate and smiled. "Plus, we were heading out this way, anyway, and I want to check in on her. She's alone."

The hill loomed on the horizon, many of the houses dry, but those closest to the bay had significant flood damage. Cannon saw sections of houses missing, and in a few cases, there was nothing left but rubble. Most of the estates were at or below the same elevation as the high school, so if the rising floodwater wasn't stopped, the hill would be consumed along with the rest of Gullhaven.

The depth finder showed eight feet of water and judging by the line of buildings, Cannon knew they were passing over the beach. The land dipped on the north-east end of the valley, and the flood was worse in this area. Cannon saw the parking lot beneath the clear water and drew back on the throttle and slowed the Whaler to a crawl. Boat wake slapped against the transom, and Nate gripped the stainless-steel handrail on the control console.

Cannon piloted the boat around debris, half destroyed buildings, and submerged vehicles. He made a left on Harris Avenue, and the big green house sat at the end of the street raised on a hill. He brought the Whaler to a stop at the flood line, which in this case was halfway up Mrs. Chandrey's driveway.

Cannon tied the Whaler off on her mailbox and jumped over the gunnel into two-foot-deep water. "You coming?"

"Should I?"

"Four ears are better than two. Just let me do the talking."

Nate nodded, and they made their way to the front door, sloshing through the water like ten-year-old boys being forced to go in the children's wading pool with their little brothers. Free of the floodwater, Cannon stomped and shook.

"Remember, let me do the talking."

Nate said nothing.

Cannon knocked.

The door opened a crack, the chain lock going taught below an old woman's face. Ms. Chandrey was a turtle of a women with thick glasses at the end of her nose, a mop of white hair in a bun, and accusatory eyes that unnerved Cannon. She didn't invite them in for coffee.

"Can we come in?" Cannon asked.

"You'll scare my cats. I'll come out." She shut the door and left Nate and Cannon standing on the porch.

Five minutes slipped away before the security chain rattled and she emerged wrapped in a blanket. "Can't imagine why you're here. I told the lady on the phone everything I saw." Copper phone lines worked without power, and crews had gotten a loose network functional above the flood line.

"I'm sorry to inconvenience you, but could you go through it one more time for me?" Cannon said.

She sighed as if she'd just been asked to hike to Seattle. "I was sitting by my front window, drinking my tea, when out of the corner of my eye I saw something over there." She pointed at a gap between two houses across the street. "A snake shot from the water, and I saw something wrapped at its end."

"Something? No idea what it was?"

"Probably a fish, because whatever it was struggled and fought," she said.

"Anything else you think of that might help us?" Cannon said.

She pursed her lips as she looked at him. "You'd be helped by a haircut, and this one could use a shave."

"Thank you, Ms. Chandrey." He handed her his card. "Contact me if you think of anything new or need any help at all in the next few days. Things are going to be tough for a spell. You have enough food? Water?"

Her face softened. "Yes, thank you, constable." Without another word she went back into her house and shut the door behind her.

"Jeez. You get that kind of treatment a lot?" Nate said.

"Naw, but sometimes. When I show up out on the bay it usually means the party is over."

"Party pooper."

"Put it on my tombstone."

Nate chuckled. "What's next?"

"We'll take a look at the scene before we head over to the Albatross."

Cannon boarded the Whaler and dropped the motor as Nate untethered the boat from the mailbox and pushed off, their dance precise and efficient.

Cannon inched the center console through the gap between houses the old lady pointed at. The smell of bleach assailed him, the scent so strong his hand went to his face and covered his nose.

"Not a good sign," Nate said. The science teacher also had his nose covered.

The Whaler eased through a destroyed house, the remnants of a family's life floating in the destruction. There were no bodies, so either the inhabitants hadn't been home, or the corpse collecting crew had already been through this area.

The Whaler came out on the opposite street that ran along the shoreline, the blacktop visible beneath the clear floodwater. Two-by-fours and broken concrete with rusted rebar protruded from the water. The bleach scent faded, replaced by the rank stink of shit.

"Head over there. What is that?" Nate said.

Cannon followed the tip of Nate's finger and turned the wheel, pointing the bow at a jumble of wood, roof shingles and broken bricks. The boat bumped into the pile of debris and Cannon dropped the boat into neutral.

"What the hell?" Nate reached out and plucked something from one of the boards.

"What is it?" asked Cannon.

Nate opened his palm and displayed a four-inch tooth.

"Shit."

"Yup," Nate said.

"That's got to be from one of the creature's suction cups," Cannon said. "Let me see."

Nate handed Cannon the tooth, and he turned it over in his hand.

"Definitely not a shark tooth," the science teacher said.

Cannon slipped the tooth into his shirt pocket and cycled up the Johnson, guiding the boat back out onto the bay. He was almost clear of the floodwater when he stopped, something in the water drawing his attention. The foul reek of waste assailed him again, and as the Whaler cut through a field of black sludge, Cannon's mind spun through a roulette of possibilities: mud from the bottom, dead vegetation covered in mud, or... Sigmund shit.

The clouds on the western horizon were closer and more menacing than they had been just an hour before. It was going to be a killer storm. The tent village would have to wait, and places would need to be found for everyone. He thought of the hill, and how many people could be packed into the huge houses there. Then he imagined the rich folks of Gullhaven bitching and complaining, but that would be minimal. The quake had hit on a Tuesday, which meant most of the transient population were down south earning the dough needed to have a vacation home, so their homes could be commandeered via the mayor's emergency status.

Cannon looked up, wondering how long he'd been lost in thought. The Whaler passed through the shit-field, and the salty sea breeze tickled his nose.

***

As anticipated, the floodwater wasn't very deep around the damaged ferry. The Albatross was tilted to port, and as Cannon killed the Johnson, he saw the flash and glow of Clint's arc welder as he repaired the hole on the boat's bottom.

The whaler nudged against the metal ferry, and a low gong reverberated over the water.

"Yo," Clint yelled.

"How you making out?" Cannon said.

"Good. I turned over the engines. One is down, but the other should start. That good enough?"

"Better. I thought we might need to tow the thing out."

"Good luck with that shit. This thing is a brick, you'd need twenty boats."

"We've got twenty," Nate chimed in.

"How much longer before we're ready to float this bitch?" Cannon said. "You want me to wait around?"

"Naw. I got another hour or two."

Cannon smiled. Clint knew the Scotty principle. "OK. I'm going on a fast rescue run and I'll be back to help you," Cannon said.

"That's a 10-4."

Cannon backed away and spun the wheel, pointing the bow west.

"Where we headed?" Nate asked.

"To Oasis lunch shop," Cannon said.

"The Minter kids?"

Cannon said nothing.

En-route Cannon called Vik on the marine radio. "American Dream, do you copy? This is Cannon."

"This is the Dream, over."

"Where you at with the disassembly?"

"One-minute constable. Mr. Singh said to expect your call." Static, then silence. "Vikram says he's on schedule. He wants to know if you'll be ready?"

"We'll be ready. Cannon out."

Cannon spun the wheel and the Johnson sputtered as the Whaler arced left toward the marina.

Oasis was a small place, set beneath an accounting office at the edge of Izzy's Boatyard where there was cheap commercial real estate. The place's front window was blown out, and Cannon had a flashback to the pawn shop. He killed the engine and eased the bow of the Whaler through the broken window.

"Anyone here?" he yelled.

Nothing but the sounds of water lapping against falling sheetrock walls.

"Anyone?"

"Here! I'm here." The voice was faint and came from above.

Rescue crews hadn't spent much time searching the wharf because it was assumed the area took the brunt of the flood surge.

Cannon looked up to see Mrs. Claudia Minter hanging out an open window. He didn't see Mr. Minter. "Can you get down here?"

"It safe? I've seen sharks."

Cannon looked around and drew his Beretta for show. "Looks clear. Come on down. Your kids are worried sick about you."

Claudia said nothing and disappeared from the window.

Cannon and Nate waited in silence, Cannon thinking about Mr. Minter. Two minutes later, Mrs. Minter was slogging through the floodwater toward the boat. Cannon helped her aboard. He didn't want to mention the husband for fear of upsetting her, but the subject jetted its way forward anyway.

"Have you seen my husband, Constable Cannon? You know Jed, right?"

Cannon hadn't seen the man, which he figured could be good or bad. He did his best to sound positive. "No, Ma'am, I haven't seen him."

A cloud passed over her face. "When the quake hit, we hid under that doorframe there." She pointed at the entrance to the backroom kitchen area. "The water separated us. I was able to hold on to the oven door handle and I wasn't washed away. He wasn't so lucky."

Cannon judged the man's chances of survival at twenty percent. It was possible he was still hunkered down somewhere, but Cannon hadn't seen him at the high school, and if he was there Nel would've known because of the children. He said, "There are many families awaiting news. Let's get you back to your kids and we'll take it from there. OK?"

She nodded.

They didn't speak as Cannon piloted the Whaler through the flooded streets of Gullhaven. For Claudia, it was her first look at her home and what it had become.

The flood line had encroached closer to Tally Street, and Cannon looked to Nate, an unspoken question there. Was the water rising faster than expected?

Once on dry land Claudia was in a hurry, and Cannon was winded when they reached the gym. Nel smiled broadly when Cannon entered like a knight of the round table returning with the grail, but when she noticed Mr. Minter wasn't with them, Nel's eyes dropped to the floor.

Claudia embraced her kids, tears streaming down her face.

"Where's dad?" asked Fred. Tears ran down the child's freckled face.

Claudia looked to Cannon, who smiled, but said nothing. Joshua stood behind Fred, the boy's eyes wide.

22

Cannon and Nate grabbed something to eat, hit the bathroom, and headed back out to meet Clint. It was 3:19PM, and soon daylight would wane and transferring the sub would become more difficult.

As the Whaler sliced through the floodwater, Nate asked, "You think Mr. Minter will turn up?"

Cannon looked at him. "One way or another."

Nate winced. Despite all the death and destruction, the man seemed unchanged by it. He hadn't built up a callus. Cannon envied him. If only he could forget what he'd seen.

The storm clouds continued their march across the horizon in the west, and he judged the storm would arrive overnight. "What do you make of this storm, weatherman?"

Nate smiled. "It's a slow mover, that's for sure. Probably be around most of the day tomorrow," he said. "When you going down you think?"

"Soon as possible. Probably first light tomorrow."

"That doesn't leave much time if you can't find the rift, or there's no way to seal it," Nate said.

"You got another option?"

Nate said nothing.

"I'll get the sheriff to start moving folks from the high school tomorrow, rain or shine. It's chilly out here, but not that cold," Cannon said.

"You think Mr. Singh will let folks camp up on his nice flat high ground up there?" Nate said, pointing to the northeast in the direction of the hill.

"I do, if it comes to that."

Cannon spun the wheel and put the Whaler on a southwest course, cutting past Izzy's and the tangle of boats in the marina and heading out onto Blackwater Bay. A slight chop rippled over the water, a northeast wind having flattened things out. The breeze was cold and bit Cannon's face, sea spray coating the boat with a layer of moisture. The gray overcast sky was draining Cannon's energy like a car with its headlights on and its engine off. He rolled his shoulders, cracked his neck, and flexed his hands, the boat pilotless for a moment.

When they'd boarded the Whaler, the floodwater had encroached another thirty feet and Cannon thought the rate of flow was increasing. The wind gusted, and the Whaler hopped across three-foot waves.

"You see the flood line when we left before?" Cannon said.

Nate nodded and said nothing. That worried Cannon. The science teacher hesitant to speak his concerns out loud for fear of making it real.

"And? Looked to me like things are picking up speed."

"I haven't checked my bayside monitoring station, but I'd have to agree based on what I've seen."

"How bad, you think?"

Nate exhaled like a deflating tire and gazed out over the bay. "Don't know. We should see if we can find my station on the way back. It was out behind Izzy's on one of his dock supports."

"OK. Remind me later. I'll forget."

"Good thing we didn't tell anyone I thought the rate was slowing. Then we'd really be screwed."

Cannon nodded. "How'd you screw up?"

"That's the thing, I don't think I did."

Cannon took his eyes off the sea and looked at Nate. "What?"

"I don't think I was wrong. Something's changed."

"What?"

"Don't know, but I do know that when water is forced through an opening it usually—"

"Expands. Jesus. What are we gonna tell everyone?"

"I think, if we're right, they'll figure things out. Even the mayor has eyes."

Cannon laughed. "That she does."

The Whaler bounced and yawed to port, and Cannon shifted his weight, his shirt flapping in the wind. "Ouch, shit," he said, his hand going to his breast pocket.

"You OK?" Nate's eyes were wide, and his hands shook.

"Easy, I'm fine." Had he made a mistake bringing the science teacher with him? Everybody is tough and experienced when they're sitting in a comfortable room, food and water at their elbow, but out in the field things were different. He brushed it off. Soon Clint would be done with the ferry and he'd have his partner in crime back. "You OK, Nate?"

Nate nodded. "I just... you looked hurt. I was scared you had a heart attack or something."

"No, it was this," Cannon said. He took the tooth from his pocket, flashed it to Nate, and slipped it away.

"Ahhh. You gonna show that to the sheriff?"

"Sure thing. First chance I get."

Cannon arced the Whaler back inland toward the supermarket. The bay got shallow, and soon the boat skipped over roads and around cars and debris. The Food King stood at the end of Halpron Street, half its yellow brick façade gone, the Albatross leaning against the building where the flood surge had placed it.

He eased back on the throttle and the boat slowed, its wake slamming against the transom, throwing spray. Cannon didn't see Clint, but the hole in the side of the Albatross had been filled with a rusted piece of steel, a silver weld line around its edges. The Whaler bumped the ferry and a boom echoed over the floodwater.

Nate stood on the gunnel in the bow, reaching up and tying the Whaler off on one of the ferry's cleats. A gray Zodiac with a five horse Merc bobbed on the floodwater at the stern of the ferry.

"Clint?" called Cannon.

No response.

"Clint?" he yelled.

"Yo. In here." The voice came from inside the flooded market. "Come on in. Having lunch."

Lunch? Cannon looked at Nate, who shrugged.

Cannon tugged on waders he'd brought. They'd been scavenged overnight, but he only had one pair. "You gonna get wet? Or wait here?"

Nate sat on the seat before the command console.

"OK." Cannon eased over the gunnel into the water and trudged through the blown-out glass double doors into the market.

Clint sat above the floodwater on the deli counter, eating a sandwich and drinking a beer. "Yo."

"Yo. You look comfortable."

"Work hard, play hard. You want something to eat? There's plenty of stuff above the flood."

Cannon surveyed the scene. "This place is going to be underwater soon. We need a scav party down here ASAP."

Clint wagged his head and lifted a radio that sat on the counter next to him. "Way ahead of you, as usual. Sheriff says there'll be a crew down here soon."

Cannon climbed onto the deli counter and sat next to Clint, his legs dangling in the water, the waders squeaking on the glass front of the display case. "What you got there?" He pulled a beer from the six pack and popped it open.

"Whatever you want. I even went and found mustard." He held the squeeze bottle up as evidence.

Cannon drew out the tooth. "Check this shit out. Found it over by the hill in a pile of shit, literally."

"Damn," Clint said, putting down his sandwich and taking the specimen from his friend.

Cannon dropped behind the counter, causing a miniature tsunami that rolled across the store, slapping walls and knocking stuff off shelves. "What do you make of it?"

"Not a shark."

"Uh huh."

"From our friend?"

"Got to be. What else attacks everything it comes across if it's not a shark?"

Clint said nothing.

Cannon made himself a sandwich and hauled himself back onto the counter. He took a long pull of his beer, bit his sandwich, and with a mouth full of food, he said, "The ferry ready to go?"

"Yup," Clint said.

"Looks like we've got enough water to get the thing going, yeah?"

Clint had a mouth full of food, so he nodded.

Ten minutes later, sandwiches and beers gone, Cannon, Clint and Nate got the ferry underway. Cannon piloted the Whaler, which had a tow line connected to the Albatross's bow. The ferry's props were still partly exposed, but there was enough floodwater to start the engines. Clint piloted the ferry as Nate watched for problems and debris in the water.

One of the ferry's engines fired right up, spitting seawater like a flailing child. The push of the ferry's engines, along with strategic thrusts and pulls from the Whaler, righted the Albatross and allowed it to float into the deeper water.

Once out on the bay, Cannon disconnected the tow rope and fell in alongside the ferry.

Cannon opened a comm channel. "Clint, you copy?"

"10-4."

"All good?"

"I'm taking on water, but it isn't bad. The bilge pumps are keeping up and the batteries appear to be in good shape. I'm running everything off the batteries connected to the dead engine. When they die, I'll switch over to the batteries being charged by the running engine. We shouldn't have any issues."

"Cool beans. I'll let Vik know we're almost ready."

"10-4."

Cannon called the American Dream and relayed that they'd be in position within the hour. The ferry chugged along puffing black smoke out its exhaust ports, but the trip across Blackwater Bay was slow. When the Albatross dropped anchor before Devil's Rip, Cannon allowed himself a breath of relief and popped a beer he'd snagged from the Food King.

He killed the Johnson and let the Whaler float west with the current toward Gullhaven. Over the next hour he watched Vik pilot the H125 over the bluffs with one of the submersible's ballast tanks dangling beneath it. With the operation underway and the day waning, Cannon cycled up the outboard and headed in.

He looked at the bay with new sight as the boat skipped over the growing chop. This was his bay, and whatever was hunting here had no right... but it had every right, Cannon knew, because this wasn't his bay. The comfort he was used to feeling as he smelled the salt air, felt the sea spray on his face, was gone.

The radar screen showed a deep red blotch to the west, and a weather warning for 6PM ran in black along the bottom of the satellite image. They swung by Nate's station at Izzy's and confirmed what they'd already surmised. The water was rising faster than they thought. The flood line had taken more ground like an invading army, and the slow creep of the floodwater was only five blocks away from the start of the high school driveway.

Cannon and Nate didn't talk as they tied off the boat and waded through the floodwater. He'd be going down in the sub in the morning, and Cannon knew how Nate felt about that. He wasn't having second thoughts about his commitment, but the reality of the situation had begun to take hold. He was going a thousand feet deep, in the middle of a raging storm, which would make visibility in the depths zero without floodlights that take battery power to run. He was to do this inside a hybrid Lexan bubble a quarter-inch thick, knowing there was a massive unknown creature hunting the bay.

When they got to the school, Nate and Cannon agreed to hookup in the morning, as Nate was going to be part of the command team on the Albatross. There were still a few hours of daylight left, but Cannon was shot.

Nel had turned over the Minter children, but she'd received five more kids as the death count rose. He and Nel sat arm in arm, watching Joshua play with the children. It was heartbreaking and exhilarating at the same time.

Cannon glanced at his watch; 6:19PM. It had been two and a half days since the quake, and they had about sixty hours before the valley was fully flooded.

23

Cold rain lashed Gullhaven as Cannon, Nate and Clint raced over Blackwater Bay toward the Albatross in the Whaler. Wind gusted at thirty-miles-per-hour, and black clouds slid east across the sky. The bay was ink, a roiling mess of whitecaps, and the boat pitched and yawed as it cut through the chop. The Johnson moaned and coughed as Spare Change sliced through a large set of waves, spraying seawater fifty feet off the bow. To the east, a faint orange glow fought through the cloud cover over the mountains as the sun tried to break through.

It was 7:18AM. Forty-seven hours to go.

Clint had arrived at the high school the previous evening, dead tired and starving, but bearing good news. Vik's submersible was almost assembled and would be ready to hit the water at sunrise. This brought a round of golf claps when reported to the mayor's advisory group, but Cannon felt anything but triumphant.

He was scared. The quake happened so fast he hadn't had time to be frightened, but with the dive he had all night to envision the small two-man sub wrapped in thick milky tentacles as they squeezed the life out of the submersible like popping a zit.

Cannon sniffed and caught the faint scent of bleach hanging in the air. He pulled back on the throttle and slowed the Whaler to twenty-five knots, the Johnson's screaming falling to a low wail. The prior night he'd broken out in a sweat while going to the bathroom, the faint scent of bleach from the day's cleaning bringing him back out on the bay like a time machine.

He lifted the binoculars and scanned the bay, moving the field glasses in an arc south to north. Something flashed off the starboard bow, something writhing in the water, or was it a whitecap? Whatever it had been was gone so fast Cannon was left wondering if he'd seen anything. He looked over at Clint, who gazed west at the bluffs looming in the distance, his face expressionless. Nate sat before the command console, eyes hanging half closed. If either man had seen anything, they weren't showing their cards.

Cannon rubbed his eyes with one hand and pushed down the throttle with his other. The Johnson roared, and the Whaler jumped over the waves at thirty-five knots.

The Albatross's lights stood out in the gloom of the rainstorm like a launch pad, the submersible sitting on the main deck surrounded by floodlights like a spaceship. All that was missing was the clouds of coolant fumes and steam.

Cannon slowed the Whaler and Nate went to the bow without being told. They each had their duties onboard, and Nate had developed into a decent mate. With the boat tied off, he killed the engine and gathered his stuff. This time he'd brought a sweatshirt and an extra pair of socks. Vik had warned him that, even though the sub had heaters, it still got cold in the depths.

"Yo!" Vikram Singh's head appeared at the top of a ladder that hung over the ferry's side.

"Morning," Cannon said. He mounted the ladder behind Clint, Nate trailing behind. He shook Vik's hand when he emerged on deck. "All good?"

"Right as rain," Vik said, turning his palm out and up, gesturing toward the rain that fell in sheets.

Vik wore a yellow rainslicker from LL Bean, its hood up, his hooked nose sticking out. Cannon stripped off his lifejacket and threw it over the gunnel onto the Whaler's deck. He wore his blue raincoat which had 'constable' stenciled on the back in big white block letters. It was old and torn, and he hated wearing the hood because it impeded his vision, but the fabric in the hood smelled like Nel, so there was that.

"You ready for this?" Vik said, motioning toward the sub.

Cannon nodded, but said nothing.

The Ocean Pearl was a two-person submersible manufactured by Seamagine Hydrospace Corporation. The cockpit bubble opened like a clamshell, and inside there were two bucket seats with large thirty-inch flat panels mounted before them. One seat was the pilot's chair, and a joystick sat idle before it.

Vikram said, "The joystick controls Pearl's yaw and pitch, along with speed and stabilization. I've piloted it many times, so you have nothing to worry about."

Cannon's eyes strayed to the bay, but he said nothing.

"In surface mode the flotation systems allow the sub to sit high in the water for easy access, but today I think we'll buckle-up while it's still here on deck," Vik said.

Cannon's face must have revealed his feelings, because Vik laughed. "Don't worry. It's quite safe. When submerged, Pearl remains positively buoyant, and should the thrusters stop for some reason the sub will slowly surface if we want it to. Once underwater, this baby will always stay horizontal, very little roll and pitch."

The screech of the air hose being removed from the ballast tanks made Cannon jump and jerk his head toward the sound. Air in the tanks would give them increased buoyancy they could release when then were ready to descend, and water could be supplied to the tanks if more weight was needed. The trapped air would then be used to blow out the tanks to return to the surface.

A man strode up to Vik, and waited.

Vik said, "Yes, ensign?"

"The sub is ready for launch, sir. Shall I call Trey and tell him to bring the Airbus?" the young man said.

"Give me a few minutes to bring Cannon here up to speed. Let's say we set drop-in time at 7:45AM." Vik looked to Cannon for approval, and he nodded. "Good." The ensign turned on a heel and retreated.

Cannon noticed a section of the ferry's gunnel had been cut away next to the sub on the port side. "We going through there?" Cannon said, pointing at the gap.

Vik nodded. "As I mentioned yesterday, the Airbus can drag us and hopefully we'll have a soft landing.

"Give me one minute. I've got to go down below," Vik said, and he disappeared through a hatch in the deck.

"You alright, partner?" Clint said.

Cannon had forgotten Clint and Nate were behind him. "I guess."

Rain lashed the three men as they examined the sub. Pearl sat on its ballast tanks, two twenty horsepower venturi thrusters positioned in front of each. The round glass cockpit was covered with a metalwork of bars that protected it in the event of a collision—or attack, Cannon's mind shouted. Behind the bubble was the sub's DC electric motor that propelled the sub at speeds up to four knots.

Vik emerged from below deck. "Nate, is it?"

The science teacher stepped forward, hand out. Vik took Nate's hand and pumped it. "You can head up to the command center in the pilothouse. You'll be able to monitor everything from up there and communicate with us."

Nate looked to Cannon, and he nodded. Suddenly Cannon felt something for the man, like he was saying goodbye to an old friend that he was never going to see again.

"Let's step out of the rain and go over the mission log, yes?" Vik said.

Cannon nodded.

They went through a bulkhead door into the main cabin of the ferry. "So, our plan today is to search as much of the bottom as possible. We've got a lot of ground to cover, but I suggest we go deep first," Vik said.

"I agree," Cannon said. "Nate and I discussed this last night, and he believes the fissure is just a continuation of an existing crack that was widened by the quake. He suggested starting deep as well."

"Good. Pearl has sufficient battery power for a six-hour mission, with almost a hundred hours of reserve power for emergencies," Vik said.

"That's a lot of juice," Clint said.

"Sure is," Vik said. "It's also got independent back-up systems for life-support. Just in case. Any questions? We'll go over the procedures and control once we're saddled-up."

"I think I'm good," Cannon said.

"Let's get on with it then."

Clint said, "Can I observe from the command center?"

"Sure thing. We wouldn't be here without you, Clint. Can you find your way?" Vik asked.

Clint nodded. "Good luck, guys."

Outside, three men stood around Pearl in the rain, waiting for Vik and Cannon. As the two-man team approached, the crewmen opened the glass clam and Cannon and Vik slipped inside, the glass dome coming down over Cannon before he was strapped into his seat. He felt claustrophobic already. His pulse raced, and pain lanced his lower back as the adrenaline flowed.

He clasped his harness and settled in his seat, the sound of rain pelting the glass bubble and drawing his attention upward. Through the blurred Lexan he watched the crew scrambling around, and he heard the *womp womp* of the approaching Airbus.

Vik leaned back in his command chair and took a deep breath, the control joystick between his legs like a helicopter yoke. "OK, as you can see you don't need to do much. The screen before you displays the rear and side cameras, and you can remove the system's status bar at the bottom with a swipe of your finger if you want the camera images bigger. The dummy lights on the status bar monitor interior and exterior pressure, battery strength, sub speed, angle of descent, depth, and life support, which has four separate icons for oxygen flow control, CO_2 monitoring, oxygen percentage, and sensor status."

Cannon said, "I'll keep the status bar right there, thank you very much. I like knowing how much air I have left."

Vik chuckled. "You're not a bay constable afraid of the bay, are you?"

"Naw, but I ain't Aquaman."

Another laugh. "Don't worry, it won't come to that."

Cannon said nothing. It sure as hell could come to that. He reached out and ran his finger along the inside of the glass bubble. All he could think about was tentacles wrapping around the Lexan and crushing it to sand.

Vik tapped on his control panel, adjusting systems as he prepared to dive.

The copter was close now, its pounding rotors blowing around the men on deck waiting to accept the hoist cable. The steel coupling at the cable's end hung before the cockpit globe, and Cannon worried about it hitting the glass. Part of him wished for that to happen. He cracked his neck and tried to relax, closing his eyes and listening to the patter of the rain.

Wind tore at the sea, and the clank of the host cable being connected to the sub made Cannon look to his partner. Vik studied him, then clapped him on the shoulder. "Worry not my young squire, we shall return victorious. Here," Vik said. "Put these on." He handed Cannon a headset with a microphone.

Cannon slipped it on and heard static, then, "You copy?"

"10-4," Cannon said.

"Albatross, do you copy?" Vik said, tapping his control screen.

"We're here, Mr. Singh," said Nate.

"Vik, my boy, Vik." The millionaire in his element now. He put his hand over the mic on his headset. "Just kept in mind that when the topside comm light is green they can hear everything we say."

Cannon gave a thumbs up.

"Mr. Singh, this is Trey. You ready?"

"Go for it," Vik said. Then to Cannon, "Hold on. This is going to get a little dicey."

The Airbus cycled-up its engines, the rotors pounding the air like a hurricane. The submersible shuddered and trembled. Cannon looked up through the glass and watched as the pilot dipped the whirlybird's nose and pressed forward.

The sub jerked and slid with the screech of metal on metal, the submersible inching toward the gap in the three-foot gunnel. A gust of wind pushed the sub to the right, and the craft veered off course, but the copter pilot corrected and banked left, dragging the sub through the gap.

The copter shrieked as it was pulled downward, but it caught air as the sub hit the bay with a splash and the hoist cable went slack.

Seawater bubbled over the glass as the Pearl settled in the bay, waves breaking over the cockpit.

24

Cannon's heart pounded as the Pearl bobbed on the storm swept sea, bay water splashing over the polycarbonate cockpit bubble. Blackwater Bay roiled, angry whitecaps pounding the Albatross and the submersible as the H125's rotors beat the air.

A frogman appeared beside the sub and climbed onto one of the Pearl's ballast tanks. Cannon saw the man's face behind his dive mask as he gave a thumbs-up and released the coupling connecting the sub to the Airbus. The sub dipped and swayed as the helicopter lifted away, water clearing from the cockpit bubble like the submersible was coming out of a car wash and going under the dryer.

"You buckled in?" Vik said.

Cannon nodded.

Vik said, "All hatches and intakes are closed." He tapped his monitor. "Pressure up." Vik released air pressure into the Pearl and Cannon's ears popped. "Opening vents."

The sub listed as the ballast tanks filled with water and the sub settled in the bay.

"Good to go," Vik said.

The Pearl lifted and fell in the swells, and Cannon's stomach ached, his nerves on puppet strings of adrenaline. A diver's mask-covered face appeared before them giving the all clear sign, and Vik gave the man a thumbs up.

Vik started the electric engine, eased forward on the throttle, and pushed the joystick down, guiding the Pearl underwater. The submersible's nose dove beneath the waves as the rudder and trim tabs angled the craft downward. Bay water washed over the cockpit and the sub leveled out, the waves no longer tossing the three-thousand-pound vessel around like a toy.

Cannon's stomach went cold as he felt the rounded clear cockpit bubble shrinking around him. He breathed, closing his eyes and mastering his fear. Everything he'd ever done in his life had brought him to this place. This was his purpose. He would help Vik save Gullhaven, feelings be damned.

Vik said, "You OK?"

Cannon nodded, but said nothing.

The radio crackled. "Pearl, this is the Albatross. Do you copy?" It was Nate.

"Why don't you handle communications," Vik said.

Cannon tapped the topside communication icon on his screen, and said, "We copy, Nate. Go ahead."

"Can we get a systems check, please?"

"Since you asked so nicely. Everything is green here, Albatross."

"Give us a status check at five hundred feet, over," Nate said.

"That's a 10-4. Cannon out."

"Enjoy the sights before it gets dark," Vik said. He moved the joystick forward, putting the Pearl into a thirty-degree descent. The sub spiraled downward, leaving a trail of bubbles in its wake.

Ten minutes passed and the gray light from above faded. Vik checked their depth and said, "Better call topside. We're at five hundred feet. Welcome to twilight."

"Didn't take long to get dark down here," Cannon said. He tapped the floodlight and spotlight icons and an array of two LED floodlights and four remote controlled LED spotlights cut through the inky grayness, scattering a school of fish.

"Even bright sunlight fades at around six hundred feet as you enter the disphotic zone. With the storm raging there's hardly any light to start with today," Vik said.

Dropping into the murky darkness was unsettling, everything beyond the LED lights' illumination a nothingness of blackness. Cannon examined his monitor, trying to get his mind off how much water was pressing down on the Lexan bubble above him.

"Six hundred feet," Vik called out.

Bubbles streamed by the sub, and Cannon turned in his seat, searching the bay.

"Kill the spotlights and leave the floods lit," Vik said.

Cannon shut down the spotlights, realizing conservation of power was important if they wanted to stay down for the full duration of the sub's capacity.

Schools of fish darted passed the nosecone, the sub's lights glimmering off their silver scales.

"You ever been this deep?" Vik asked.

Cannon shook his head no.

"Don't worry. It's very safe."

"Says you."

"You sound like my mother. Always looking for problems before they arrive, creating them in a way."

Cannon needed to talk to sooth his nerves. A thin smile spread across Vik's lips. Cannon said, "Are your parents still around?"

Vik drew back on the joystick and the Pearl leveled out as it dropped into the abyss. The millionaire laughed. "Around? Yeah, they're around alright. Giant pain in my ass is what they are."

Cannon was surprised to hear Vikram speak of his parents this way.

"Don't get me wrong, I love them both, but damn did they both change when my life took off."

"How?"

"The old man wanted me to be a doctor, surprise, surprise. I didn't know what I wanted to do and when I left university, they practically disowned me. 'You're not living here. Don't come to us for money.' Yada yada," Vik said. "Then as soon as my first company hits and I'm making serious dough they come to me. Tell me they don't want the same things anymore and they're splitting up. Getting divorced. Same things? Are you shitting me, I say. You've been married forty years, of course you don't want the same things. Now I'm carrying two separate estates for them and I have to deal with boyfriends and girlfriends."

A large snake-like eel wriggled before the sub and Cannon jumped, the creature turning its luminescent eyes his way and flashing its teeth before disappearing into the darkness.

The water temperature outside the sub was fifty-six degrees, a drop of ten degrees from surface temperature. Cannon rubbed his hands together, but the interior of the sub was a balmy seventy degrees, the life support system measuring and treating their cabin air. His mind was making him cold. The thought of all that water between him and breathable air. Cannon's hands trembled and sweat dripped down his back as panic waged war on common sense. Everything was fine. He was fine.

Cannon talked to hide his unease. "What's that do?" He pointed at a robotic arm that was bent over itself and tucked against a ballast tank.

"We can control that from in here. See the basket below it? We pick-up specimens and shells and drop them in there," Vik said.

"Seven hundred feet and dropping," Cannon said. He glanced at his watch. 8:05AM. They'd been wet twenty minutes. He rolled his shoulders and tossed his head side-to-side to crack his neck. Vik watched him, the thin smile fading from his face.

The cabin was tight and reeked of body odor. The hum of the electric motor and the pop and rush of bubbles played rhythm to the buzz of the thruster's lead guitar. Propellers churned, and the sub vibrated as it lumbered through the sea. He tapped the pressure icon. Exterior pressure was over three thousand pounds per square inch and rising as the submersible continued its dive to the bottom.

"Eight hundred feet. This is the deepest I've ever had her."

Cannon wished Vik had kept that little nugget of information to himself. He stared into the blackness, his lower back screaming with pain, nerves jumping. His eyes slid from the dark water to his control panel. He toggled through all the exterior camera images, but there was nothing except the sea and streaking bubbles.

"What about you? You're from down south, right? Not from here," Vik said.

"LA. Dad was a cop, mom a teacher. She died when I was sixteen. Cancer. Dad was never the same. We were never the same," Cannon said. That was more than he'd told anyone other than Clint and Nel since arriving in Gullhaven.

"Sorry, didn't mean to pick a scab."

"No. No. It's alright. I see dad occasionally. Usually go down there at Christmas time. It's just we…"

"Don't have much to talk about? I hear that. My father watches FOX news all day. I don't even know who he is anymore."

Cannon laughed. Did he ever know his father? An LA detective who cracked some of the biggest cases of the last twenty years and his son wrote tickets for people speeding through the inlet and taking twenty-inch halibut. "I hear that. At least your…"

"It's OK. You can say it. I'm rich. It isn't a dirty word. You're right. The money certainly changed their opinion of me, but I think that bothers me more than anything else. I'd expect that from strangers. But from my mum and dad?"

"Everybody has an anchor to carry," Cannon said.

Something flashed in the darkness ahead and Cannon flipped on a spotlight and adjusted its beam to illuminate the area.

"What?" Vik said.

At first there was nothing, just bubbles and whitewater churned up from the thrusters, blackness beyond.

A shark glided from the darkness like a stealth submarine, the great white's slick gray body shimmering under the LED light. With a wag of its caudal fin the beast came forward, mouth flexing open, flat dark eyes peering through the polycarbonate glass at them.

The great white slithered through the bay, circling around the sub, as if sizing it up. "It'll move on," Vik said. "I've been feet away from ones bigger than this guy. He's curious. He won't—"

"Whoa," Cannon said.

The shark drove its snout into the submersible's nosecone, opening its jaws, trying to take a piece out of the Pearl.

"Damn. I've never seen that before." Vik drew back on the throttle and pushed the yoke left, and the sub arced away from the shark.

"Eight hundred feet," Vik said.

The shark kept pace with the sub as it descended, as if waiting for backup. Then the great white got bored and darted upward out of sight with a wriggle of its tail.

Cannon studied the sub control lights at the bottom of his screen. Everything showed green.

"Coming up on nine hundred feet. Let's get all those lights back on and check in topside," Vik said.

Cannon activated the four spotlights, angling them to give each camera a chance to pick something up. Water refracted the LED light and the bay depths were still. He called Nate and gave the OK.

"Cannon, can we keep this channel open? The camera feeds aren't showing much. Over?" Nate said.

Cannon let static fill the channel as he looked over at Vik, who shrugged.

"That's a 10-4, Albatross."

Seawater pushed the sub around and Vik struggled with the yoke, trying to keep the submersible on course. "Getting some strong currents rising from the bottom to the east. Bring up your SONAR and take a look. Icon's in the upper right."

Fear washed over Cannon, Nel's face filling his mind's eye, his father's voice admonishing him for his stupidity. "What kind of dumb shit goes a thousand feet deep in a soap bubble?" He rubbed his hands together, breathing in through his nose and out through his mouth.

"Nine hundred feet. We should reach bottom shortly. Anything unusual up there?"

"SONAR looks clear, Pearl," Nate said.

Specs of organic material glistened under the LED lights, and the bay got cloudy and visibility dropped.

"Dang. We must be getting close to the bottom. Kicking up silt. Turning off thrusters."

The whine of the propellers ceased, and the swirling bubbles cleared. Cannon undid the clasp on his harness and leaned forward in his chair. His back was cramped, and he did his best to stretch in the confined space. He took a pull of water and offered the bottle to Vik, who took it and drank deeply.

"Not much to see yet," Vik said. He tapped his display and SONAR covered the screen.

Nothing moved in the darkness. No giant stalks of kelp. No seaweed. Here in the darkness, photosynthesis wasn't possible, and the hydrothermal vents were too deep to support chemosynthesis.

The cabin grew hot, and Vik turned up the air scrubbers and lowered the cabin temperature. The bay water outside the sub was forty-eight degrees and rising.

"Odd," Vik said. "Albatross, what's the normal bay temp at this depth this time of year?"

"Unknown, Pearl," said Nate.

"Guesses?"

"Colder than forty-eight degr—" Nate said, his final word cutoff by static.

The water cleared, and Vik pulled back on the yoke, leveling out the Pearl, the bottom visible through the murky water.

25

A thousand feet down in the darkness, the Pearl's exterior LED lights illuminated a world that resembled a desolate planet. Sand and silt blurred the water as strong currents ran along the bay bottom, dark patches of black mud like blemishes. No vegetation swayed, and no coral formations teemed with life. Only shards of stone stuck out like teeth, the bottom of Blackwater Bay barren.

Cannon panned around the sub's LED spotlights, looking for anything unusual. The bay floor rolled on into the blackness, not so much as a bump or dip.

"Anything?" Vik asked.

"Hard to see the bottom with all the swirling silt, but there's nothing of significance yet."

"You can see well enough?"

"To find the rift? Yeah."

"Ok. I'm gonna run a basic grid pattern until we have something better to go on," Vik said.

Cannon nodded. He peered through the clear cockpit bubble, searching the bay. Something glinted in the distance off the port bow and Cannon adjusted the spotlights.

"Got something?" Vik eased the yoke to the right and the sub changed direction.

"I think… what are they?"

"Viperfish," Vik said. "Very common at these depths. They usually migrate toward the surface at night to feed."

The gang of viperfish changed direction as one and came at the sub. The green and black fish were a foot long and sported fang-like teeth used to kill its prey. Vik said, "They can live for forty years, but die in captivity within a few hours. See that dim light blinking from them?"

Cannon nodded.

"To entice prey, they flash that light on and off, and twist their dorsal spines like a fishing reel." Vik pulled back on the throttle and slowed the sub. "Looks like it's covered in scales, doesn't it? But it's not. We don't know what the Viperfish's skin is made of. They normally hide deep, so there isn't much information on these creatures beyond the basics."

The group of seven fish circled the Pearl, their unhinged jaws revealing rows of white teeth. They passed the sub, fins slithering through the water.

"These things normally like warmer water. Might explain why they're here," Vik said.

Cannon's brow knitted, then he remembered the water temperature increased when they'd passed nine hundred feet.

"Like many things that live in the abyss, viperfish can go long periods without food," Vik said.

"You ever see one before?"

Vik said, "Only pictures. They rarely enter the twilight zone and never the euphotic zone."

The fish scattered and disappeared into the blackness, the sub's searchlights creating patches in the darkness like spotlights on center stage.

The Pearl trembled and was pushed off course. "Shit," Vik said. He struggled with the yoke and eased back on the throttle. "The current is really strong. We're getting pushed west."

"Cause?" Cannon said. He'd brought up his SONAR, but nothing showed above the rolling blue-black pixelated smudge that marked the bottom.

"Unknown. Feels like water pressure," Vik said. When he realized what he'd said he looked at Cannon. "The fissure. Setting an easterly course." He pulled back on the control stick and the sub listed to port as the Pearl turned in a wide arc.

The thrusters stirred up silt, and visibility went to zero. It was like they were in a sandstorm. Bubbles streamed through the murk and Cannon adjusted the angles of the exterior cameras, but clouds of sand and whitewater filled the screen.

The sub cruised fifty-feet above the bottom, diving nose-first into the wall of pressure. Cannon worked the cameras and examined every shadow. The rift was most likely large, but Vik had said they couldn't rule out several smaller tears.

"So you're with Nel? She seems great," Vik said.

"You know her?"

"Don't know anybody, but our paths have crossed. I see her in The Bean sometimes."

"Really?" She'd told Cannon she'd given up her obsessive coffee habit.

Vik looked at him, eyebrow lifted, eyes squinted.

"I just… I thought… She told me she didn't drink coffee anymore."

"Ahhh. Relationships."

"You don't know the half of it."

"Really? Nel is a beautiful woman. You're single. She's single. What the hell is the problem? You're not one of those needy dudes, are you?"

Cannon considered this. Was he needy? He didn't think so, but maybe he was wrong. Cannon spilled it all to Vik, telling him all about Sherri, her death, his feelings of responsibility. How Nel was the first women he'd been with since.

"Damn. How many years? You're like a virgin again."

"Thanks for the thought."

"What's holding you back? Sherri? She's been gone a long time."

"I know, but it was my fault, and now I just get to live on? Have a nice life?"

"Are you shitting me? Come on, man. You're no more responsible for her death than I am."

Vik tapped his control panel and adjusted the floodlights. The flat brown nothingness of the bay floor slid by below, not so much as a shallow hole visible.

"I was the one that made her jump. The one—"

"Made her? Did you throw her off the cliff? She decided to swing on the rope. Next you're going to tell me it was your fault the rope broke."

"If she hadn't been on it…"

"Bullshit. Get over yourself. You think you control your life?" He chuckled, tapping his screen and adjusted the temperature of the air flowing into the cabin. It was getting hot.

"Water temperature is up to sixty-one degrees," Cannon said. "How can that be?"

"Flow from a thermal vent," Vik said. "Don't change the subject. You don't control your life. All you can do is make decisions based on what you think is best. Control? It's an illusion, even for someone like me. Like right now, for example. It appears that I have full control of the sub, right?"

Cannon nodded.

"But I don't. Not really. What if an earthquake hit right now? The Lexan bubble over our heads cracked? Or the bay bottom opened and swallowed us? All these things could happen right now. What control? We have no control. Therefore, there's no way you can be responsible for Sherri's death. You loved her. I get it. But you need to move on, buddy. I don't know you well and even I can see that."

Cannon said nothing. He'd said too much and now he felt like a fool, but was Vikram right? Had Cannon been carrying the weight of the world on his shoulders? Maybe he was wrong about everything. "What about you? You and Mrs. Singh happy?"

He laughed. "Happy? Shit. That word is worse than control."

Both men laughed.

"Didn't know you were an amateur psychologist."

"Intro to Psych in college. Guess some stuff stuck, but yeah, Priva's alright, most of the time."

Cannon hadn't seen the woman since she and Vik had arrived on the Airbus. She'd retreated to the American Dream and was waiting things out in luxury. "Where did you meet?"

Vik scowled. "This is going to sound strange, but it was kind of arranged by our parents."

"Really? Wow, uh... I didn't think..."

"It's OK. Untie your tongue. We weren't forced to get married, our parents introduced us and encouraged our relationship... convenient. Over time we came to love each other."

Water bubbles snapping around the sub, oxygen leaking through the life-support vents, and the faint rumble of static filled the silence.

Vik piloted the Pearl along the bottom, fighting the current that pushed silt at them like a sandblaster. Through the cloudy water, tiny pinpricks of light shone in the darkness ahead. Cannon looked to Vik to see if the man had seen the lights, and he had. Vik was transfixed, gazing through the cockpit bubble. His hand drifted to his display and he tapped off the exterior light array and the Pearl was plunged into complete darkness.

Lights glowed in the distance like stars at the edge of interstellar space. Unlike real stars, these lights moved, zigzagging and darting through the water.

"Anglers," Vik said. "These bad boys have been around since the early cretaceous."

A fish swam into view and Cannon let out a slow breath.

The brown angler had long raised scales along its back and tiny black eyes that were so recessed Cannon couldn't see them. A long fleshy growth stuck out from the top of the fish's head like a fishing pole, and its tip emanated light to entice prey. The fish's large head had a crescent shaped mouth full of fang-like teeth angled inward to make it easier to snag small fish.

"Remarkable," Cannon said. He knew things lived in the darkness of the deep, but not being a biologist, Cannon had always believed life wasn't possible without sunlight. Even in one of the most desolate spots on Earth, nature had found a way.

His nerves eased, and he no longer obsessed about the thousand feet of water sitting atop him. He'd never be comfortable in the sub, but he no longer feared for his life. A large bubble snapped against the cockpit and Cannon jumped, the sound reminding him anglers and viperfish weren't the only things in the depths. What else swam in the darkness? He knew, and the thought brought back all his fears and worries.

"There are many types of anglers and they can be found in most deep seas. Their modified dorsal ray is different for every subspecies, but they all light up. Survival in the abyss requires these types of odd bioluminescent adaptations."

The sub's electric motor whined as it fought the intense current driving everything west.

Show over, Vik turned the floodlights back on, but left the spotlights off. The sub glided through the darkness, a cone of light before it.

Cannon rubbed his hands together, chasing away an imaginary chill. "Let's find this rift and get the hell out of here," Cannon said.

"Yeah. I think you're right."

Cannon said, "Time?"

"Elapsed mission time is 157 minutes. Plenty of time left. I'm a bit concerned about the rising water temperatures, but it won't affect the sub."

"Power is at 61%," Cannon said.

"We're burning juice fighting the current."

"Should we break off and come in at another angle? Maybe use the current in our favor?"

Vik rubbed his chin. "Last thing we want is to get caught up in the flow of this thing. Lose control of the sub and end up rolling around on the bottom like a stone. I'm gonna bring her up a bit. Give us a little more space." Vik pulled back on the yoke and the sub's nosecone rose, driving clouds of silt and whitewater.

"You seeing this?" Cannon said. He pointed at his screen where the local SONAR image filled his screen.

A massive blue shape dropped on them from above. The heat signature shifted and changed, the image going from red, to blue, to yellow and back to red.

"What do you make of that?" Cannon said. "School of fish?"

"Too big for that," Vik said. He looked over at Cannon and for the first time he saw fear on Vik's face.

The current jerked the sub around, the cloud of pixels on the display slowly closing the distance from the surface to the bottom. The sea shook, like an explosion had detonated.

The SONAR cleared, and the giant shape was gone.

26

The monster darted through the darkness, all its warning senses reading danger. Its tentacles and arms flayed about, ripping at the bay. It had passed above the lit thing, evaluating, preparing to strike, but then it felt the sea tremors, the vibrations in the water warning the beast that another predator was near. The strange light had a clear carapace, and the creature sensed prey within.

The grey form of a great white appeared in the dark water, and the beast hung in the darkness, waiting, fearing nothing as sea water surged around it. Its tentacles and arms floated loose, twisting and writhing like vipers.

The shark knifed through the sea and struck the giant beast a glancing blow, the shark's teeth tearing into the beast, but not taking hold.

The leviathan's whips coiled and struck, reaching out for the shark as it faded back, preparing to take another bite.

The light from the strange clear creature holding its prey disappeared into the darkness below.

The beast moved, trying to throw off the attacking shark, but the twelve-foot fish was like a heat guided missile, and it changed direction along with the beast.

The shark thrust downward with its tail, accelerating, scything through the sea toward the monster.

The creature jerked backward, and a shock wave of water rolled through the depths and pushed the shark off course. The beast flushed its ink sac and a black cloud filled the water, further confusing the shark's small brain. The leviathan lashed out with all its appendages, coiling around the shark and dragging it down.

The beast was no longer the prey, but the hunter.

Tooth-filled suction cups fastened to the shark and blood filled the water, pushing away the ink. The whips tightened, pulling the fish in, drawing the great white toward its open maw.

The shark buck and rolled, twisting in the beast's grasp, but the creature held on, attached to its enemy in several spots. The beast's skin shifted color as it attacked, and the shark struggled, but it was a losing battle. The monster drove its prey into the depths, water streaming from its siphon.

The shark spasmed. It was drowning, deprived of oxygen as the beast held it still. The shark stopped struggling, and the beast spiraled downward with its prize, tearing chunks of flesh from the great white with its whip claws and feeding its beak.

As it fell, the odd lit creature reappeared in the darkness below. Even as the beast ate the shark, hunger consumed it and its primal thoughts shifted to new prey.

27

It was 11:19AM and the two aquanauts were starting to tire. Cannon saw it in Vik's face; his normal laugh lines smooth, lips flat and absent their smirk curl, and a focus that told Cannon things were getting real. His own stomach had informed him of this some time ago, and as the Pearl glided along the bay bottom, he felt nauseous.

The radio crackled. "Pearl, this is the Albatross. Status, please." Nate sounded concerned.

"All systems green. We're working our way around some stronger currents we think are blasting from the rift. We should have it in our sights soon. Over," Cannon said.

"Copy, Pearl. Things are getting dicey up here. Check-in at fifteen-minute intervals, please. Albatross out."

Cannon felt Vik's eyes on him and turned. The man had a look of consternation on his face, and Cannon said, "What?"

"I've had an idea. Open a channel."

"Albatross, do you copy?" Cannon said into his headset microphone.

"We copy, Cannon. Go ahead."

"This is Vikram. Maybe it's best if you take the Albatross and its crew to a safer location. You're not doing anything for us where you are. Copy?"

"Stand by, Pearl." Low, consistent static like the hum of an old radio filled the line. "Vik, you've got a plan for the sub?"

"Since the H125 can't lift the Pearl, I figure I'll surface in shallow water, tie it off, then Cannon and I can get out without waves pounding us. Once the clamshell hatch is open, the sub is susceptible to sinking," Vik said. Then reading the silence, "The thing has insurance, but we might need it again, right?"

"10-4, Pearl. We'll wait around as long as we can then move inland. Continue with status reports every fifteen minutes."

"10-4, Pearl out."

Vik navigated south and turned east once when the current lessoned. "We're getting steady resistance again. Anything on the SONAR?"

"Big depression at three-one-three."

"Setting course." Vik tapped his control display and gently pushed the control joystick to the right. The sub effortlessly changed direction and drove nose first into the current.

The submersible glided through the dark abyss, the floodlights catching nothing but small specs of silt and vegetation shining like tiny stars under the harsh LEDs.

Vik shivered and shook himself. "So, why'd you become a cop? 'Cause of your dad?"

Cannon gazed into the depths, the lifelessness reminding him of his own life, a barren wasteland with no color, no variety, and no future. "That was part of it. I was in the Navy, but I was an electronics tech. Never saw any real action except once."

"Do tell?"

Cannon sighed. "It's the wrong kind of story. One I'm not proud of because of the end result, but still..."

"Ah, you sacrificed to do the right thing?"

Cannon jerked his head toward Vik, eyes wide.

Vik laughed. "You think I got where I am by not being able to read people? You're an ethical man. Doesn't take much to see that."

The electric engine whined as the sub drove into the current, Vik straining with the yoke to keep the Pearl on course.

"I don't know. It's one of those things I look back on and ask, what if I had handled things differently."

Vik stared into the blackness and said nothing, knowing Cannon would continue.

"I was supposed to be on leave. I was stationed on the Enterprise. Bridge RADAR technician. Anyway, I'm onboard when most folks are onshore partying and having fun. Me? I'm going to the bridge to check on a diagnostic when I hear yelling. Sounds to me like a struggle. So, I follow the sound."

"Don't tell me, let me guess. The sounds were coming from an officer's cabin?"

Again, Cannon was amazed. "Yup. Care to finish the story?"

"What was the asshole doing? Taking, um, liberty with a crew member?" Vik said.

"Sure sounded like it. I put my ear to the door. I knew what I needed to do. The woman was whimpering. To me it sounded like a child was being beaten. It was the Chief Engineer's cabin. A guy I knew to be an... asshole."

"So, what'd you do?" Vik's eyes never left the blank watery expanse before him.

Cannon sighed. "Actually, what you'd think. I burst into the room and found him on top of her. He turned on me and told me to get out, but I held my ground. Then she started yelling for me to get out."

"Oh, boy. It was consensual?"

"No, but I found out later she didn't want to report the incident because she didn't want anyone to know."

Vik shook his head. "I've read the military has a sexual assault problem. Women are afraid to report."

"Very common in general. Makes my blood boil just thinking about it."

Vik nodded agreement but said nothing.

"I spent the rest of my enlistment driving people back and forth to the airport down in Alameda."

The fissure appeared out the murky water like a giant shipwreck. A dark gash fifty feet wide disappeared into the darkness to the south and north. Cloudy water streamed from the rift, waves of heat visible on the SONAR. Blackness filled the void.

"Damn," Vik said.

Cannon opened a channel topside. "Albatross, this is the Pearl. We've found it."

There was a delay, then, "Well done, Pearl. Document everything you can. We're moving off spot. The Albatross is taking on serious water."

Cannon said, "Clint still there?"

"Here, Cannon."

"Your patch fall off?"

"Partly, but this tub's got leaks everywhere and a few more have sprouted in these harsh conditions."

"That's what you say. Remember, paperwork, Clint. Paperwork."

Vik maneuvered the sub south, moving around the crack. The fissure's edges were already covered with tiny white tube worm-like stacks with black tops. Seeing Cannon's fascination, Vik said, "They're probably eating the algae that lives off nutrients proved by thermal vents deep below."

The fissure reminded Cannon of cracks in the ground he'd seen out in the desert when every trace of moisture had been removed. The cut was a jagged scar, the sand and silt having been cleared away by the current revealing stone.

"Cameras on and recording," Cannon said. He adjusted the angle of the forward camera, pointing it downward and did the same for those on the stern and both sides.

"The current is crazy. This is as close as I can get," Vik said as he struggled with the yoke.

"Are you seeing this, Albatross?"

Static. No response. Cannon lifted an eyebrow and looked at Vik.

"Don't worry. They said the storm was getting bad. They're probably out of range or the weather is messing with things."

"Or both." Cannon tapped buttons on his display, but nothing changed. The bay was cloudy with silt and the maw of the fissure opened before them.

"I'd love to go down there," Vik said.

"You crazy?"

"A little. You have to be to be a submariner." Vik adjusted the Pearl's levels and temperature controls. "Look, I think we've reached the end."

The fissure was narrowing and closing as they went south. The gap closed to ten feet, and the current lessened considerably. Vik said, "Changing course so we can find the other end." He drew the joystick toward him and to the right, and the sub spiraled away from the fissure as the submersible turned around.

"Submariner?"

Vik laughed. "We all have our war stories. Mine are just as boring as yours. Locked up in a tin can for months at a time, with only men and their failing mental states and increased body odors. I hated it."

"Ever see any action?"

"Yup. Just not the good kind. Twice we thought we were launching our missiles only to be called off."

"Missiles? Nukes?"

"One of them was nukes. Imagine that? I thought the world was done."

"Yet here you are."

The sub purred on and Cannon closed his eyes, breathing deep and settling his nerves, which had reasserted themselves.

When the sub reached the opposite end of the fissure, Vik said, "How the hell are we going to close something that big?"

Cannon didn't answer at once. He tapped his screen, looked over his shoulder at the whining engine, then said, "Explosives? Strategically placed detonations that would cause a cave-in?"

"I don't know. With the water pressure and currents fighting us, we'd need a lot of explosives. Could we even get what we need?"

"Now that is the question. I know Tim Leppers has some dynamite he uses to blast up in the mountains when he's working in the mine, but that wouldn't work here. Could we make something?" Cannon said.

Vik shook his head. "We'd need a hell of a lot of pipe bombs. And we're underwater. Igniting them and keeping things dry would be impossible given what we have at our disposal."

"How big you figure the fissure is?" Cannon was talking to keep his nerves from shaking him apart.

"At least a half mile long. Fifty feet across at the widest point, but as you saw at the end, it's still widening." Vik's face clouded with pain.

"That's it then. Gullhaven is lost," Cannon said.

"Maybe not. I think we're looking at this all wrong. Maybe instead of trying to close the fissure, we should try and open Devil's Rip."

Cannon jerked back in his seat like he'd been punched. "Above water we could use the dynamite."

"Detonation wouldn't be an issue, and we don't need to clear the whole mess, just make it so water can flow," Vik said. His console beeped.

A red blob with blue arms dropped from the top of the screen and filled the frame. The thermal coloring of the anomaly shifted as it descended.

"This image isn't a bunch of smaller organisms. It's like before, one giant mass, and it's coming down on us fast," Vik said. "The current and turbulence it's causing is pushing us around. You better hold on."

The submersible pitched backward, the Pearl fighting to maintain speed and course. "You think we should get out of here?" Cannon said.

Vik looked unsure. He peered upward through the Lexan bubble, searching for answers.

The image on the SONAR grew, filling the screen. In the darkness there were no shadows and their LED light made the sub stand out like a cockroach on an infant's ass. "Killing exterior lighting," Cannon said.

Darkness filled the bay outside the sub, the glow of their cockpit lights leaking into the blackness like sewage.

"Shutting down interior lights," Vik said.

The cabin went dark save for the glow of the helm monitors. Vik's face looked haggard behind his lit screen. "Shutting down engine."

"What? Why? Shouldn't we run?"

Vik shook his head. "Haven't you ever seen Empire Strikes Back?"

"Of course, what the hell—"

"Remember when Han and crew escaped? You remember how they got away?"

Cannon had a vague memory of the Millennium Falcon with his landing claws affixed to the side of a giant Star Destroyer. "Then they floated away with the garbage," he muttered.

"That's it. I'll let the current carry us away and hope the creature doesn't notice us."

"Didn't work very well for Han. They ended up getting caught anyway and Han got stuck in a block of carbonite."

The hum of the electric motor died, and silence pressed in on the sub as it was pushed away from the rift. Vik tapped his control screen and turned off the emergency ascend system. Darkness pressed in on them and the silence was unnerving. Cannon thought he heard his blood coursing through his veins, but it was only bay water rushing past the sub as it was pushed away from the fissure.

The massive anomaly descended, filling the SONAR screen.

28

"It's almost on us," Vik said, the glow of his control screen casting blueish light on his face.

The oily darkness pressed in on the Pearl as it sat on the bay bottom, and claustrophobia rose in Cannon like a storm tide. He didn't like tight spaces, and he'd been sealed up in a mason jar a thousand feet down for almost four hours. His undershirt was wet with warm sweat, but he was chilled. His hands trembled, his nose ran, and his lower back responded to the adrenaline running through him with sharp pain that made Cannon stiffen in his seat.

SONAR showed the massive anomaly three hundred feet above the submersible. Cannon looked up, straining to see anything, but there was only blackness with an occasional streaking bubble. Cannon fought the urge to turn on the cabin lights, but fear kept the urge at bay. His heart raced, and he felt an overwhelming urge to scream.

Cannon opened a channel topside, though he didn't expect to get a response. "Albatross, do you copy?" Static. He tried three more times as the multicolored unknown object from above closed in and filled the SONAR. Cannon turned to Vik. "How big do you think this thing is?" Cannon had his own theories based on what he'd seen, but he needed to talk, or he might lose it.

"Big. It's your monster. Has to be. There's nothing even close to this size in these waters. A fifteen-foot great white would be a dot about the size of a golf ball at this magnification. It's real big, and it's homing in on our location."

"That makes me feel so much better." The question Cannon wanted to ask, but was afraid to hear the answer to, was, "How will we defend ourselves if the beast attacks?" Instead he said, "It senses something. Vibrations in the water?"

"We haven't moved in ten minutes. It could have sensed our position before we shut down. Sharks can sense vibration in the sea miles away. If this thing is from the deep like Nate thinks, it's probably extremely sensitive of sound, light, and vibration like most abyssal creatures."

"Again. Not making me feel better. Shouldn't we be worried here?" Cannon said.

The anomaly was almost on them.

Cannon and Vik peered upward as something massive hovered in the murky water. Cannon's hands shook so hard he sat on them. The monster moved, and the currents it created pushed the sub across the bay floor.

"Oh, shit," Vik said.

The creature blended into the overwhelming blackness and in the absence of light it was difficult to see the leviathan, but Cannon felt it.

A tentacle reached out and probed the Pearl, and Vik jumped and yelled.

Cannon griped the armrests of his chair so hard his hands hurt. Something Vik had said was fighting to get to the surface of his mind, struggling to be heard. Abyssal animals... what was it? "Lights," he blurted.

The tentacle had withdrawn, and nothing could be seen except the swirling water and bubbles left in its wake.

"What? Light what?"

"You said it before. Abyssal animals are very sensitive to vibration and light, and—"

"And if we blast it with our lights, it might lose our position and be startled enough to let us get away," Vik finished.

"Better than waiting for it to pulverize us. You saw how thick that tentacle was. If it wanted to, the monster could crush us like a grape."

Vik breathed deep and closed his eyes. "Firing up lights." He tapped the icon on his command screen and the bright LED lights lit the abyss with a flash of white light.

The massive beast jerked back, sending a wall of strong currents in the sub's direction. In that fleeting moment, Cannon caught a glimpse of the monster.

It was a hideous prehistoric looking beast that resembled a giant mutant squid, but with several notable upgrades. The deep-sea monster's two basketball-sized eyes stared out from an armored carapace that tapered back over a teardrop torso with stabilizer fins and a tail ending in a thin caudal fin. Its eight serpentine tentacles were covered in spikes and suction cups filled with teeth. The two longer whips ended in claws with white tooth-like serrations along the inside edges. The claws snapped and cracked, searching for prey.

The beast was forty feet long, and as it writhed from the lights, Vik fired up the electric engine and spun the sub around.

The creature shot through the water like a torpedo, tail first. The mutant, like its relative the giant squid, had been designed to move backward with greater speed and efficiency than forward. It attacked, with its tail and caudal fin thrust before it, two giant whips looped back in attack position, eight serpent arms reaching for the sub as it sped off through the bay at five knots.

"We can't outrun it," Vik said.

"You think of this now!"

Vik pulled hard on the yoke, and the sub listed sharply to port. "I'll make a jagged course. Maybe it'll throw the thing off."

Tentacles writhed and whipped around the Lexan cockpit bubble.

Cannon was sure he had only moments to live. Seconds passed as the sub raced through the bay, the electric motor moaning, the twin thrusters digging into the bay.

"Why hasn't it attacked us?" Vik said, eyes focused on the empty seafloor.

"It's still sizing us up, trying to figure out if we're edible," Cannon said.

"You'd think it would be pissed off because of the lights. Maybe—"

The sub was pushed to starboard, and Cannon was jerked in his seat harness.

"Pearl. Do you copy? Vik? Cannon?" The Albatross was back online.

Cannon said, "We're being chased by the creature."

The monster's dark shadow passed overhead, its arms hanging around the sub like a living cage. The massive creature blossomed into the light, its torso and flaying arms filling Cannon's view. Its beak-like mouth opened and closed, rows of white razor-sharp teeth glinting in the LED light.

The creature surged upward, and the resulting concussion wave drove the submersible backward, and it spun and twisted as it tumbled through the bay. Cannon squeezed his eyes closed, thinking about praying but not doing so. What good would it do? He hadn't been to church since he was a boy and he'd learned there that God only helped those who worshipped him.

Cannon heard Vik's heavy breathing. The man didn't look so confident anymore. Even if the beast didn't manage to eat them alive, when the Lexan bubble cracked, the pressure would crush them, and maybe that was for the best. He said, "Vik, should we scuttle the ship?"

Vik turned to look at him like he was insane, and in that moment, Cannon did feel nuts. What the hell had he just suggested? Suicide?

Vik didn't answer, but returned to his controls.

The beast lowered itself onto the sub, and the vessel creaked as tentacles wrapped around the submersible. It was only a matter of time now.

Vik spun in his seat, grabbing the joystick that controlled the robotic arm. The claw at the end of the arm opened and flexed, then reached out for the creature. Vik clamped the claw onto a tip of one of the tentacles, severing it.

Pale yellow blood filled the water and turned light blue as the beast spasmed. The impact wave drove the sub into the bay floor and silt and sand obscured their view as the vessel's nosecone drove into the bay bottom.

The sound of rending metal and the tinkle of cracking Lexan filled the cabin. A thin crack appeared in the nosecone to Cannon's right, a white line that ran to the cockpit hasp. The submersible lost power, plunging the sub into complete darkness and blinding them. All systems were down, including life support.

Vik spun in his seat and threw open a service panel on the port bulkhead. He pulled wires free and began separating them, rerouting power.

Cannon sat, stunned. Even though he'd expected this he still couldn't believe he was going to die a thousand feet down where his body would never be found, and he and Vik would forever be interred in their watery grave.

Vik cursed as he messed with wires. "One of the batteries is damaged, I think. I'll disconnect it and reset the bus."

Cannon waited and watched the leviathan as it brought its claws around and grabbed the sub by the ballast tanks.

The interior lights came back on, then the exterior floodlights.

The creature bucked and heaved, a low bellow vibrating through the water.

Vik started the electric motor and dropped the throttle, kicking up silt and making visibility zero. He pulled back on the yoke and the sub rose from the bay bottom and fought through the sea, passing between writhing tentacles.

With a battery down, mission time had been cut in half, and they were now running on emergency power. Vik guided the sub upward, bubbles streaming by the cracked cockpit bubble that so far hadn't leaked.

Cannon said, "Should we blow the ballast tanks?"

"Negative. That will send us straight up, but I wouldn't be able to maneuver the sub as well. I'm thinking evasive action is crucial at the moment."

The beast was behind the sub, and the rear camera showed the creature pulling itself along the bay bottom, its tail slithering through the water. The two long arms with claws reached out for the sub and in moments the Pearl would be in the creature's grasp again.

The surface hailed them, and Vik said, "Turn that noise off."

Cannon stabbed his screen and the Albatross's hail fell silent. His head pounded as he watched the beast float over the sub. Metal grinded and the sub jerked as Cannon was pulled in his harness. He moved the rear camera view to the top of his screen, watching as the claws closed the last few feet. Just as the claws were about to bite down on the ballast tanks, Vik threw back the throttle and the sub slowed. The long arms flew past the cockpit bubble and Vik let the sub slam into the beast's face.

He dropped the hammer and the thruster propellers spun, kicking whitewater into the creature's eyes. Another crack appeared in the Lexan, and the engine faulted, but didn't stop. Vik maneuvered the robotic arm toward the monster's eye as it struggled to bend its arms and grasp the sub, but the submersible was too close. Vik turned to port, and the beast swam upward, disappearing in the silt filled water.

Vik tugged on the joystick as a surge of water slammed into the sub and the Pearl yawed. The submersible's electric engine whined, and the sub tumbled through the sea out of control and landed on the bay bottom.

Cannon adjusted the angle of the rear camera with a tap of his index finger. Clouds of white bubbles streamed over a black background.

"What in God's name is that?" Vik said.

The rear camera showed a line of circles, pink and white, each rimmed with teeth.

"Our death," Cannon said.

The rear camera was ripped from the submersible and the top of Cannon's screen went dark.

29

Vik drew back on the throttle. The thrusters slowed and stopped driving the submersible's nosecone into the bay bottom. Clouds of silt filled the water as Vik worked the yoke, trying to get the Pearl off the bottom.

The status display icons at the bottom of Cannon's screen were mostly red, but it was the thirty-two percent battery power that worried him. With one battery down, the remaining power cell was struggling to provide the juice needed for the thrusters, life support, LED lights and a slew of other ship systems, each of which took a slice of the electrical pie.

The Pearl shuddered as it broke free of the bay bottom, rising through the cloudy water. The beast was nowhere to be seen, and Cannon breathed a sigh of relief. Maybe the thing had gotten bored and moved on. Or it wasn't hungry or didn't like the taste of Lexan.

The white underside of the beast and its serpentine arms blossomed from the darkness into the glow of the LED lights.

"Oh, shit," Vik said.

The creature's claws clamped down on the sub and pulled it toward its open mouth.

Cannon screamed as Vik pulled on the control stick, but the sub wouldn't budge. The sound of rending metal sent spasms of pain down Cannon's back and two more cracks appeared in the cockpit bubble. Whitewater and bubbles streamed around the nosecone as the sub was dragged toward the creature's open maw.

"This isn't working," Vik said. He brought the throttle to neutral, then dropped the hammer, using the sub's momentum and the strength of the beast's pulling tentacles to drive the sub at the creature's face again.

Vik raised the robotic arm like a lance, positioning it to impale the beast's eye.

The creature's jaw flexed, its teeth white under the LEDs. Vik pulled back on the yoke with a primal scream of fury, and the nose lifted just enough for the sub to crash into the leviathan's carapace above its eyes. The robotic arm missed its mark, and the tentacles wrapped tighter around the sub. The Pearl creaked and moaned, metal flexing, plastic breaking.

With a thrust of its tail, the beast pushed the sub downward and slammed it into the bay floor. The thrusters stopped, the lights went out, and their screens went dark. Bubbles popped as they streaked around the sub, and Cannon felt a soft puff of air from the vent next to his seat. Life support was up thanks to emergency backup systems.

Otherwise, the Pearl was dead in the water.

"You OK?" Vik said.

"I think so." Cannon felt his head where a thin stream of blood slid down his forehead from a gash. He stretched his legs and his knees hurt badly.

The two men sat in the still darkness, staring up into the blackness through the spidered Lexan, waiting for the bay or the beast to finish them. Cannon's eyes adjusted to the darkness, but there was nothing to see.

"We've got a flashlight, but I'm thinking we should stay dark," Vik said.

The bay bottom settled, covering the submersible in a thin layer of sand and silt. The water was still, and Cannon saw nothing moving in the blackness.

"We can't stay down here forever. Rescue is out of the question and we're running out of air and power," Cannon said.

"All excellent points."

"Why aren't we rising? Didn't you say if the sub crashed it would ascend?"

"We're stuck in this silt pretty good and the ballast tanks are still full. Plus, I'm fairly certain I forgot to turn the system back on. Remember I turned it off when we wanted to be sitting on the bottom? As a last resort we can blow the ballast, but I'd have little control as we go up," Vik said.

"If you can't get the power back on, what choice do we have?" Cannon looked up at the cracks in the Lexan, but he could barely see them in the complete darkness.

"Another excellent point."

Silence save for the sound of bay water sloshing around the disabled submersible.

Vik clicked out of his harness. "Let me see what we've got."

In the darkness, Cannon heard Vik snap open the access panel on the starboard bulkhead. He chanced a short burst of light that filled the cabin like a camera flash.

"Shit," Vik said.

Cannon smelled burnt rubber.

"The panel is fried. Emergency back systems are controlled by a relay, so we've got life support, but nothing else," Vik said.

"So you can't get the thrusters going?"

"Might be able to, but it will take time."

Cannon said nothing. Every minute they waited was one less minute of air. Cannon thought the best plan was to take their chances, blow the ballast, and start heading up. On their way, Vik could try and restore some of the sub's systems. He said, "Look, I know blowing the ballast is risky, but what choice do we have? Either the thing gets us, or we asphyxiate. Why not try?"

With communications down there was no way to get other opinions and Vik sighed. "I don't like it, but I see your points. I'll dull the flashlight beam with a cloth and maybe I'll be able to get us some juice."

"We're good then?"

Vik sighed in the darkness. "I just don't know."

A faint bioluminescent light floated through the blackness to port, and Cannon gazed through the cracked cockpit bubble, transfixed. Something glinted to his right, and a tentacle hung in the water next to the sub, but it wasn't writhing or searching. It simply hung in the water, content to sway with the current.

Cannon whispered, "Can you get the emergency comm up?"

"That I should be able to do once I have a bit of light. It's part of backup systems."

"Do we risk it now?" Cannon peered upward, waiting for the monster to descend through the darkness.

"No. What can they do for us? We're on our own until we get closer to the surface," Vik said.

"If," Cannon said. "Only one way to do that, and that's go up."

The beast passed overhead; Cannon could tell because the currents rocked the sub around, kicking up more silt and sand.

The toggle switch for the ballast tanks was on a control bar beneath Vik's dark display screen. There were four manual relays there that didn't require power. A switch to release compressed air into the ballast, one to flood the tanks, another to open the cockpit bubble, and a fourth to open the vents.

"OK. Let's do it." Vik sounded like he was trying to convince himself, but it didn't matter.

Vik flipped the toggle, and there was a loud *pop* as air was forced into ballast tanks, evacuating them of seawater. Whitewater and massive bubbles slid by in the blackness. The sound reverberated through the sea, notifying all the creatures of the deep that there was prey available.

The Pearl started to rise, sluggishly at first as the craft struggled to free itself from the bay bottom, then faster as it escaped in a cloud of bubbles and started the thousand-foot ascent to the surface.

Cannon held his breath, waiting for the leviathan to swoop down and finish what it had started. The submersible leveled out as it rose, gaining speed. Minutes ticked by, and the beast didn't show itself.

A drip hit Cannon on the nose, and he wiped it away with his middle finger and tasted the water. Salt. He reached out in the blackness, running his hand over the cracked Lexan until he felt a bead of moisture there. "Damn," Cannon said. "The cockpit bubble is leaking through one of the cracks."

"I figure we're at about eight hundred feet. As we go up the pressure will lessen. We might make it," Vik said.

Might. That was the first time either of them had acknowledged out loud that this may be their final ride. Cannon said, "Got any duct tape?"

"As a matter of fact, I do. There is no mix-up duct tape can't fix-up. Behind you in the storage container. Also, there's a bottle of emergency air under each seat. Get them out. We might have to abandon the sub at some point when we reach the surface."

"Planet of the Apes style?"

Vik laughed.

Cannon snapped out of his harness and felt around his seat. He unclasped the hasp on the container and reached blindly inside. His hand hit plastic, a box that was most likely the first aid kit, bottles of water, medicine, then he felt the sticky edges of the tape and pulled the roll out.

The tear of the tape sounded like an avalanche in the silence of the deep. Cannon placed several pieces of the silver universal problem solver over the hole, then taped up the cracks as best he could. Not being able to see in the dark was growing frustrating.

A faint glow filled the cabin as Vik turned on the flashlight and dulled it with a rag.

Gray light appeared above.

Static burst from the headset Cannon had forgotten he was wearing.

"Got it. We're on the emergency channel. Go ahead."

Cannon said, "Mayday. Mayday. This is the submersible Pearl. We are in need—"

Nate stepped on Cannon's transmission. "Thank God. We thought we lost you."

"Not yet. Do you have our position?"

"Negative, Pearl. We are off site. Over."

"Send as much help as you can to our last known surface location ASAP. Sigmund is on our tail," Cannon said.

Nothing but stuttering static.

"Do you copy, Nate?"

"Yeah, we copy. Sending everything we've got your way."

"Copy that."

Cannon and Vik looked at each other, the faint light from above getting brighter.

"We're halfway, I figure," Vik said.

Like the coming of day, the pale surface light leaked into the bay, and fish, debris and kelp took shape in the haze. Bubbles streamed past the submersible as it rose, the battered sub creaking under the strain.

Cannon ran his hand along his duct tape repair. It was damp, but with the pressure easing, he no longer worried about the bubble breaking. In the growing light Cannon stared down between his feet, the clear cockpit bubble revealing the dark shape of the beast as it hung in the water below.

"Holy shit," Cannon said.

Vik's head jerked toward him and Cannon pointed.

The creature's long whip arms came at the sub, claws snapping.

"Jesus, what can we do?"

"Nothing," Vik said.

As they passed what Vik guessed was the three-hundred-foot mark, the beast was fifty feet behind the Pearl.

Cannon closed his eyes and breathed. His hands were rock steady. He hadn't come back from the depths of hell only to be eaten with the surface in sight. Pain cut through him and he forced himself not to watch the beast as it came at them. Waves broke on the surface above and sound returned to the world. The distant rumble of an outboard, crashing whitecaps, and the wonderful screech of gulls.

The Pearl broke the surface, bay water frothing over the cockpit bubble. The submersible rocked and jerked in the four-foot swell, the gray storm-filled sky like the bright sunlight of the Caribbean. Relief flooded through Cannon, the pain in his back easing, but it was a short-lived peace.

Tentacles rose from the bay like serpents, writhing around the sub as it bobbed on the storm-torn sea.

30

Teeth scraped against the Lexan as suction cups locked onto the Pearl, the pink anus-like mouths gnawing on the sub. Metal bent, plastic cracked, and fiberglass splintered as the submersible heaved and pitched, waves pounding the clear cockpit bubble. The monster's white carapace rose from Blackwater Bay, claws snapping and searching. Rain lashed the Pearl as it rolled, and lightning lit the world like white fireworks.

Cannon clutched his emergency bottle of air, his stomach screaming, lower back pounding with pain.

"Here," Vik thrust an inflatable life jacket at Cannon, who stared at it like he didn't know what it was.

Through the blurred cockpit bubble, within the writhing tentacles, the creature's dark eyes floated above its tooth-filled mouth. Beyond, three boats bounced over whitecaps, throwing spray. The Pearl creaked and bent as the leviathan crushed it. The Lexan bubble finally gave up the ghost and shattered, shards of tiny dull plastic pelting Vik and Cannon.

Waves broke into the open cockpit, slamming Cannon in his seat. Salt stung his eyes as wave after wave pounded the Pearl and the cockpit filled with seawater. The scent of bleach filled the air, burning Cannon's nostrils.

"We need to get out of here," Vik yelled over the rising tumult.

The beast had clamped down on the ballast tanks with its two claws and was dragging the submersible relentlessly toward its mouth while its other eight arms crushed the sub. Steam and fog rose from the bay like genie's breath, the rain easing to a drizzle.

The tip of a tentacle snaked over the broken Lexan bubble, coiling and stretching as it searched, suction cups flexing, the tiny mouths within chomping.

Vik pulled a dive knife from its sheath on his leg and sliced the tip of the tentacle off with a powerful stroke.

Blood splattered the cockpit as the beast jerked, and the sub trembled as a shockwave of bay water crashed into the open cockpit. The creature bellowed, and tentacles flailed, searching for purchase, twisting and thrusting and grabbing.

Vik snapped out of his harness, the listing sub sinking beneath the surging waves. Vik pulled on his PFD and retrieved a handgun from a cabinet on the port bulkhead. When he looked back and saw Cannon still sat strapped into his chair, he said, "What the hell are you doing? You want to die? If not, get your ass in gear." He reached across the cabin and swatted Cannon on the head.

The starboard side bulkhead cracked open as tentacles squeezed the Pearl and bay water rushed in. Then the sub was in two pieces and the aft section fell away. Vik brought up his gun and fired as the cockpit was sucked into the beast's mouth.

Bullets ricocheted off the monster's carapace, thumping into the water. The sea rose around Vik and he disappeared in a mound of whitewater.

Cannon put the mouthpiece for the emergency air tank in his mouth. He snapped free of his harness and jumped, but his foot caught on the destroyed gunnel and he faceplanted, his shins slamming against a twisted ballast tank as he hit the water. He lost his grip on the air tank, and it fell from his mouth and was lost in the tumult. Waves and whitewater pounded him and dragged him under. Saltwater stung his eyes, and he pasted them shut as he got tossed and pulled like he was in a clothes dryer. He twisted in the cold water, not knowing which direction was up. Panic seized him, and he opened his eyes.

Something soft slithered across his legs, and Cannon started. The remains of the sub sank into the abyss, sucking Cannon down with it. He swam hard, lungs burning for air, a field of tiny stars twinkling in the water before him. His arms ached, and his legs cramped as he fought upward, the gray light of day shining like the north star.

Cannon broke the surface, sputtering and coughing as waves pounded him. The sound of approaching outboards brought hope, but the serpentine legs of the beast searched all around him. He looked for Vik in the chaos, but he didn't see the millionaire in the turbulent water. Cannon reached for the red clasp that would inflate his lifejacket, but paused, bay water spraying his face, waves crashing around him. Bobbing around on the surface in a bright yellow vest might not be the best way to avoid becoming kraken chow.

A guttural scream of fear snapped Cannon's head around and he saw Vik struggling to stay afloat on a piece of fiberglass debris. Blood ran down the man's face and one arm hung limp.

Shots rang out, and the beast's carapace sank back into the bay, its squirming tentacles and snapping claws hesitating as it considered the new threat.

Nate led in the Whaler, followed by two other boats. All three vessels had men firing at the beast. Bullets slapped the water and cracked against the creature's outer shell, but this only enraged the monster. The creature heaved in the bay, tentacles and attack arms whipping wildly, its claws grabbing water and air.

Nate brought the Whaler to a stop fifty yards back, and the other two boats moved around to flank the beast.

The rain stopped, leaving a thick mist that hung over the surface of the bay. The pop and snap of gunfire was deafening, and smoke filled the air, the scent of gunpowder thick.

For Cannon, time slowed as he sank beneath the waves. He wasn't drowning, not yet, but with all the commotion in the water he figured his best bet was to stay still and let the people with guns do the fighting. The beast would flee, and they'd pick him and Vik from the bay and the aquanauts would be drinking beer and eating hot food by nightfall.

A piece of the submersible struck Cannon and drove him under. He sucked in a breath and took in bay water, coughing and choking as he sank, his arms and legs heavy with weariness.

As the whitewater tossed him around, Cannon thought of Nel and Joshua. Since he and Nel weren't married she couldn't collect his pension. It would go to his father, who didn't need it, and when he died, his deadbeat sister would reap the benefits of his hard work... well, work anyway. As the bay took him the dark sentiments were like a parting gift, a freeing realization that would let him go to the beyond with a clear conscience.

He looked up as he sank, his worries fleeing. Joshua filled his mind's eye and his peace was disturbed. What would the boy do without him? Who would be the father figure the boy desperately needed? He was that person. That was his job now.

He stroked toward the surface, life surging in him as his survival instinct kicked him in the ass. If he died, so be it. Drifting to the bottom like a stone wasn't his fate. He wouldn't let it be.

Cannon broke the surface to the sound of Vik screaming. His fellow aquanaut was twenty feet away, treading water and trying to stay above the pounding surf. The gunfire had ceased, and only three tentacle-arms searched above the water, suction cups puckering. The beast's head had eased back into the sea, but Cannon saw its white carapace floating just below the surface, black basketball eyes watching.

Cannon was exhausted and could no longer tread water. He pulled the red clasp dangling across his chest, and with a *whoosh* his PFD inflated. The waves tossed him around like a cork on a rising tide, the smell of bleach suffocating the scent of the sea.

A piece of the creature's severed tentacle floated by, the anus-like mouths within the suction cups searching for something to latch onto like a worm that'd been cut in half. Blood turned blue as it leaked from the appendage and the severed limb sank beneath the waves.

Nate was circling back with the Whaler, and a blue sport fisherman moved in from the south, and a sailboat under power came from the north. They had the creature surrounded, or so Cannon thought. Nate maneuvered the Whaler toward Cannon, but it was getting pushed around in the rough seas. The blue fishing boat moved in for Vik, but the wind howled, and the boat was blown off course.

Seeing the rescue attempts failing, the captain of the sailboat brought the vessel around and knifed toward the center of the chaos to provide cover and support, its small outboard rattling.

Blackwater Bay erupted.

Tentacles shot from the water all around the sailboat, the white appendages glistening in the gray light. A knot of water surged from the bay, two claws shooting from the whitewater like bullets, two long attack arms coiled and flexing to strike. The creature roared, and hot sea spray hit Cannon in the face. His face felt like it was covered in blood, but when he checked he found only yellow-tinged slime.

Tentacles wrapped around the sailboat, squeezing and crushing it. Fiberglass shattered and cracked, and men dove in the stormy sea. Crunching and cracking rose above the pounding sea as the sailboat was pulled underwater. Men screamed and shouted, and one-by-one tentacles rose from the bay and ensnared the men.

A tentacle found Vik and lifted him from the sea. He dangled there, struggling to free himself as suction cups burrowed into his chest and legs, tearing away flesh. He screamed, a blood boiling wail that made little spiders run down Cannon's back. With a final rending like meat being torn from bone, Vik was squeezed in two. His legs and lower torso hung lifeless for an instant, then fell in the bay. The last thing Cannon saw of the millionaire was the look of utter shock on his face as the tentacle pulled him under Blackwater Bay.

Cannon floated in the swell, rolling with the waves as he was lifted up and down, mind spinning. Men screamed, and through the fog of shock, Cannon saw Nate spinning the Whaler's wheel, trying to bring the boat around, but the vessel was getting beaten back by the swirling winds and vertical sea.

He closed his eyes and thought of Sherri. Was she looking down on him? Would she welcome him? Or blame him?

Something tugged on his PFD. Cannon shook his head and looked up to see Nate trying to gather him in using a boat pole.

A searching tentacle surged from the bay directly between the Whaler and Cannon, but it wound itself around Vik's lower half as it sank, and the extra seconds saved Cannon's life.

The leviathan surfaced, all its tentacles writhing like spider legs. Nate leaned over the gunnel of the Whaler, the beast forty feet away, its snake-arms slithering through the sea, searching, always searching. Then Nate had Cannon by the shoulders, and both men fell sprawling onto the Whaler's deck.

It was 2:19PM. Forty-one hours until Gullhaven was underwater.

31

Cannon lay on the fiberglass deck of the Whaler, panting and staring at the cloud-filled sky. Seagulls wheeled overhead, their mournful cries a welcome sound after the silence of the deep. The trusty Johnson rumbled to life and he heard the *pop* as Nate dropped the throttle. The engine roared as the propeller clawed at the bay, the bow lifting. Cannon stayed where he was, his head pounding, limbs numb, eyes stinging with seawater.

Vik. The man's face filled Cannon's head, his laughter, the way he made fun of himself. He'd have to tell Priva. People who go through intense situations together form bonds much faster, and Cannon felt he owed the dead millionaire something. He didn't know what, but something, and telling his wife and trying to help her through her grief seemed like something.

The Whaler hopped and skipped over Blackwater Bay. Cannon didn't have the strength to lift his head and peer over the gunnel. What did it matter? He coughed, bay water dribbling from his mouth, his throat stinging, ears popping, lungs still burning from lack of air. He'd just go to sleep. Leave his worries behind. He closed his eyes, letting the cool sea spray coat his face, the bounce of the boat jarring him.

"Cannon! Cannon!" Nate's voice rose over the pounding waves and the roar of the motor. "Are you alright? Cannon, I need you."

It was those last three words that stirred him from his pity party. He so loved hosting those. He was always the center of attention and it allowed him to bring his misery and self-flagellation to new heights.

Cannon rolled on his side and spit out the last of the bay water. He propped himself up against the bench seat before the control console, gazing through the rising mist at Gullhaven on the eastern horizon. He peered around the center console. Vapor obscured his view as the churning Johnson kicked up spray and mist. He pulled himself onto the seat, rubbing his eyes and flexing his arms and legs.

A mound of whitewater trailed behind the Whaler, the surge of water cresting.

The blue fishing boat peeled off and headed west, forcing the beast to choose which vessel it would go after.

The kraken chose the Whaler.

Waves broke before the beast as it shot through the bay like a missile, tail first, long arms with claws extended forward like a gun array.

"Take evasive action," Cannon yelled.

"What? I don't—"

Like he'd been prodded with one of the creature's arms, Cannon vaulted to his feet and moved around the command console.

Nate stepped aside, and Cannon took the wheel. He spun it hard to port and the engine whined as it sucked water and air. The Whaler bounced over the chop, leaving a white trail of bubbling water.

The beast changed its course and stayed on their tail.

The Whaler leveled out and Cannon spun the wheel in a slow arc and set course for the wharf.

"The marina?" Nate said.

"Where else? It'll chase us all round the bay if we let it. We need to get to dry land and I don't want to lure the thing near populated areas. There's that big—"

The Whaler slammed through a set of waves and Cannon gripped the wheel with both hands. Nate reached out and grabbed Cannon's arm. Cannon glanced at the science teacher and couldn't help but smile, and Nate let go and grabbed the stainless-steel handrail.

"As I was saying, there's that warehouse down at Izzy's and there's all kinds of debris in the water. I think we can lose it in there. At least delay it while we get away," Cannon said.

"Why not head straight for closest shallows? Razor Point? This thing needs water to swim, no?"

Cannon said nothing. He didn't know how much water the monster needed, but he didn't think it needed much. It had stayed on the surface of the bay for several minutes and swam in the flooded streets of Gullhaven. If the creature was what they thought it was, a giant mutant octopus-squid, the beast most likely drew in sea water that passed over gill filaments, absorbing oxygen and releasing carbon dioxide via diffusion, which meant it couldn't live out of water long.

Cannon said, "I don't know, man." He sighed. "Thing's been down there a long time I figure."

Nate said nothing as he stared astern, mist rising from the churning propeller like smoke.

Cannon jerked the wheel to starboard and continued his zigzag across Blackwater Bay. Pain leaked through his arms as he held the wheel, the vibration inching through his body like a disease.

"Cannon," Nate said. He was pointing to the west.

He didn't see what he was showing him at first. Only the inky water and the rolling waves covered in mist marked the surface of the bay. Then he saw them, two three-foot dorsal fins knifing through the bay, flanking the leviathan on both sides.

He looked at Nate, and the science teacher shrugged. "A marine biologist, I'm not."

Cannon had seen sharks defend their territory in the past, and Blackwater Bay was certainly theirs. With the red triangle only three hundred miles to the south, the bay served as an important respite for great whites making their way up and down the coast of California, and he was familiar with their habits. He'd never seen anything like this.

The beast didn't appear to notice the sharks, or if it did, was ignoring them. Cannon chuckled to himself. Ignore great white sharks at your own peril, squid-boy.

They were three miles out from Gullhaven; the wharf and its pile of destroyed boats taking shape in the mist. He checked the depth finder: two hundred feet and dropping. In the distance the blue fishing boat had come along the port side and was running a lateral course, keeping pace with the Whaler.

"Who's piloting the blue sport fishing boat?" Cannon said.

"Clint."

Cannon smiled and hailed his friend. "Clint, you out there?"

"10-4, partner. What's the plan?"

"You see these sharks stalking the thing?"

Static. No response.

"Clint, you copy?"

"Yeah, I see them now, Cannon. Looks like they're hunting."

"What do you say we help them out?"

Clint laughed. "Us help great white's hunt? There's a first. I'll come in from the south. Copy?"

Cannon smiled. His friend understood Cannon's plan without him having to say a word. "Got it."

He arced the Whaler to the north as Clint moved his vessel south. For a few harrowing moments Cannon couldn't see the creature and he feared it had submerged, but when he resumed his easterly course the now familiar fist of whitewater surged toward them. Sharks still flanked the creature, their dorsal fins throwing spray, caudal fins snaking through the sea. Cannon nudged the wheel to starboard, putting the Whaler on course to circle the beast. Clint did the same in the opposite direction, and within minutes they surrounded the sharks and the beast.

As if they'd been consulted, the sharks attacked the creature. The leviathan slowed as dorsal fins rose from the bay on both sides of the beast.

"Let's go. It's Miller time," Clint shouted over the radio.

"Boom!" Cannon shouted. He spun the wheel with his finger, the boat choking and sputtering as it made the sharp turn and headed back toward the wharf. Clint did the same, and the two boats raced for cover as the sharks bought them some time.

"Take the helm," Cannon said.

Nate took the wheel and Cannon looked to the stern, bringing binoculars to his eyes.

Through the mist and dull gray light, Cannon watched the beast defend itself. Great whites are patient hunters, and they circled the monster as its tentacles shot from the sea.

One of the sharks went in for a bite, but the dorsal fin disappeared before it reached its target. He watched as the beast tore the shark apart, tentacles pulling pieces of the great white's gray flesh into its mouth. A second shark vanished beneath the waves, and so did the leviathan's carapace.

Cannon let the binoculars drop to his chest as he gaped at the tangle of white appendages jerking through the water.

"It's coming at us again," Nate yelled.

"I see."

The leviathan had resumed its pursuit, a mound of whitewater surging through the bay. It was moving faster than it had been. The sharks pissed it off.

Reading his mind, Nate asked, "Can you get any more out of this thing?"

The RPM gauge said the Johnson was already spinning at 4400RPM, and the throttle was pinned.

The knot of water flattened, and the creature dove, its tentacles disappearing into Blackwater Bay. Cannon jerked the wheel and made several erratic turns as the Whaler bounced over the bay. Thunder boomed, the echoes rolling over the water. In the west the storm thinned over the mountains, gray patches where sunlight fought to break through the clouds dotting the horizon. Cannon judged they were a mile out from the wharf, and he hoped the shallow water would discourage the monster.

The depth gauge showed fifteen feet as the center console sliced across a flooded beach, through a maze of submerged cars in the wharf parking lot, and threaded the needle, passing within feet of Izzy's warehouse and a sunken yacht next to it.

The monster didn't even slow. It rose from the floodwater, using buildings, sunken cars, and demolished boats as footholds for its tentacles as it pulled itself through the floodwater. Its bulbous eyes focused on one thing: the Whaler.

A shot rang out. The blue boat sport fisherman sliced through the floodwater, and Clint stood on the bow, peppering the creature with rifle shot.

The beast kept coming, pulling down a section of the giant metal warehouse as the Whaler passed through the open bay doors going thirty-nine knots. The outboard screamed in the close confines of the warehouse, and the grunts and chuffs of the beast as it followed resounded off the metal walls.

The large set of double bay doors on the opposite end of the warehouse stood closed.

At his current speed, Cannon figured they had ten seconds to either turn around, get the doors open, or go through them. Panic filled him as he scanned the floodwater. His palms sweating, his lower back spiking with pain.

Behind the Whaler, the creature tore and broke everything its tentacles attached themselves to, the sound of splashing as metal and wood plummeted into the water rising like a hurricane in the metal building.

With no space left, Cannon spun the wheel hard, trying to turn the boat around. The Whaler bounced off something unseen in the floodwater, and the Johnson whined and stalled.

32

The Whaler careened into a row of outboard motors that sat below the waterline like a shoal, and the sound of crunching fiberglass and grinding metal made Cannon wince. Using the boat's remaining momentum, he continued to turn the vessel around as he fumbled with the ignition key. The flywheel spun, and metal scraped on metal, but the motor didn't start.

"Nooooo," Nate yelled. He'd been knocked to the deck and blood covered his face.

The leviathan lifted its carapace from the floodwater as it tore apart the warehouse, pulling itself along, tail dragging behind. The stench of bleach and rot pervaded the air as the creature huffed and bellowed, water shooting from its siphon.

Cannon closed his eyes and counted to five the way his dad had taught him. He breathed, blocking out the commotion, letting the gas settle in the engine. He turned the key and the Johnson sputtered.

The beast's tentacles searched the floodwater. The monster was forty yards away.

He spun-up the motor and the Johnson screamed to life. Cannon slammed the throttle lever down and the Whaler leapt from the floodwater, bouncing off something below the surface. He struggled with the wheel and brought the boat level, but the Whaler was heading straight for the creature.

"You got a gun?" Cannon yelled.

Nate still sat on the deck, rubbing his head and staring at the open maw of the leviathan as it rose from the water, preparing to accept its prey. The beast's claws came around on their long arms, searching and snapping.

"Rifle," Nate sputtered.

"Get it. Fast!"

Cannon turned the boat sharply to starboard, cutting in front of the beast as its arms reached for the Whaler.

Nate appeared at Cannon's side holding the rifle.

"Its eyes. Shoot at its eyes!" Cannon yelled.

The floodwater in the warehouse had become a maelstrom as the Whaler churned everything up and the monster destroyed the building. The boat skipped beneath outstretched tentacles and Nate fired.

The leviathan rocked back, sending a shockwave of water rolling across the warehouse. It slammed into the Whaler, kicking the boat to port. The propellers dug, and the boat turned sharply. Nate fell, and

Cannon's feet slid out from under him and he clung to the ship's wheel to stay upright.

A gray rectangle of light marked the open bay doors they'd come through. Ahead a pile of crates rose from the water, the faded brown metal wall beyond. Cannon turned the wheel over, pulled the throttle to neutral, waited a heartbeat, then slammed the boat in reverse.

The Johnson bucked on the transom, smoking and throwing sparks, but old reliable didn't stall. The prop clawed the floodwater and caught the tip of a tentacle as it snaked through the water.

The beast screamed, flailing its arms as it fully breached.

Cannon jerked the control lever forward and the boat lurched, the turbulent water splashing over the bow and flooding the deck.

"Hold on!" Cannon said.

He set course for the open bay doors, slicing over a tentacle, the engine coughing as the propeller severed the appendage.

The beast lunged forward, throwing itself at the Whaler as it passed, and the leviathan's torso landed twenty feet behind the boat, its tentacles falling around and on the Whaler. Suction cups grabbed the hull, and Cannon kicked at an arm as it twisted its way toward the command console.

The Whaler was moving fast, and it tore free of the beast's tenuous grasp as a shockwave of water lifted the fleeing boat and launched it through the open warehouse doors like a child spitting out vegetables.

The nineteen-foot center console landed with a shuddering jolt that sent Cannon to the deck and Nate overboard. The science teacher hit the water hard and disappeared beneath the raging whitewater and dirty foam.

The Whaler powered on out of control, darting across Izzy's marina, nobody at the wheel. The Whaler hit a sunken boat, was pushed to port, and listed sharply as it ran into a pile of debris. The engine didn't stall, but instead drove the Whaler into the pile, spitting floodwater behind it, crushing the fiberglass hull.

Cannon's head ached. Nate. He needed to help Nate. He got to his feet and drew back on the throttle and the Whaler stopped driving forward. The monster pulled itself from the collapsed warehouse, tentacles hauling the beast's girth, eyes searching the destruction. Nate was nowhere to be seen.

The radio crackled to life. "Cannon! Cannon! Do you copy?" It was Clint.

"I copy. What's your position?"

"Running low on fuel so I peeled off. What's your status?"

"I lost Nate."

"On my way."

"No. Head back. There's nothing you can do here right now." He put the Whaler in reverse and eased the boat off the debris pile and brought the vessel about.

"Nate! Nate!" he called. The cacophony caused by the beast drowned out his voice and sorrow seeped through Cannon like sewage.

"Here!"

Cannon's head jerked toward the scream. Fifty yards away, between the beast and the Whaler, Nate struggled to stay above the floodwater. He quickly did the math in his head and concluded he couldn't reach Nate before the beast did. His hand hovered over the throttle, the rational side of his brain waging war with his heart. Duty and honor, those things that make you who you are. What good was being alive if you were a coward?

He dropped the hammer, spun the wheel and headed for Nate. The teacher must have heard or seen Cannon coming, because he stopped yelling and splashing about, and hid himself by clinging to a piece of a fiberglass hull that still had some of its filling attached to it.

The Johnson screamed and caught the beast's attention, and it hesitated as the creature's giant eyes adjusted to light. It had been dark in the warehouse, and the beast's sensitive eyes surely weren't accustomed to rapid changes.

Cannon brought the boat to a stop by jamming the throttle from forward to reverse. The boat shook like it had been hit with a rock as the outboard's inner workings slammed, slipped and ground, sending a stream of dark smoke out the exhaust port.

Still old faithful didn't stall.

Cannon lifted Nate onto the gunnel and let him pull himself the rest of the way into the boat as Cannon piloted the Whaler toward open water.

Nate lay on the deck, panting.

Cannon wove in and out of sunken cars, debris, and destroyed boats, heading for the flood line. The Whaler bounced and whined, a thin trail of black smoke leaking from under Johnson's cover.

"You alright?" Cannon said.

Nate leaned against the gunnel, rubbing his head, eyes glazed. "I think so."

"Well, we're not out of this yet. I need you to keep an eye out for—"

A tentacle shot from the sea, just missing Nate where he sat. The teacher butt-inched toward the command console, his eyes never leaving their trail of whitewater.

Above, the clouds thinned, like a child pulling apart cotton candy. Sunlight peeked through, golden spotlights highlighting parts of the devastation.

Cannon turned to port and headed up Lancaster Avenue, two and three-story buildings rising on both sides of the flooded road. Cannon spared a glance over his shoulder. Debris crashed in their wake, but he saw no sign of the beast.

He arced the Whaler north, turning sharply onto Bayside Lane, the depth gauge showing the floodwater at eleven feet. Second story windows just above the flood line reflected the jetsam, but he saw no people, and that made him feel a brief twinge of relief. While he'd been wasting time at the bottom of Blackwater Bay, rescues had continued.

"No!" Nate yelled.

Cannon spun around and looked to the stern.

A tentacle slithered over the gunnel, oozing like a giant white slug, its tip curling and searching the deck. The arm rose and two more crawled over the gunnel, hungry little puckering mouths chomping within the suction cups. The stench of bleach and decay washed over him, and Cannon's stomach went cold.

Nate fired, the .22 caliber bullet going through the thick appendage and continuing through the fiberglass hull. Water geysered from the hole, spraying Nate and Cannon and filling the boat. The bilge pump snapped on and a steady stream of water shot from the side of the boat like a giant taking a piss.

Tentacles thrashed around the Whaler as the beast's mouth rose from the floodwater, its tooth-filled maw opening and closing. Its eight legs snaked over the gunnel on all sides, and suction cups attached to the boat and nearest building. The Johnson whined as the monster held the Whaler. The propeller tore at the water, shooting a twenty-foot rooster tail across the street, where it slammed into a window, shattering it.

Fiberglass cracked and bent as the giant mutant squid squeezed the Whaler. Cleat screws popped, the Johnson broke free of the transom and went silent with a sputtering cough and fell into the water. The deck cracked down the middle, and the center console was torn from its screws and tossed aside. Stainless-steel side rails twanged and rang as they flexed and broke free of the hull. The smell of gasoline mixed with the scent of bleach filled the air.

Cannon ran across the deck and dove off the port bow, covering his head as he crashed through a window into the building beyond. Shards of glass tore at his clothes and ripped his skin as he landed and rolled, coming to rest on a shard of glass that impaled his thigh. He screamed as he pulled the glass knife free and held his hand over the wound.

Nate's jump was easier. He threaded the needle, stepping off the bow through the window Cannon had cleared. "Are you OK? Can you walk?" Nate said.

"Yeah." Nate helped him to his feet. Cannon's knees grew weak and he staggered, but Nate took him by the arm.

A section of the outside wall and ceiling disappeared as the creature tore off a piece of the building. Through the dust and smoke Cannon saw the remains of the Whaler lifted from the water as the beast crushed it and let the pieces sink below the floodwater.

Anger rose in Cannon. He and that little center console had been through a lot. He headed for the beast and Nate grabbed his shoulder. "And what the hell would you be doing? You got a death wish?"

The look Cannon gave the science teacher must have been brutal, because Nate's hand fell away, and his eyes grew wide.

The building was coming down around them and a chunk of ceiling landed on Cannon's head, breaking his trance, anger turning to fear.

There was a door on the far wall, and he ran to it, Nate in tow.

33

The hallway was dark and filled with shadows. Cannon looked both ways like he was crossing the street, dark blue carpet and off-white walls stretching into darkness in both directions. Nate panted behind him, his breathing harsh and erratic. The scent of mold mixed with bleach filled the hall and smelled oddly of French toast.

A bulletin board filled with flyers hung from the wall before him, and closed doors lined the walls every ten feet. The red glow of an exit sign cut through the darkness to his left but leaving the protection of the building wasn't something he was interested in, so he went right.

Bricks broke and cracked, and the hallway walls buckled, but didn't come down. A white tentacle wriggled through the open door, its suction cups puckering and searching like there was an eyeball at the end of the arm.

Cannon pressed on and didn't look back. The sounds of breaking stone, splintering wood, and breaking glass erupted behind him. Dust and pieces of the ceiling rained down, and the hallway behind them collapsed as the front of the building gave way.

Cannon spared a glance to see if Nate was still with him, and he was. The science teacher's face was smeared with dried blood, his hair had pieces of glass in it, and dirt covered his wet clothes like he'd been dipped in flour and readied for frying.

They came to the end of the hall and the red glow of another exit sign cut through the gloom. Cannon threw open the door to the emergency stairs and stood on the landing, the building shaking beneath his feet.

He looked up and down the dark staircase, mind racing, heart pounding. Going down would mean going closer to the creature, but going up had its own perils. If the building came down, they'd be buried. Cannon headed up, jumping steps two at a time.

"The roof?" Nate said. He was panting hard, but he was right behind Cannon.

Cannon had to figure out what came next. From the roof he'd have a view of the road below, and with any luck they'd lost the creature.

As if the beast could read his mind, the monster shrieked like a thousand cats hissing at once. The staircase trembled, and Cannon clung to the handrail as he ran, the top marked by an emergency light that lit the landing. There he paused.

Nate wheezed like he'd run a marathon, hands on knees. "What... now?" he said between breaths.

Cannon put up a finger. He was listening hard, blocking out the sound of falling bricks, the splash of water, and the rumble of destruction. He heard a low moan just below the surface noise, a grunting and breathing. He laughed to himself. This damn thing wasn't giving up. It had chased him from the depths and passed up other prey to stay on his trail.

"What's the plan?" Nate asked again.

"Don't get eaten."

Cannon pushed through the door onto the roof, and salt air tinged with bleach assailed him. Beams of sunlight broke through the clouds, selectively illuminating the destruction like flashlight beams. The front of the building was gone, and below in the street, the monster's arms probed and tore at the structure, its carapace floating on the surface, its siphon sucking in water as the creature breathed.

"We need to get off this roof, fast," Cannon said.

With the front of the structure gone, and no building behind, Cannon was again forced to make the most basic decision; right or left.

The gap between buildings to the right was fifteen feet. The left looked slightly shorter, so he ran that way, pausing before the parapet wall and gazing at the department store's roof below. Klingman's was as old as Gullhaven and had been the town's general store when the town had been no more than a fishing village.

Cannon turned to Nate, who stared at the gap between buildings as though it were the Grand Canyon, eyes wide, mouth hanging open. Could the science teacher make the jump? Could he?

Another section of the building fell away, and a white tentacle snaked through the debris. They didn't have any time left. If they didn't get off the roof soon, they'd be crushed in the collapse that was seconds away.

The beast pulled itself into the alley between the buildings, and Cannon saw the monster's baseball-sized eyes staring up at him. The beast's arms tore at the alley and the roof pitched.

Cannon backed up to get a running start.

"You're really—"

Cannon didn't hear Nate. He ran as fast as he could, his feet slipping on the gravel roof, legs aching, lower back pounding. If Nate didn't follow, he didn't. What else could Cannon do?

He jumped, trying to catch a cloud.

Below in the alley the albino leviathan struggled to reach him as he sailed overhead, the snake-like arms coming within ten feet of Cannon's legs. Halfway across he realized with a sinking dread that he was going to come up short.

He hit the side of the Klingman's Department Store, hands grasping for purchase on the parapet wall. One hand managed to grip the top of the wall, and for several harrowing seconds Cannon hung there, struggling to pull himself up as his fingers cramped and lost their hold.

Nate flew overhead, landing on the department store roof and going into a roll. Then he was grabbing Cannon, pulling at his arms as Cannon fought to get over the bulwark and onto the smooth black rubber roof.

With a final surge backward, Cannon and Nate fell in a tangle, both men winded and pulling for air.

The sound of rending stone and breaking wood rose from below, but Cannon didn't look. He got up, helped Nate to his feet, and bolted for the door on the opposite end of the roof.

"Thanks. I owe you one," Cannon said.

"I think we're even."

Cannon threw open the door, but paused. Going into the store meant being confined again, and if the beast found them... They couldn't go back, or to the front or rear, which left west. There was a building there, but it was a low structure and the jump to its roof was impossible. With no options, Cannon plunged into the darkness of the emergency stairwell.

He paused on the landing, Nate beside him, both men stinking of fear.

"What now?"

Cannon looked at Nate, but said nothing.

The sounds of destruction echoed up the stairwell, and Cannon considered staying put. If the beast didn't see them, surely it would give up. But could it smell them? Sense the vibrations in the air as they moved?

Seconds passed, then minutes, as an uneasy silence spread through the building like fire. Cannon closed his eyes, hoping the creature had given up, or been distracted. To that, the rational part of his brain reminded him the beast had lain in wait before, biding its time and waiting for him to make a move.

They sat, the silence deepening, Cannon's unease dissipating.

"Did you know my parents wanted me to be a cop? Can you imagine?" Nate said.

Cannon said nothing. He needed to think.

"I had no interest. Dad always told me how much money police made. That true? I mean, you're not a cop... well, you are but—"

"Not now, Nate. I know you want to talk to ease your nerves, but we're not out of this and I need to figure out how the hell we're going to get to the waterline without being eaten by this thing. So, give me a minute, yeah?"

Nate pressed his lips together and looked at the floor.

Now he'd hurt the man's feelings. "I'm sorry. It's just, I'm not—"

"No worries. I understand." His hands shook as he bit his nails.

A half-hour passed, the two men sitting in the dark, Cannon's imagination conjuring multiple scenarios, each of which ended with their corpses being sucked into the monster's beak-mouth.

"Sorry about before," Cannon said. Now *he* wanted to talk to pass the time. "Why didn't you become a cop?"

The teacher sighed. "Just didn't seem like me. I'm not good at delivering bad news, and from my viewpoint, that's what law enforcement people spend much of their time doing. Plus, all the things they see and must do? Seems like a tough way to earn a living. Don't get me wrong, police are needed just like firemen and teachers, but I just didn't see myself arresting people and breaking up domestic disturbances, which is what? Eighty percent of what they do?"

"Sounds about right to me. That's why I went the constable route. Less shit to deal with. You married?"

Nate laughed. "I was. High school sweethearts, but we grew apart and she left me for a... get this, a cop."

Cannon laughed. "Sorry."

"Don't be. It's funny. She lives down in San Francisco now. Haven't spoken to her in years."

"Nobody in your life?"

"The singles scene in Gullhaven isn't what it used to be, as I'm sure you're aware... or maybe not, you're with Nel Stevens, right? Lucky you. She's a catch."

"That she is. When all this is done, maybe she has a friend... we can..."

"Double date?" Nate finished.

"Sounds high school, but yeah."

"I'd like that."

Another half hour passed, and Cannon got to his feet. "Ready? I'm going down and see if we're clear."

Echoes of sloshing water, and the occasional plop and splash caused by falling debris filled the stairwell, but the low moaning was gone. The floodwater had reached the lower stair landing and it lapped gently against the cinderblock walls.

"Now what?"

"We swim."

Nate stared at the water, fear and pain cutting across his dirt and blood smeared face.

"Wait here. I'll check things out and come back for you."

He nodded.

Cannon dove in, arms stretched before him as he slid into the water. He opened his eyes, but the floodwater was cloudy, and oil, salt, dust, and pollutants stung his eyes. Opening the stairwell door was difficult because of the water pressure, but he managed.

Mr. Minter's bloated corpse hung in the floodwater, his vacant eyes staring into the next world. Cannon made another mental note. His list of bodies to retrieve was growing long.

Cannon swam for the front of the store. Stray beams of sunlight cut through the haze, and mannequins stared at him from their watery display cases. He dove and passed through a broken window and out onto the flooded street where he surfaced, coughing and spitting water.

The flooded street was deserted. The remains of the Whaler littered the water, and small waves slapped against what remained of the building he'd fled into.

A mighty roar jerked Cannon's head around, and a tangle of serpentine legs surged from the water.

Cannon dove underwater and tried to go back through the window he'd come through, but it was blocked by one of the beast's arms as it searched the lobby of the department store.

Nate. How would he get back to Nate? These thoughts fled as his survival instinct kicked in and he swam for his life.

34

Cannon's face slammed into a submerged Honda Civic. He bounced off, kicking hard, his lungs exploding from lack of air. He couldn't see in the brackish water, and panic raked its icy claws down his back. He surfaced, bobbing within the flotsam and jetsam, the creature's appendages tearing at buildings and searching the water.

He dogpaddled to the nearest building and put his back to a brick wall. A tentacle attached to the wall above him, ripping off several bricks that splashed into the floodwater.

Something wound around Cannon's ankle and yanked him under. As he went down, an image of Luke Skywalker ran through his head, the young hero being sucked under by the one-eyed snake monster in the trash compactor.

Cannon struggled to free himself, the teeth within the suction cups clawing and digging into his skin as the arm pulled him toward the beast. Pain ran up his leg as he bucked and twisted as he was dragged through the water. Another tentacle latched onto his arm, and Cannon screamed, sucking in water and choking.

Several booming cracks resounded through the water like thunder.

Cannon was free. Both tentacles released him, just like Luke. He floated just below the surface, his body tingling as his nerves danced on hot coals, bite marks throbbing with pain. His face was above the water, and Cannon took shallow breaths as he surveyed the scene.

Nate stood in an open second floor window below the Klingman's Department Store sign. He was blasting the monster with a pump action shotgun, firing and pumping shells into the breach, not hesitating between shots. Gun? Where the hell... Klingman's sold hunting equipment, some basic firearms, and ammo.

The giant mutant squid lifted its carapace and heaved itself at the store, crashing into the facade, its tentacles and claw arms climbing up the side of the building toward Nate as he fired. When the gun clicked empty, he dropped it and picked up another and continued his barrage. Cannon smiled through his fear and pain. Nate had loaded multiple weapons. Well done, Poindexter, well done.

As the tentacles closed in, Nate backed away from the window, and three of the beast's naked white arms twisted through the window. Two heartbeats, and an explosion rocked the street. Glass, dust, black smoke and pieces of tentacle missiled from the window and littered the floodwater.

The beast wailed, throwing itself backward and slamming into Gus's Grub luncheonette. The ends of two tentacles spouted blue blood where they'd been shredded by... what?

Cannon dove into the floodwater, stroking hard for the entrance to the department store. He bounced off debris, eyes stinging, muscles cramping, pain gripping his leg and arm like bracelets of tiny knives.

He surfaced and looked back. The creature pulled itself from the debris of the restaurant, shaking off wood, twisted metal, and garbage. Its eyes focused on the department store as wounded tentacles pulled its albino bulk across the flooded street. Cannon took a deep breath and went under, swimming through the department store entrance to the emergency stairwell. The door was propped open with a chair. Nate had been busy. He wriggled through the opening into the stairwell and climbed up the remaining steps to the second-floor landing on his hands and knees.

Nate stood waiting for him, holding two shotguns. "Thought I'd lost you." The science teacher leaned the guns against the wall and helped Cannon up.

"Need to catch my breath a second." He propped himself against the wall, the sounds of destruction filling the stairwell. "Nice job. Owe you one. How'd you blow it? Gunpowder?"

"Yup. While you were gone, I looked around. I think we can get on the roof of the apartment building to the north," Nate said.

Cannon harrumphed. "It's forty yards away and it's higher, so unless you have some type of superpower I'm not aware of, there's no way we can jump that distance."

"Who said anything about jumping?"

Cannon's eyebrows rose.

"Come on." Nate handed Cannon a Benelli five-shot pump-action and climbed the stairs.

Warm light drenched the partners as they exited onto the roof, a cone of sunlight leaking through the dispersing cloud cover. White tentacles snaked over the parapet wall, searching, suction cups puckering like so many little assholes. Blood oozed from the tip of the severed appendage, but the wound didn't slow the tentacle as it searched.

Nate ran to the northern wall and looked up at the roof of the apartment building. Cannon followed, but when he came to a stop before the parapet wall, he still couldn't understand how they were going to get across.

"See those cable and electrical lines? You think they can hold my weight?"

Noticing the mound of climbing gear procured from the department store, Cannon thought he understood Nate's plan. He leaned over the short wall, gripping the cables and flexing them, testing their strength. He learned nothing

A section of the building collapsed as the beast tore at the structure, and the roof pitched.

"Now or never," Nate said. He grabbed a carabiner and attached it to the cables that spanned the gap. He secured a safety line to the building, then around his waist and through the binger. Because the apartment building was a little taller than the department store, Nate was forced to pull himself hand-over-hand across the black wires, his safety line dangling below him.

A section of roof caved in.

Cannon snapped on his own carabiner and pulled himself onto the cables, which now held the weight of two men. The cables sagged and danced as Cannon inched out, the black wire slippery in his hands. For every foot he went forward, he slipped back six inches.

The department store roof caved in, collapsing on white tentacles and tugging on the cables. One by one the wires twanged and snapped like piano strings.

Cannon held on as he swung over the alley, the brown brick façade of the apartment building coming at him like a tidal wave. Nate was twenty feet above him, holding onto the wires, legs swinging as his safety line tugged him backward.

Cannon slammed into the wall, lost his grip on the cables, and plummeted toward the floodwater twenty-five feet below. He smacked the water hard, his leg and arm wounds screaming.

Nate scrambled up eight feet of wire and pulled himself over the parapet wall onto the roof.

The sun had started its descent to the horizon and a purple-bruised sky shone through the maelstrom in the west. Cannon went under, swimming for the apartment building's lobby. Two of the four large windows that had looked onto a pristine entrance garden had broken and Cannon swam through easily. Plants swayed with the push and pull of the floodwater like kelp, and lobby furniture sat undisturbed, as if waiting for potential renters.

Cannon let the last of his air leak from his mouth as he swam up the wide staircase to a second-floor common room. Floodwater lapped against the stairs as he crawled the last few steps, collapsing with exhaustion on the large second floor landing.

"Cannon! Cannon!"

A metal door slammed, and a miniature tsunami rolled across the space, slapping the walls. Nate emerged from the emergency stairwell.

Blood pulsed from Cannon's leg and arm, both wounds looking like tiny sharks had bitten him. The leg wound was the worst, and blood leaked through his fingers as he covered the gashes with his hand.

"Shit," Nate said. He searched frantically, his head jerking side to side.

An emergency defibrillator was mounted on the wall next to an elevator with shiny gold doors. White and black shadowy waves reflected on the shiny surface like a mirror. Nate opened the plastic cabinet and pulled free a first aid kit.

As Nate bandaged his wounds, Cannon listened to the thunder outside as the beast brought down Klingman's. "You OK? Any lightheadedness?"

He did feel dizzy, but what did it matter? "I'm good." He got up and fell back on his ass.

"Let's rest a few."

There was a thump from down the hall.

Cannon and Nate looked at each other, then got to their feet. They'd both lost their weapons, but the two men followed the sound anyway. A door was thrown open at the end of the hall, and flickering candlelight spilled into the hallway.

Cannon put up a hand for Nate to wait as he eased through the open door like a wraith.

An old woman stood there, gazing across her apartment, the breeze pushing back her long gray hair. Her head spun around as a hand went to her mouth, but her face softened when she saw Cannon in his blue uniform shirt.

"Are you OK? Do you need help?"

The woman said nothing. She stared at Cannon, her hands moving.

"Nate."

The science teacher was at his side in seconds.

"Sign language. She's deaf." Nate made the gestures for 'are you alright?'

Her hands moved so fast Cannon didn't make out the individual symbols, not that he would've understood them if he had.

"She said she's been waiting here. Doesn't understand what's happened."

Cannon nodded. "Tell her to sit tight and we'll be back for her."

The woman read his lips and leapt to her feet, shaking her head, and gesturing wildly.

"It's dangerous out there right now. You could—"

The building shook, and Nate took the woman's arm and led her from the apartment.

Her name was Mira, and her husband had gone out to get donuts and never returned. Cannon didn't know what Nate told her, but based on the expression on her face it hadn't been the version he would've told. Her husband was most likely dead in the flood, yet the woman looked hopeful and relieved.

The party went single file down a fire escape on the back of the building, the beast pulling its pasty girth over the rubble pile that had been Klingman's a block over. The three companions went building to building, and when that wasn't possible, they swam, the monster tearing down buildings and destroying what was left of Gullhaven.

Cannon's stomach bitched, and his muscles complained. Nate said nothing, trailing behind, following Cannon's every instruction, while Mira appeared grateful just to be on the move. The floodwater got shallow as they fought through the destruction. They were determined to make the flood line by nightfall. The water on Fredrick Street was knee high, and the party waded out onto the flooded blacktop to make a final dash to the flood line.

35

Cannon led Mira away from the collapsing buildings, and through the floodwater toward a cross street. Nate trailed behind, and Cannon smiled. They'd been going non-stop, balls to bone, since 7AM. They needed a breather, and Cannon climbed onto a pile of rubble and sat. He let his head fall in his hands, breathing through his nose and out through his mouth, fighting back the nausea that spread through him. They needed food and water, and they needed it now.

Across the street, Mario's Italian restaurant sat forlorn, its front window blown out, much of the furniture that had adorned the dining room sucked away by the flood. But like all restaurants, Cannon figured Mario's had a cold box, and there might be food therein.

Cannon got up. "Wait here. I'm going across the street to see if I can find us some grub."

Mira gazed across the street and hugged herself. Nate said nothing. The science teacher, who that morning had been gung-ho to be the hero, looked whiter than the monster, his face pink in places where blood hadn't been fully washed away.

Cannon waded across the street and climbed through the broken plate-glass window. Furniture and debris were piled in one corner of the room, and shadow waves danced on the walls. Menus floated on the surface of the floodwater like lily pads, the week's special of three meat lasagna proudly displayed in red lettering atop the white paper. Art prints depicting Rome, Venice, the Coliseum, and other Italian landmarks adorned the walls, and white linen table cloths floated just below the surface, marking the tables like flooded islands.

He went into the kitchen, and the silver ribbed walls of a walk-in cold box sat in the far corner. The floodwater was up to Cannon's waist, and when he opened the walk-in, water rushed into the cold box.

The lower shelves were lined with plastic containers full of marinating meats, fresh chicken, and fish, gutted, but yet to be filleted. The vegetables were sodden and inedible, but there was one container on the top most shelf that looked promising.

Cannon stepped on the lower shelf, holding onto the steel legs that supported the shelving system. Using the tips of his fingers, he worked the container forward and let it fall into his hands. It was heavy, and as Cannon tried to catch it, the foggy plastic box slipped from his hands and fell into the floodwater, bobbing and swaying, waiting to be unsealed.

Cannon wasn't disappointed, nor was he thrilled. The plastic food container held pounds of cannoli filling speckled with chocolate chips. Not real food, but sugar, and that would get them by.

Like Winnie the Pooh with his paw in the honeypot, Cannon scooped the sugary cheese filling from the container with his hand, eating as he made his way out of the restaurant and back to his friends.

The companions sat in silence for a time, eating the cannoli filling, licking their fingers and trying to forget about the monster. That was hard. All Cannon's bumps still hurt, his cuts still bled, and the sounds of the retreating monster reminded them all the beast could turn around and head back. Strangely, Cannon didn't care if it did, and neither of his companions appeared to either.

Mira licked her fingers, the faint edges of a smile curling her lips. Nate looked the worse for wear, but he'd live, and that was saying something given what they'd been through. Cannon's thoughts drifted to Nel and Joshua, and he looked to the western horizon.

The sun was falling fast, and soon it would be dark. He wiped his hands on his pants and got up. "We better get on our way. Don't want to be walking around in this shit in the dark."

Mira was on her feet before Cannon finished speaking, but Nate sighed and rubbed his neck.

The sun went down, leaving a black and purple sky that spread over Blackwater Bay like a bowl of spilled sorbet. New life surged through Cannon as the sugar spread through him, providing the temporary energy needed to make one final push. When he crashed it would be epic, and thoughts of sleep made his eyes flutter as he struggled to keep them open.

The three companions turned west and waded up Udal Lane toward the flood line.

***

Floodwater lapped on the blacktop at the end of the long driveway that led up the hill to the high school. The three weary companions stopped to catch their breath, darkness and the hum of crickets pressing in on them. The lower bowl of Gullhaven was flooded, and the water inched up the hillside, slowly consuming the valley and everything in it.

It was 8:47PM. Thirty-four hours until the entire town was underwater.

"Hey! It's Cannon!" A group of people rushed down the driveway, yelling and screaming for help. Cannon and his crew must have looked like death warmed up. Nate was led away with Mira, the old woman mouthing 'thank you' at him as she was taken away to be fed and examined, and maybe reunited with her husband. Cannon walked like a zombie, eyes forward. When someone took his arm, he jerked away.

Deputy Sheriff Day stood waiting, arm still held out where it had clasped Cannon. "Just trying to help."

"I know," Cannon said. "Sorry, it's just I've got one more thing to do before I can rest."

Day said nothing.

"Have you seen Mrs. Singh?"

Day's eyes strayed to the ground. "I think she's up in the cafeteria with Nel and the kids, helping out."

"Does she know?"

"She hasn't been told anything. We were waiting for you. Figured it was your call, plus we wanted to hear the story from you first. Make sure we got everything right. She might sue, and the mayor—"

"Is a nitwit," Cannon said. He brushed past Day, who watched him head up the driveway, leaving a trail of water and footsteps, soaked shoes squeaking.

A cool breeze came down from the mountains, the scent of rot and stagnant water filling the air. Moonlight cut through the thin cloud cover and stars twinkled like a million eyes. Everyone cleared out of Cannon's way as he passed, like he was diseased, and nobody wanted to touch him. In truth, he looked like he'd been through a war, and the amazed and shocked faces he saw as he made his way to the cafeteria raised his spirits.

He hit the head and drained the main vein, splashed water on his face and washed off the top layer of mud and blood. Then he scrubbed his hands, trying not to think of what might be under his nails.

The cafeteria was organized mayhem, and when Joshua saw Cannon he screeched and bolted in-between tables and leapt into his arms. Cannon hugged the boy so tight he thought he might hurt him. Nel wasn't far behind, and as they embraced, Cannon felt eyes on him. Over Nel's shoulder, Priva Singh watched them, her eyes filling with tears.

Cannon broke away, kissing Nel on the forehead and telling her he needed a moment. Nel's face clouded in response to the forehead kiss— he had to stop doing that—and she glanced over her shoulder and saw Priva watching them. She let go of Cannon and took Joshua by the hand. Nel pecked Cannon on the cheek, and said, "See you in the gym. Don't be too long."

Cannon said nothing.

She didn't leave, as though she was waiting for him to tell her something. When he said nothing, she asked, "Are you going to the meeting at ten with the sheriff?"

"Didn't know there was a meeting, and no. I'm done. I'll join in you a few minutes."

"Ok," she said. She rubbed his shoulder and turned to leave.

"There is one thing you can do for me," he said.

"Anything."

"Grab me some food?"

"Sure."

Cannon turned to Priva, who had been watching the exchange between he and Nel, her mind seeing what she thought she'd never have again.

"Priva, I—"

She fell into his arms, wailing. "What am I going to do? What am I without him?"

Cannon didn't know who he was anymore and had no advice to give her, so he said nothing and held her tight.

36

The beast didn't understand the frustration it felt, so the beast processed it as pain and hunger.

It had never failed to catch its prey. Had never been beaten back by any creature. The pain it felt deep within knifed through the leviathan each time it breathed, its many wounds confusing the creature. It had been out of the water for too long because of this alpha… it would get it. That single purpose consumed the beast.

The creature pushed and pulled itself into deeper water, the strange square rocks crumbling in its wake. The beast's eyes drew in more light as familiar darkness settled around it. Its olfactories detected no prey. The beast had expended a great amount of energy in its ravenous rage and had gotten little for its efforts.

The new sensation of frustration burned through the creature as it darted through the bay, the ends of its severed tentacles stinging and throbbing, bullet wounds aching.

It would rest. Build its strength.

And hunt the alpha.

37

Cannon had never been so exhausted in his life. As soon as his head hit the rack, he'd nodded off as Nel rubbed his neck. His dreams were troubled; floating corpses, Joshua staring up at him with lifeless eyes, the town he'd come to love in ruins, but the surreal images weren't all bad. Nel and Joshua were alive.

He woke and lay with his eyes closed, listening to the stirrings of humanity as the gym came awake with the sunrise. Coughing, sneezing, and the occasional fart reminding Cannon he was in a room with three hundred other people. The stale smell of feet and onions hung over the room.

He felt a stare on him, and he opened his eyes to find Joshua watching him in the half-light of dawn. Cannon stuck out his tongue and the boy chuckled. Nel turned over on her cot and smiled. He took a mental snapshot; Joshua and Nel smiling at him, eyes bright and full of hope. They were looking to him for that hope, and he would do everything he could to make that hope reality.

"You're awake," Nel said. She leaned across the gap between cots and pecked him on the cheek.

"Morning," he said.

Cannon sat up and swung his legs off the bed. "Coffee," he said, getting up like a zombie. He smelled bacon and coffee coming from the cafeteria and his stomach grumbled so he followed his nose.

In the cafeteria, the sheriff dropped her plastic tray next to Cannon. Nel sighed, but offered her creamer for her tea.

"Where were you last night?" Tanya asked.

"Sleeping."

She sighed and looked at Nel, as if to say, "Men, am I right?"

"Why? What did I miss? The mayor's plan to drain Blackwater Bay?"

"Don't be ridiculous. You and Vik came up with the plan when you were in the deep. We've been thinking about this the wrong way. Instead of stopping the water flow, we'll change where the water goes."

Cannon shook his head and his face scrunched-up. "You're going to have to be a bit more specific."

"It was Vik's idea. Remember?"

Cannon said nothing. The last two days were a blur.

"Instead of trying to close the fissure, we're going to try and open Devil's Rip," the sheriff said.

Cannon sighed. "Your nuts. Vik and I were just spinning shit. Have you seen the inlet? It would take more explosives than we've got times ten to open the inlet and we'd probably bring down the bluffs in the process."

"Ah, but we don't need to clear Devil's Rip, we just need to get the water flowing out of the valley."

"How do you plan to do this?"

"The mayor has had crews working through the night. We've got an armada of six ships, and there are forty cases of TNT. Tim Leppers just received a shipment for the mine, so we were lucky there. We strategically place explosives and set them off in a cascading timed detonation."

Cannon chuckled. "What about the monster? It's still out there. What? You think it's just going to let us go about our business?"

"There has been progress there as well," Tanya said.

Cannon noticed Joshua was listening intently, the boy absorbing everything that was being said. He whispered to Nel, "Do we really want him to hear all this?"

Nel kissed him and gathered Joshua in her arms. "We're done eating so we're going to hit the playground for some fresh air. Catch you down at the flood line?"

Cannon nodded. When they were gone, Cannon said, "What progress?"

"A group of fishermen have sewn together a bunch of nets and put explosive charges sealed in wax along its length. They think if we can get the beast caught in the net, we can blow it to high heaven."

"Sounds ambitious."

The sheriff said nothing.

"Where do you want me?"

"Lead boat directing the armada and supervising the placement of the explosives. Take any help you think you might need. Maybe Nate? He seems to know a lot about the geological makeup of Gullhaven."

Cannon nodded. "If he's up for it. He was in shock when I last saw him."

"Nothing some food and sleep didn't fix, as you know."

"Not everyone is me."

"You got that right."

***

The flood line had inched halfway up the hill overnight, and Cannon's breath caught at the sight of the village under the light of day. The lower bowl of Gullhaven, including the wharf, was underwater.

171

Roofs, chimneys, and the tops of light poles stuck from the floodwater, forlorn reminders of what lay below the surface.

The boats were moored at the flood line. It was a ragtag fleet; Clint's blue sport fisherman, captained by his friend, the Bus for backup, a Parker with twin Yamahas, a Bayliner with an inboard/outboard motor, and two center consoles, one eighteen feet long, the other twenty-one.

Cannon chose the bigger center console for himself and Nate, and had the net laid out on the forward deck. The science teacher had agreed to accompany him, but he wasn't the same jovial, eager beaver he'd been the prior day. This Nate had seen things. Things he had no desire to see again. He'd made that very clear. He'd also made clear that he wouldn't be left behind like a coward as Cannon saved the valley.

Cannon had the same discussion with Nel, who felt she was being left behind like a damsel. He'd mansplained, "When this story is told down the line by the kids who survived, you know who the hero of the tale is going to be? Not the fools who almost got themselves killed by a giant octopus-squid. No. It will be Ms. Nel. The nice lady who got them through the most difficult part of their life. That's your job. Let me do mine." The speech hadn't appeased her, but the argument that she and Cannon both couldn't go because of Joshua finally got her to relent.

Nate gathered his bravery and built a shell around himself. He sat on the bench in front of the command console, staring out at the flooded town, saying nothing. Cannon worried that when it really mattered, Nate might not be able to act, but what choice did he have? He needed the man's knowledge and expertise, and who the hell was he to tell the man he couldn't come after all they'd been through?

Sheriff Locke commanded the other center console with Deputy Sheriff Day on the Parker and Tim Leppers on the thirty-two-foot Bayliner. He, along with a group of volunteers as support crew, would set-up the dynamite in Devil's Rip.

The armada was armed to the teeth; Cannon had an M9, two spare clips, and a shotgun with two pockets full of shells. The other boats were stocked with rifles, shotguns, and a selection of fireworks, and four hand grenades provided by an old timer. They'd salvaged an old harpoon gun from the whaling museum and mounted it on the bow of Clint's sport fisherman, and they stocked the boats with harpoons that ranged the entire historical spectrum from wooden handles and hand pounded tips, to diecast aluminum bolts.

The mayor stood at the flood line, water lapping at her shoes, wind blowing her long black hair. Dark bags hung beneath her racoon eyes, and her face sagged.

The mayor whistled, and everyone turned her way. A crowd had formed on the high school driveway, like everyone had come out to see off the fellowship of the ring. The mayor cleared her throat. "First I want to thank everyone who worked so hard through the night. We would be lost if it weren't for your efforts." A smattering of light clapping. "As you can see, the water is rising a bit faster than predicted, so today we'll try and open Devil's Rip enough to let the water flow out. Those not directly involved in this mission should report to Gloria for an assignment. We must assume our efforts to unblock the inlet will fail, so we need to be prepared to move out of the school by tomorrow morning at the latest. I've asked Gloria to coordinate the evacuation."

Some murmuring, but nobody spoke up. It was a little odd for the sheriff's assistant to oversee such an important task, but if there was anyone in Gullhaven that could get it done, and fast, and without brawls, it was Gloria. She was like the mother of Gullhaven, and nobody, the mayor included, would cross her. Though he'd never admit it to the mayor, Cannon liked the decision.

"Let's get to it then," she said. "The Bus will hang back since it's slow and will serve as the command ship. That's where I'll be."

Flood water popped and cracked as tiny waves broke on the blacktop and gulls squawked overhead, as if volunteering to help. "Ok, Godspeed."

Cannon went to Nel and Joshua who stood with the silent crowd. "You get setup with Joshua. There's a tent and—"

She put a finger to his lips. "I've got things covered here. You worry about you, OK? I'm sorry about before. Don't throw your life away, Lee. If the valley floods, it floods. There are other places we can live together, but I can't live without you." She paused and looked down at the floodwater that lapped on their shoes. "I love you."

Intense heat washed over Cannon and his stomach went cold. Sweat dripped down his back and he felt like he did when he was handed a bill he couldn't pay. He leaned forward to kiss her on the forehead but stopped himself. He took her in his arms, pulling her close and kissing her neck. Then he surprised himself, and her. Cannon said, "I love you."

He turned to leave, and she grabbed his elbow. "Promise me, if you have to, let the thing go. Give it up; you will, rather than risk your life."

Cannon said nothing, bile reaching up his throat.

"Promise me."

"I promise."

The roar of outboards screaming to life was like the start of an auto race, and the crowd waved and cheered as the armada backed away from the flood line, turning west and heading for Main Street.

Cannon followed Clint, and Nate and Cannon didn't speak as their center console glided through the devastation. Cannon thought of Venice, though he'd never been there. The pictures he'd seen showed canals as streets, and he remembered thinking how cool it would be to live in a city like that, taking your boat from place to place instead of a car. He closed his eyes and let the sunlight warm his face, imagining he was in a gondola on his way to a bottle of red wine. Someday. Maybe someday.

His center console was a Century 909, and its name was Bitter Sweet. The vessel was old, the registration tag saying it was first commissioned in 1984, but the motor was a 150HP Mercury that looked no more than five years old.

Cannon's brow furrowed as he gazed at the net stretched over the deck in the bow. Whoever had come up with the idea hadn't faced-off against the monster. Getting a net around the thing was going to be difficult. The beast seemed to sense their presence, know their movements before they did. Did it matter? If they could get the inlet open enough to let the overflow leak into the Pacific, then the floodwaters would recede, and they could take on the monster on their own timeline. It was best to leave apex predators alone, and they'd move on, but this situation was different. This beast was trapped, and cornered animals are the most dangerous kind.

The line of boats trailed through the wharf, moving around sunken cars, light poles, and destroyed boats. Cannon pushed down on the throttle and the Century skipped over Blackwater Bay, throwing spray as it bounced over the light chop.

"Look!" Nate pointed off the port bow.

The dorsal fins of orca knifed through the sea alongside the armada like wingmen; sea predators and man coming together with a shared purpose in a rare moment of detente.

Cannon smiled. He'd take any help he could get.

38

The orcas moved in closer, encircling the armada like they were protecting a group of calves as the six boats powered toward Devil's Rip.

Blackwater Bay was calm, and jagged white lines of foam streaking the green was all that remained of the storm. The sky was a deep oxygen rich blue, not a cloud in sight. Mist floated over the bluffs in the west and trailed across the valley, pulling apart like cotton. The air was warm, but the spray kicked up by the group's passage cooled things down. Cannon wiped a coating of water from his sunglasses and rolled his shoulders.

He was sore, his leg and arm wounds pounded, and the numerous cuts and bumps covering his body ached with renewed vigor. He'd pushed himself harder than he should've—like most in the Gullhaven— but the lack of rest and food would eventually catch up with him.

Nate's chin lifted as the twenty-one-foot Century sliced through the water. Gulls and egrets soared overhead. After everything that had happened in the last three days, the chatter and singing of the wildlife proved animals were more resilient than people. Or was it their lack of worry for tomorrow? Either way, the animals had already moved on while the people of the valley hadn't even started picking up the pieces of their lives.

The radio crackled to life. "Cannon, this is Clint on the Blue Whale. Copy?"

The Blue Whale. Cannon chuckled. "Yeah, I copy."

"Nothing showing on your SONAR?"

"Fish finder's showing some striped bass, maybe some dogfish, nothing else of note. You?"

"Negative," Clint said.

"Keep me informed. Out."

Nate got up and came around the command console, taking the binoculars from where they hung from the throttle arm. He put the field glasses to his eyes and studied Devil's Rip for a long time, sighing and harrumphing.

"Problem?" Cannon said.

"Don't know." He let the binoculars fall to his chest where they swung on their lanyard. "There's so much debris—dirt, trees, rock, sand, gravel—an explosion may cause everything to collapse in on itself."

"Making the clog worse."

Nate nodded. "I think the key will be to focus on one spot and let the water do the rest."

"Like putting a pinhole in a dam."

"Yes. I don't know how much pressure the flood water is putting on the blockage, but when seawater starts to flow, the gap should widen. Fast. It will cascade as the opening gets wider," Nate said.

"So where do I tell them to put the charges?" Cannon asked.

Nate sighed. "Directing from a ship on the bay is going to be hard. I think I need to go with them. Really examine the terrain and show them exactly where to put the charges to maximize their effectiveness."

Cannon lifted an eyebrow, but didn't protest. If that's what his friend thought needed to be done, who the hell was he to question him? Nate was on the mission because of his expertise, and Cannon wasn't one of those people who went to the doctor for advice and then didn't follow it.

The bluffs loomed in the west, and the downdraft of wind rolling over the cliffs was strong and steady. Cannon drew back on the throttle and let the center console drift toward the inlet, the newly risen sun over his shoulder in the east. He didn't like the idea of losing his partner—friend—but Cannon saw little choice. "OK. I'll transfer you to the Bayliner." Cannon got on the radio and informed the mayor and sheriff of his plan and relayed the instructions to the captain of the Bayliner; Tim Leppers, the explosives expert.

"Nate, do me a solid, will you? Just check the net before you split. Whoever I end up with won't know what to do with the thing."

"No worries. There isn't much you need to know."

As the Century skipped the final mile to Devil's Rip, Nate examined the charges strung all along the fishnet like Christmas tree lights. When he was done, he joined Cannon behind the command console, the science teacher's blonde hair blowing back off his face, his cheeks rosy red. "Here," he handed Cannon a TV remote control. It said Samsung at the top in white block letters.

Cannon took the remote, staring at it as though it were an ancient artifact. He looked around comically. "Don't see my big screen around here, mate."

"I think the cable's probably out," Nate said.

"Nothing ever on anyway," Cannon said.

The remote had black tape holding it together, and all the buttons were covered except the red power button and the up arrow of the channel selector. Nate said, "Be careful with that. You have to hold the power button and the up arrow at the same time to detonate the net, but make sure you don't do that before you're ready or…"

Or he'd blow himself and the Century sky high. Wouldn't that be a laugher? Cannon would become a permanent addition to the Devil's Rip blockage.

The armada reached the inlet and Cannon powered down and dropped anchor. Chain rattled over the bow as the Bayliner moved in alongside the Century.

The orcas kept their distance, circling, waiting.

"Yo!" yelled Tim.

Cannon waved and shut down the Merc.

Nate stood along the starboard gunnel, looking back at Cannon like a child that was going off to school for the first time.

Cannon smiled. "Go on, now. You'll be back under my wing by lunch."

Nate laughed and stepped over the gap between boats.

"Who's helping me?" Cannon asked.

Tim turned around, surveying his crew as if he hadn't considered who he was trading to get Nate. After a moment's consideration, he picked the biggest and youngest lad, Fred Green. The kid worked as a mate on a crab boat, and his thick arms and legs were the product of hauling crab pots from the ocean most of his life.

The young man climbed aboard. "Aye, Constable Cannon. Where do you want me, sir?"

"Cannon, or Lee is fine." He pointed to the bow.

The kid nodded, but said nothing as he made his way to the bow and sat on the forward gunnel.

With Nate in position, it was time for the team placing the explosives to go ashore. This would be tricky because of the abundance of debris in the water and the unstable nature of the blockage. Climbing ropes would be used to assist Nate and Tim as they placed the charges, and these lines would provide some safety should the clog shift or collapse while they climbed on it.

The Bayliner eased through the water, and Tim killed the motor and let the old cruiser bump against a debris pile.

Cannon scanned Blackwater Bay for the monster. Nothing.

Nate and Tim slid under the bow railing and dropped to the unsteady ground. Nate went ahead with the guide rope, tying off as he went, creating a path for Tim who carried the duffle of explosives.

Time bled by as Cannon watched Nate and Tim move up the debris pile. Fred coughed and wiped his nose with the back of his hand, but said nothing.

Nate directed Leppers, Nate carrying a spool of blue wire and connecting each charge as Tim set them. There would be eight charges on each strand, and there would be ten strands, detonation controlled by a master remote constructed from a wireless soundboard donated by a local DJ.

A low bellow resounded over the bay, and Cannon scanned the western horizon. A mound of water pushed over the bay, two thick white tentacles with claws at their tips hovering above the surface in attack formation.

"Shiiiitttt," Cannon said.

He opened a channel to the Bus. "Mayor, we've got company on the way."

Static, then, "10-4, Cannon."

The beast's timing was perfect. Nate and Tim were almost done setting the charges, but might not be finished before the leviathan arrived.

The mayor hailed the armada. "To everyone on this channel. Prepare to be attacked. All hands-on deck with weapons at the ready."

Cannon pulled anchor, started the Merc, and moved the boat closer to Devil's Rip for cover. "Come on." He coaxed Nate and Tim, who appeared unaware of the encroaching danger. "Ready that net, Fred." Cannon had almost forgotten the boy was there.

The monster was a mile off.

"Cannon, should Tim and Nate stay on the bluffs?" It was the sheriff.

Nate and Tim could climb the bluffs to get away from the creature, but the armada could only run, and as Cannon had learned the hard way, there was nowhere to hide. "No. Hold position and prepare to fight. I'll give the order to scatter as soon as the net is on the thing. Over."

"10-4." Tanya sounded scared and irritated, but she didn't argue.

If it's on the water, it's on you. Cannon grimaced

"Cannon, it's Clint. I'm going to move into the point position. I've got the harpoon gun. Let me see if I can stick this bitch before it gets a chance to nosh on us."

"Go for it, Clint. We'll be right behind you." Cannon rubbed his chin. "Mayor, on second thought, it might be best for you to move the Bus away from us."

"You sure?" The mayor sounded much happier than she had on her last transmission.

"Yeah, that thing is so slow there's no way you'd be able to perform evasive maneuvers. Move off and sit tight. You're our backup."

"10-4."

The fist of whitewater grew as the monster rose from Blackwater Bay.

"Tim, you copy?" Cannon said.

"Yo!"

"We've got company. Pick up the pace."

Nate and Tim did, and when they were done setting the charges, they rushed down to the water line, where they were picked up by the Bayliner. Once Nate and Tim were safely onboard, Cannon breathed a sigh of relief.

"Coming in to get Nate," Cannon said. He inched the Century alongside the Bayliner and Nate and Fred returned to their original posts.

Nate stepped aboard, and Cannon hugged him.

The science teacher stared in surprise, eyes going wide.

The leviathan roared, and surged from the sea, mouth flexing open, all its arms shooting at Clint's boat.

Cannon heard the twang of the harpoon gun and the thump as the metal spear hit the monster's carapace. The beast didn't squeal or buck. Its white tentacles snaked over the deck of the sport fisherman, suction cup mouths chomping. Clint jerked the ship's wheel side-to-side, trying to shake the beast, and his friend and the sport fisherman disappeared under a writhing pile of white.

Fury burned through Cannon, and he pinned the throttle control. The Merc wailed, and the center console jumped from the water as Cannon turned the wheel over and put the bow of the vessel on the beast's head.

The radio crackled, Nate yelled, but Cannon tuned them out. He'd ram this bastard, and if he went down with the monster, so be it. Nel's voice filled his head, "Don't throw your life away." He saw Joshua's face. He put his hand on the throttle and eased it back.

An albino tentacle bigger than an anaconda speared from the bay, hung in the air, then lashed out and wound itself around Nate's waist. The science teacher looked at Cannon and screamed as he was yanked over the gunnel and disappeared beneath the waves.

39

Cannon froze, holding his breath, waiting for the science teacher to pop through the dirty whitewater and bloody foam. The bay water swirled where Nate had gone under. Panicked cries squawked from the radio, men screamed, and fiberglass cracked.

Nate didn't come up.

A tentacle slithered over the gunnel, and anger burned through Cannon. He drew down, the Berretta barking, 9MM parabellums thumping into the transom and the tentacle.

The beast roared and surged from the bay, a knot of whitewater breaking across the Century's bow, washing Cannon down the deck.

The orca moved in and attacked the monster, taking bites and backing off, circling the leviathan. Tentacles searched the sea. A mangled fish was tossed through the air, and blood sprayed across the bay.

The beast wrestled with the orca, and Clint was free of tentacles. He had one foot on the Blue Whale's gunnel, firing into the water, white splashes marking the buckshot's entry. The bay roiled, and blue blood mixed with red as the orcas fought the monster.

Cannon eased down on the Century's throttle, moving in close. He'd use the orca as cover as he deployed the net.

Tanya moved her vessel across from Cannon, staying back. The other boats fired on the creature, and the sea exploded as the beast was peppered with bullets.

"Cannon, you copy?" It was the mayor.

"Little busy."

"Doing what? Trying to kill yourself?"

"I'm going to deploy the net."

"We're ready to blow the inlet, Cannon, and you don't want to be anywhere near here when it goes. If things work the way we want, the bay will empty, and that'll create strong rip currents."

Cannon didn't answer. The roar of the beast, the push of the wind, and the sound of splashing water filled the world, but Cannon stayed focused. The Century was almost on the beast and he saw the creature's dark eyes through a cloud of blue blood and bay water.

He ran to the bow and began throwing the net overboard, tentacles writhing from the bay all around the boat. An arm attached to the Merc, another the port gunnel, and the boat listed.

The net was half deployed, small floats keeping it on the surface. Cannon heaved and pulled at the netting, tossing it overboard. When he was done, he retreated to the command console.

Tentacles tore at the Merc and it coughed and stalled.

"Shiiiiitttttt." He pulled his knife and went to work slashing the engine free of suction cups, the bay erupting around him, tentacles crawling over the Century's deck, tiny mouths biting and searching.

Blue blood streaked the deck and the beast roared. Cannon cranked the engine. "All boats, net is deployed. I repeat, net is deployed. Move away from the scene at once. Detonation in twenty seconds. Tim, you still with us?"

Static. "I'm here. Waiting on the order."

"Move back. I'm going to try and lure the thing toward the inlet, and we'll blow both at once."

"But, you need—"

"Those are my orders. Standby."

Two corpses floated in the jetsam, one was Fred Green, the young man's arm gone, face crushed almost beyond recognition. How many had died this day? How many more would die before the day was through?

The monster surfaced, its carapace and several of its arms tangled in the fishing net. The beast didn't appear to notice the net, and it came at the Century with renewed fury, a wake of blue foam trailing behind it.

Cannon dropped the throttle and put the bow of the Century on the inlet. From the corner of his eye he saw the Bus, the Blue Whale, and the sheriff's center console moving away. Clint and his Bayliner bobbed on the turbulent sea, waiting. The table was set and now it was up to him.

The monster changed direction, and as it came at Cannon, the orcas moved in behind the beast, driving it forward.

Cannon scanned ahead. He was getting close to the inlet, and rocks and debris made the bay a minefield. The netting didn't appear to be slowing the beast, but it was clearly visible clinging to the monster's carapace.

Sea spray coated his face and Cannon smiled. If he had to die, being on the water with a sea breeze blowing in his face was how he wanted it to happen. He remembered Nel's words, but reminded himself he wasn't throwing his life away, he was saving the town, and he wasn't done yet.

"Cannon, it's Tanya. What the hell are you doing?"

Cannon didn't answer.

The red buoy marking the channel that led to the inlet hung just beneath the surface, and Cannon pinned the throttle, spinning up the

Merc to full power. The motor screamed as the blocked inlet loomed ahead, the tall bluffs obstructing his view of the Pacific.

Cannon waited until the last moment, the pile of rocks blocking the start of Devil's Rip only two hundred yards off, and he turned hard to port. The Merc coughed and popped as it clawed at the bay and struggled to pull in the water necessary to cool the engine, but the outboard didn't stall. The motor shrieked as the Century jerked and bounced through the maelstrom, the monster's tentacles wiping and searching, claws snapping.

Cannon was almost around the beast when a tentacle attached to the transom, six feet of the milky appendage grabbing the gunnel and dragging the boat to starboard. He drew his Berretta and fired, his last three bullets thumping into the tentacle. The white snake-like arm slithered back into the sea.

Cannon pulled the remote Nate had given him from his pocket, the boat swaying and listing, the monster roaring, the bay a turbulent mess of debris, corpses, and blood.

The Century bounced over an uprooted bush floating in the water, and the boat rocked hard. Cannon fell, and the remote slipped from his hand and clattered across the slick deck, sliding back to the transom and coming to a stop against one of the aft drain holes.

Cannon blocked out the wail of the creature, the squawk of his radio, and Nel's voice telling him not to throw his life away. He thought of Vik, bay water surging over the gunnel and swamping the boat.

His fingers wrapped around the remote and he braced himself against the aft gunnel, bay water filling the Century. Water shot from the boat's side as the bilge pump worked overtime. The Merc stalled and Cannon sat there for a five count, panting hard, pain shooting down his back.

A tentacle snaked over the bow and the boat was lifted from the bay, listing sharply to starboard.

Cannon unclipped his radio and opened a channel. "Tim, blow it."

A series of low pops, like far-off cannon fire, rumbled across the bay. Black smoke, mist, and white plumes of dust and ash clouded Devil's Rip, but there were no sounds of cracking stone. No splashes from falling rocks.

The detonation hadn't done a thing.

Cannon pressed the power button and up icon on the remote, and the sea exploded. The Century was tossed across the bay, and the twenty-one-foot center console landed with a smack, bay water surging over the gunnels.

A cry of pain that sounded like the largest tire ever made losing all its air at once pushed over the chaos. Specs of white skin fell like snow, and fat, suction cups, and pieces of tentacle and white skin floated on the bay's surface, a large chunk of the beast's carapace sinking beneath Blackwater Bay.

It was over.

A loud crack snapped in the distance.

A stream of water cascaded through the blockage, and the current pulled the sinking Century toward Devil's Rip. The motors were underwater, and the rest of the armada had moved away and was out of range. Even the Bayliner, which had stayed close to ignite the land charges, was plowing through the bay at top speed, black lettering on its transom reading Tip Top.

"Mayday. Mayday," Cannon called.

Static.

A growing stream of water pushed through Devil's Rip and stones and debris fell as the gap widened. The Century was pulled toward the inlet and Cannon had no way to stop the vessel. With nothing left to do, he sat behind the command console, watching as the hole in the debris clog grew bigger and more water rushed from Blackwater Bay.

Orca swam by, falling in with the current and heading for the Pacific. Cannon smiled as he watched them go, knowing the next time they crossed paths, things would be different.

The water level dropped fast as the debris in the inlet got washed out to sea. As predicted, only a fraction of the blockage had been cleared, but it was enough. Water flowed into the Pacific again.

What was left of the Century slammed into a rock as it was dragged out of control into Devil's Rip. The crunch of fiberglass didn't even register with Cannon. He was in another place, another time, and he called up the mental picture he'd taken of Nel and Joshua just the day before. Their smiling faces looking to him for support and guidance.

There are moments, though rare, where Cannon felt his world was in perfect order, everything falling into place the way he'd planned. The last four days had been unlike anything he'd ever experienced, but even though the town was destroyed, and it might never again be what it was, Cannon felt relief at having survived.

The boat wedged itself between two boulders, the current pulling the vessel under as it was driven on the rocks. Cannon jumped in the water to avoid being sucked under with the boat and swam hard for the base of the bluffs. Waves broke over him, and the scent of bleach stung his nose as he pushed through the blue blood tainted sea.

A corpse floated in the inlet beside him. It was Nate.

Cannon grabbed his friend, hugging him and apologizing, the horror of his death rushing back. He dragged his friend's body onto the rock shoreline at the base of the bluffs and collapsed. Tears came then, the sun shining, a warm breeze sending ripples over the bay water as it poured through Devil's Rip into the Pacific, sunlight sparkling off the sea like diamonds.

40

The epicenter of the earthquake that ravaged Gullhaven was a hundred miles to the north, just east of Eureka. Tremors were felt as far as San Diego, but other than a few falling bricks and some cracked roads, San Diego and Los Angeles had been spared major destruction. Despite this, all communication was knocked out and emergency services had been swamped for days helping the injured and getting the metropolitan areas back up and running. San Francisco hadn't been as lucky. Fires, collapsing buildings, tsunami waves and extreme tides had battered the city, and it would take years to recover.

Army and Coast Guard support arrived in Gullhaven shortly after the death of the beast, and crews of skilled construction tradesmen eager for work had come from all over the country to help clean up and rebuild.

Cannon sat in his lawn chair on Razor Point, Blackwater Bay gently lapping over his toes. The crash and ring of metal resounded over the bay, a payloader moving rocks or gathering debris. The rumble of construction was constant, and it bounced around inside the mountain valley day and night. The roads through the mountains had been cleared, and food and supplies were provided via state and federal emergency agencies. The Army Corps of Engineers would determine if it was feasible to reopen Devil's Rip for boat passage, but based on the destruction along the bluffs, Cannon didn't think Devil's Rip would ever be navigable again. The problems this created were troubles for another day, but Gullhaven was in for tough times without the fishing trade and rich folks from San Francisco coming up the coast in their boats.

Vik's widow, Priva, made a substantial contribution to the local hospital, which allowed residents to get back on their feet without having to worry about medical bills. The death count was at 137, which Cannon didn't think was bad, all things considered. A single loss is felt, but given the suddenness of the disaster and the ensuing chaos, 137 was better than what he'd imagined. There were still people missing, so the body count was likely to go up, but he couldn't stop thinking how much worse things could've been.

Services were held for Vik, Nate, Cindy Becker, Trevor Krisp, Mr. Minter—all the people who'd been lost in the disaster. Again Mrs. Priva Singh came to the rescue, and a monument was to be constructed in a park by the wharf that would bear the names of those lost, including her husband. All the ceremonies had been difficult for Cannon, saying goodbye, but it was also a way of moving on. He hadn't known Vik or

Nate very well, but he considered both men close friends in death, and sorrow tugged at him, regrets for not getting to know both men better when he'd had the chance.

A chill breeze gusted over the bay, and his temporary patrol boat, another Boston Whaler center console, slapped against the sandspit. The tides had returned, though he'd seen no sharks or orca in the bay. He figured it might take some time for the beasts to forget, or feel comfortable venturing into the bay, but he hoped someday they'd be able to get through Devil's Rip.

He pushed off the top of a cooler that sat in the sand next to his chair and dug out a beer. The can was cold, and condensation dripped on his uniform shirt. He was technically off duty, but these days he was always working. The sheriff had given him more authority, and he acted on the mayor's behalf in many matters concerning the rebuilding of Gullhaven. The mayor had buried her hatchet, and she and Cannon had been working together without incident.

In the aftermath of the explosions that killed the beast and opened Devil's Rip, Cannon was found at the base of the bluffs holding Nate's corpse, rocking back and forth in a daze, asking for Vik. The loss of Nate was an unhealed wound, and no matter where Cannon's life went, he would always think of his friend and remember it was partially his fault the man was dead.

The sun fell below the horizon behind him, leaving a bruised sky. He fished out another beer and waited for Nel's kitchen light to come on. She and Joshua still lived in their apartment on the second floor of the old house on Long Island Avenue, but that would be changing soon. He'd asked Nel to marry him and offered to adopt Joshua and legally make the boy his son.

Nel hadn't said yes right away, in fact she'd asked Cannon the hardest question he'd ever been asked: are you over Sherri? He was, but he didn't know why, or how, and he'd done a terrible job of explaining that. This had led to an argument, and Cannon had gotten no answer to his question.

In the days that followed, Cannon realized he could lose Nel and Joshua, and it became clear that was the worst possible thing he could imagine. That's when he knew he really loved them both, and wanted to spend the rest of his life, whatever that would be, taking care of them both.

When he told Nel that, it did the trick, and the wedding was set for later in the month.

Cannon took a pull on his beer and smiled.

Nel's light came on and Cannon saw a shadow pass before the window, and he lifted his binoculars. Nel stood at the window, staring out at Blackwater Bay. Knowing Cannon was probably watching her, she waved.

Cannon waved back, though he knew there was no way she could see him. She knew he was there, and what mattered more than that at the end of the day?

Nel had it rough in the aftermath of the quake. Seven of her children were orphans, though four had family in Gullhaven who had agreed to look after them. The other three stayed in town with various foster parents, and eventually Nel would work with the state to find their relatives or arrange their permanent care.

Even with all the death, the plight of Gullhaven wasn't without miracles. Mira's husband, AKA the donut man, had been found alive and well. He'd been in the bakery when the earthquake hit, and he, the baker and his staff were able to scramble to the second floor before the ground floor windows imploded and the store was flooded. Cannon had been there for their reunion, and the sight of the old couple hugging and kissing had pushed Cannon that last inch he needed to commit to Nel forever. He wanted that. He wanted to grow old with her. Never leave her side.

Cannon's SAFE boat was removed from the roof of Century One Office Plaza, but as predicted, the vessel and motor weren't salvageable, so it was junked. A new SAFE boat was ordered, but Cannon stripped some parts from the old patrol boat and would make the new one his own by carrying the memory of his old vessel close.

A low rumble settled over the valley, and the still water that rolled over Razor Point jiggled and shook.

It was a tremor, the sudden release of energy in the Earth's lithosphere creating seismic waves. There'd been several in the last week as the broken and cracked tectonic plates settled.

Cannon lifted his beer to the sky and said, "To you, Nate and Vik." He finished the beer with one long pull, and crunched the can. He put it in the cooler and reached for another, but hesitated. He was off duty, but with no backup he was always on call. He decided two was enough and closed the cooler.

It was getting late, and it was time to head in. He got up, folded his chair, and went back to the Whaler. It was bigger than the boat he'd inherited from Krisp, and newer, but when he looked to the bow, he expected to see Nate, and when he didn't, sorrow washed over him.

The sound of hydraulics echoed over the water as Cannon dropped the motor. The 200HP Honda choked as it started, pulling for water as the Whaler eased off the sandbar. Though the tides had returned, they were running higher than normal thanks to the limited flow through Devil's Rip, so Razor Point wasn't visible as often. He made a point of sitting on the sandspit when he could, and it was a ritual he planned to continue.

He reached up and felt the beast's tooth where it hung from its leather necklace. He fingered its sharp tip, the rough serrated edge. It had almost gotten him.

Almost.

41

The hatchlings break free of their egg cocoons and cling to the underside of the rock their mother hid them under. Swirling seawater disturbs the creatures, and more than five hundred larva mutant squid dart around the tiny cavern beneath the stone, the frenzy stirring sand and silt.

A hunger burns in each small creature, a need to hunt and feed, yet they're no more than smudges getting pushed around by the slightest of eddies. They wait in the water, thin and almost transparent, their gelatinous bodies floating on the shifting currents.

One in the group wags it microscopic tail, driving forward, mouth open and catching plankton and other nutrients, its forming gills puffing in and out. Others follow, and soon all the creatures are swimming through the sea.

Darkness gives way to gray twilight, and above light fills the sea. The beasts are drawn upward. The hatchlings swim toward the light, their tentacles thin as fiber-optic cable.

The tiny beasts are cannibals, and as hunger consumes them many feast on their siblings. So many cloud the water a culling of the herd is necessary, but many survive and continue their ascent to the light from the cold abyss. Most will die or be eaten in the next twenty-four hours as the creatures evolve and grow, but this is a necessity for those who might survive. Their chances now lay in secrecy and remaining unseen.

As if on cue, fish and turtles knife through their ranks and the animals eat many of the hatchlings as they fight to survive. Most should already have been eaten, and its only by random chance of the changing tides and the shifting of the world's foundation that allows a chosen few to go where their kind had been unable to go for eons.

Everything is out of balance; the sea temperature, the light, the dark cracks where its kind live.

There are only two hundred left as they cross the twilight zone and enter a world filled with color and life. In a foreign habitat, instincts useless, the creatures separate, each an individual and becoming less part of the group with each passing second. These are solitary creatures, and as they triple in size over the next day many break free of the pack and stray off. Most will be eaten, crushed, or starve to death.

As they grow the beast's turn a blueish-black, taking on an appearance not seen on Earth for millions of years. There are muffled sounds from above, and tentacles writhe and read the vibrations in the sea.

Four great white sharks knife through the group, feeding, and the remains of the creature's kin are scattered through the bay, a mess of torn gelatinous tissue that will be eaten by the small fish and crabs.

One remaining creature hides beneath a dead stalk of kelp.

Something gnaws at its insides, a feeling it has never experienced, a primal warning telling it to be cautious, even as the overwhelming urge to feed washes through it. A burning and longing that constantly eats at it like another leg. It always feels the pull of starvation, the unease that comes from never being satisfied, never feeling whole. It knows no other way to live, as if part of it was always missing, a piece that can only be replaced with flesh and blood.

It hovers and waits.

THE END

Edward J. McFadden III juggles a full-time career as a university administrator, with his writing aspirations. His novels Shadow of the Abyss, Primeval Valley, THROWBACK and The Breach were recently published by Severed Press, and his short story Doorways in Time appeared in Shadows & Reflections, an estate authorized Roger Zelazny tribute anthology with an introduction by George R.R. Martin. His other novels include AWAKE, The Black Death of Babylon, and HOAXERS. Ed is also the author/editor of: Anywhere But Here, Lucky 13, Jigsaw Nation, Deconstructing Tolkien: A Fundamental Analysis of The Lord of the Rings (re-released in eBook format Fall 2012 – Amazon Bestseller), Time Capsule, Epitaphs (W/ Tom Piccirilli), The Second Coming, Thoughts of Christmas, and The Best of Pirate Writings. He lives on Long Island with his wife Dawn, their daughter Samantha, and their mutt Oli.

 SEVERED**PRESS**

 facebook.com/severedpress
twitter.com/severedpress

CHECK OUT OTHER GREAT DEEP SEA THRILLERS

THE BREACH
by Edward J. McFadden III

A Category 4 hurricane punched a quarter mile hole in Fire Island, exposing the Great South Bay to the ferocity of the Atlantic Ocean, and the current pulled something terrible through the new breach. A monstrosity of the past mixed with the present has been disturbed and it's found its way into the sheltered waters of Long Island's southern sea.

Nate Tanner lives in Stones Throw, Long Island. A disgraced SCPD detective lieutenant put out to pasture in the marine division because of his Navy background and experience with aquatic crime scenes, Tanner is assigned to hunt the creeper in the bay. But he and his team soon discover they're the ones being hunted.

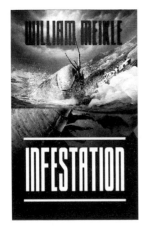

INFESTATION
by William Meikle

It was supposed to be a simple mission. A suspected Russian spy boat is in trouble in Canadian waters. Investigate and report are the orders.

But when Captain John Banks and his squad arrive, it is to find an empty vessel, and a scene of bloody mayhem.

Soon they are in a fight for their lives, for there are things in the icy seas off Baffin Island, scuttling, hungry things with a taste for human flesh.

They are swarming. And they are growing.

"Scotland's best Horror writer" - Ginger Nuts of Horror

"The premier storyteller of our time." - Famous Monsters of Filmland

CHECK OUT OTHER GREAT
DEEP SEA THRILLERS

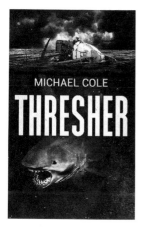

THRESHER
by Michael Cole

In the aftermath of a hurricane, a series of strange events plague the coastal waters off Florida. People go into the water and never return. Corpses of killer whales drift ashore, ravaged from enormous bite marks. A fishing trawler is found adrift, with a mysterious gash in its hull.

Transferred to the coastal town of Merit, police officer Leonard Riker uncovers the horrible reality of an enormous Thresher shark lurking off the coast. Forty feet in length, it has taken a territorial claim to the waters near the town harbor. Armed with three-inch teeth, a scythe-like caudal fin, and unmatched aggression, the beast seeks to kill anything sharing the waters.

THE GUILLOTINE
by Lucas Pederson

1,000 feet under the surface, Prehistoric Anthropologist, Ash Barrington, and his team are in the midst of a great archeological dig at the bottom of Lake Superior where they find a treasure trove of bones. Bones of dinosaurs that aren't supposed to be in this particular region. In their underwater facility, Infinity Moon, Ash and his team soon discover a series of underground tunnels. Upon exploring, they accidentally open an ice pocket, thawing the prehistoric creature trapped inside. Soon they are being attacked, the facility falling apart around them, by what Ash knows is a dunkleosteus and all those bones were from its prey. Now...Ash and his team are the prey and the creature will stop at nothing to get to them.

CHECK OUT OTHER GREAT DEEP SEA THRILLERS

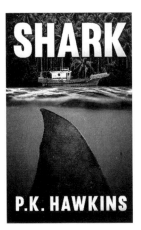

SHARK: INFESTED WATERS
by P.K. Hawkins

For Simon, the trip was supposed to be a once in a lifetime gift: a journey to the Amazon River Basin, the land that he had dreamed about visiting since he was a child. His enthusiasm for the trip may be tempered by the poor conditions of the boat and their captain leading the tour, but most of the tourists think they can look the other way on it. Except things go wrong quickly. After a horrific accident, Simon and the other tourists find themselves trapped on a tiny island in the middle of the river. It's the rainy season, and the river is rising. The island is surrounded by hungry bull sharks that won't let them swim away. And worst of all, the sharks might not be the only blood-thirsty killers among them. It was supposed to be the trip of a lifetime. Instead, they'll be lucky if they make it out with their lives at all.

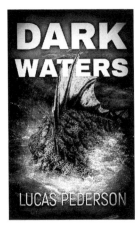

DARK WATERS
by Lucas Pederson

Jörmungandr is an ancient Norse sea monster. Thought to be purely a myth until a battleship is torn a part by one.

With his brother on that ship, former Navy Seal and deep-sea diver, Miles Raine, sets out on a personal vendetta against the creature and hopefully save his brother. Bringing with him his old Seal team, the Dagger Points, they embark on a mission that might very well be their last.

But what happens when the hunters become the hunted and the dark waters reveal more than a monster?

Printed in Great Britain
by Amazon

28069478R00112